CH01521149

Where the Gulls Fall Silent
By Lelita Baldock

ISBN: 9798486845697
(Amazon Paperback Edition)

Disclaimer
The characters in this book are entirely fictional. Any resemblance to actual persons living or dead is entirely coincidental.

Editing by Lucy Skoulding - Starlight Editing
Cover Art by Kimberly McMahon of @creatively_kimberly

First published October 2021
Visit: lelitabaldock.com

Other novels by Lelita Baldock

Historical Fiction
Widow's Lace
https://www.amazon.co.uk/dp/B086BDLP3X

Crime Fiction
The Unsound Sister: Book one of the Bell Cases
https://www.amazon.co.uk/dp/B08ML8QS7H

Glossary

Chipples - the green heads of shallots, spring onions or scallions. Used in Chipple pie in early spring.

Cloam Oven - a stone oven built into the wall of a stone hut. It had an oven section and open coals on which food could be boiled or fried.

Crowdys Crawn - a drum.

Drift nets - lighter nets used to fish in the open waters off the coast of Cornwall. Typically less expensive, allowing fishermen to own their own nets and control their catch.

Hevva - the cry the Huer makes to announce fish have been sighted.

Hevva Cake - a celebratory cake baked after the first 'Hevva' cry. Made from flour, lard, milk and dried fruits. Known for its distinctive criss-cross pattern over the top, to symbolise the fishermen's nets.

Huer - young man employed to watch for schools of fish.

Potfry - a clay pot that was placed on the open coals of a cloam oven to cook food.

Porth Gwynn - The town of Port Quin on the Cornish Coast was known as Porth Gwynn (its Cornish name) in the years this novel describes.

Seine - a large net made of twine, used to fish in bays along the coast of Cornwall. Seine's required multiple boats to string the net between. Typically a very expensive net type, owned by a wealthy sponsor of a town or region, who then took a percentage of the profits.

Semaphore Bushes - wooden sticks painted in white and black stripes that the Huer waves to indicate fish have been sighted.

Trevithick Boiler - a steam engine used to power pumps that pump out water from mines that track under the sea. First used off the coast of Southern Cornwall.

Troyls - a dance or celebration, usually held in the fish cellars.

Tulls - hard felt hats worn by miners to protect their heads while working.

Yarg - traditional Cornish cheese, covered in nettle to help it keep. Soft and creamy in texture and flavour.

PART 1

Prologue

You were born in high summer, as the trade winds blew the stench of fish guts and rotting seaweed up from the shore. You were born in sweat and blood and fear. Meraud never left my side, my husband Cubert sat in the dust of the street, our son Enyon at his knee.

You were late, very late. I'd joked to my Cubert you'd be a late sleeper. He didn't laugh.

It was like you knew what was coming, what you would bring. So when the cramps that dragged down my belly came to rack my body, I already knew you'd take your time, make me fight. Fight to push, to breathe, fight to hold you, fight to live. And I knew I deserved it. Like you, I knew what would come.

But fight I did, as I had from the day I was sure you lay within me. Tiny, barely anything but blood of my body, and seed of his. You brought sickness like I had never known, days, weeks in bed, I could stomach nothing but thin broth, your brother made it. He was a good boy. The house-keeping suffered, but Cubert never chided. Only worried as I paled and thinned while my belly swelled with you. I was older I told him, the years of my quickening almost done, that was why I suffered so. I knew it was a lie. So did you.

Finally, you relented, and as the last rays of the long days of August faded from the sky your cry, fierce and furious, a proclamation that you had arrived and you would not be cast aside, pierced the gathering gloom and brought Cubert rushing in, Enyon on his heels.

You were cradled in Meraud's arms, slick with blood, red with anger, as she carried you to a bucket of fresh water to wash you down. But Cubert's eyes sought only me. He loved me then, perhaps still… in two strides he was by my side, eyes wide. I answered the question that swam within those deep blue pools. Hands clenched as one, at least for this moment, I brought his palm to my lips and kissed him gently, I would take what I had left.

"I am well," I whispered. "She is well."

"A girl?"

Would you believe his face brightened further, then softened with truest love at the announcement of your sex? It's true. For that moment he loved you best of all.

Know that. I think it matters.

Enyon went straight to your side, as was his want in the days he was with us. Tall and lanky for his age, calm beyond his meagre years, he took you from your god-mother, swaddled in a scratchy woollen blanket and held you close.

"Bring her," Cubert said, and he did.

Cubert went to move away, move to you, but I held firm his hand. Forgive me little one, but these were my last moments too. He looked to me, a shadow crossing his face. I smiled, too tired to confront that shadow.

Enyon held you out, pride shining from his features. I released my husband's hand.

Cubert took you, gently. Tears filled his eyes at your perfect eyes, perfect nose, lips and cheeks. The light downy hair upon your crown. He swallowed and turned to wipe the moisture from his eyes, before laying you down on my chest.

I took you, and forgive me, but I paused, in that moment, in the glow of family, my family. I paused.

And then I pulled your swaddle aside. You wiggled at the touch of the cooler night-time air that still carried the stench of scales and death, but did not cry out. You knew who you were even then, it was up to him to decide.

And he did.

Cubert looked at you. At your tiny body, your perfect arms and hands, torso, legs, at your feet...

He stiffened, it was slight, but I was watching for it. He knew.

Our eyes met, the truth was told. I held his gaze, I would not turn away, not from you, never from you. He looked down at the swept dirt floor. The warmth and love and joy of the moment dimmed. As I'd known it would

Enyon shuffled over, I covered you quickly. Meraud rested her hands on his shoulders, just starting to broaden with adolescence, he would be the image of his father. He still glowed with wonder, the light of your coming condensed down to just his face, his energy.

It gave me something to anchor to.

I love him for that.

It was his surprise that told me Cubert had moved. That and the cold air that suddenly flooded the space beside me.

"Father?" Enyon called, confusion furrowing his brow. Cubert didn't turn. Stride steady, he cleared our humble cottage, heading out the door to the pebbled streets of the port. He shut the door gently though. That was for you, a kindness, the only one his heart could spare.

Enyon looked to me, fear now creeping across his features.

I should have smiled at him, should have beckoned him to sit beside us, to talk, to explain, so he could understand.

But I was... tired. And you began to fuss... and, nothing forgives my selfishness but I ignored the plea in his eyes and brought your lips to my breast. I turned from my first born. He was still a boy.

He deserved more.

"Go to your father," Meraud gently prompted him. "Go on."

He paused, caught in the knowledge that there was something amiss. Young enough to still be loyal first to his mother. I felt his gaze searching me, seeking my eyes, my words, my explanation. Mother always made things right.

But this I could not.

You began to suckle, gentle butterfly fingers on the fat of my breast, pressing softly. I smiled. At you.

I heard him leave, the slight scuff of the floor his feet made lately, they'd grown faster than his mind could compensate for, leaving him prone to drag his gait. He opened the door. It banged shut.

I closed my eyes, lips trembling.

They were gone.

You suckled.

The bed creaked as Meraud perched herself at my feet, her hand warm on my knee.

I lifted my face to hers, eyes red-rimmed with unshed tears. And smiled.

It did not matter, not one bit. Because you, you were perfect... you were worth it all.

Mackerel Pasties

Porth Gwynn, Cornish Coast 1852

The high noon sun beat down on the port, a gentle breeze swirled about the rippling currents of the bay, and the children ran.

The white sand of low tide puffed beneath their feet, their squeals of laughter pealing out across the water. Two mothers, skirts hitched to their thighs, arms wet with the sea they'd walked out to meet, looked up from their nets, sun-browned hands shielding their eyes to watch the children pass, then, heads shaking, bent back to their task. The men did not look up from the slimy silver flash of pilchard bodies that squirmed within their catch.

Back on the shore the children closed in. The leader, Rewan Lobb, a boy of about ten summers, dark of hair and eye, whirled a kerchief above his head in defiance and grinned, before leaning to his task and putting on speed. He loved to tease the little ones. Near the back of the pack Kerensa Williams, small and fair, loped, her uneven gait hindering her pace, but not her determination. Gerens, a smaller, lighter version of the boy with the kerchief, kept pace beside her, uninterested in defeating his older brother and claiming the kerchief, just happy to be part of the group. Suddenly, Derwa lunged, hand brushing along Rewan's untucked shirt, almost catching him. Rewan spun, running backwards for a few steps, taunting. Then, without warning, he spun round, feinted left then darted right up the naturally rocky outcrop that lined the bay. Long legs cleared the rocks quickly, landing on the pebbled streets of Porth Gwynn. On the top he paused, jogging on the spot, watching his pursuers as their shorter legs navigated the rocky climb. Derwa cleared the gap first, Rewan let out a laugh of delight and shot ahead towards the cluster of stone cottages that hugged the bay's edge. Just coming to the rocks Kerensa looked up, a heavy frown on her face. She watched Rewan gliding fast along the foreshore, his eyes checking over his shoulder periodically, focused only on those upon his heels. The rocks would slow her, the pebbles too. Sand was more forgiving to her uneven gait.

Kerensa decided.

She shot left, running as fast as her mismatched legs allowed, skirting the line of the rock barrier. Confused, Gerens paused, one foot already placed to climb. He watched. The shoreline before him curved in. He saw Rewan moving along the curve, saw Kerensa matching his direction, but from the inside of the curve. He understood. Slowly Kerensa came up closer to Rewan, then in line, then, amazingly started to slowly pull in front. Rewan did not look down to the beach, his eyes saw only Derwa, closely followed by Cardor and Treeve. Letting loose a whoop of delight, Gerens set off along the beach, following Kerensa's path.

Kerensa's breathing was ragged and her right foot ached abominably, but she would not stop. Ahead of Rewan now, the end of the bay was approaching, changing suddenly from flat sand to rocky cliff face. Rewan would veer inland, circling through the cottages and huts, back towards the centre of town. She had to intercept him before then. It was time to make her move. Taking a deep breath and bracing herself for the pain, Kerensa bolted right, leaping onto the rocks, hands and feet splayed to scramble up the incline. A sharp edge caught her hand, slicing the tender skin of her outer palm. She didn't notice, didn't stop, eyes fixed on the top of the climb, on the street, on her goal.

Scrabbling she cleared the rocks, pulling herself up to standing. Rewan's head was turned, watching the other children, his loping stride bearing down on her fast. Kerensa braced herself, feet planted firmly, hands out ready to snatch the kerchief.

She didn't see Kenver, running down from the fish sheds, but Gerens did. Eyes wide he tried to call out a warning, but it was too late.

It all happened at once. Rewan looked forward and saw Kerensa standing in his path, shock loosened his mouth as he tried to slow his forward pace. Seeing his body twitch, anticipating his next move, Kerensa lunged to the side, arms reaching, just as Kenver hit the pebbled streets, the momentum of his downward run affording him no opportunity to change direction and then - bam!

All three children came together at once in a ball of limbs, bones, scrapes and cries of shock.

The pebbled street came up to meet Kerensa's cheek bone. She rolled with the impact, the wind knocked from her lungs, coming to a stop on her side, the weight of someone else's legs sprawled across her waist. The legs moved and Kerensa sat up. Kenver, whose legs had landed on her, stood up, shaking with rage.

"What the hell Rewan?" he shouted. "Look where you're bloody going!"

Sat in the dirt of the street Kerensa brushed down the front of her cotton dress, checking for tears, her nimble fingers finding one just above her knee. She inspected it quickly, it would need a patch. Something to do before mother comes home…

Kenver looked over at her, "You all right there Kez?" he asked, offering her his hand to stand. Kerensa ignored him, pulling herself to her feet, wobbling slightly. He looked away, back to Rewan, laying on his side, face away from them. He hadn't moved.

The rest of the children arrived, circling around the trio, Gerens coming up the rocks behind Kerensa. Silently he stood by her side, eyes quickly scanning to check she was all right. A small graze on her cheek was slowly welling with blood. He knew better than to say anything, though.

Still Rewan hadn't moved.

"Rewan?" Kenver called again, voice wary now, his initial fury replaced with a twinge of fear. Slowly the children stepped forward, inching towards their leader. Rewan, the oldest of their group by at least two summers, son of the town's most successful fisherman, who would inherit the fine boat known as the Silver Sea, whose last summer of childhood was now waning… what if?

Kenver reached down, gripping Rewan's shoulder, "Rewan, say something," he pleaded, then rolled his friend's body onto his back.

Rewan's face was split wide in a huge grin of amusement, his body shaking with mirth. He was laughing, laughing uncontrollably. And he laughed, and laughed, and laughed and laughed.

The children dusted themselves off and dispersed, their morning games finished by the call of hungry bellies. Rewan bent down and scooped Treeve up onto his shoulders, his smallest brother giggled with delight, still young enough to thrill at the height, not conscious of the indignity of being treated as a child.

"See you tomorrow Kez," Gerens waved to Kerensa as he fell in behind his brothers.

Kerensa waved, watching her friends seep into the streets of Porth Gwynn. Her own tummy grumbled loudly, ordering her home as well. She made her way through the streets slowly, her limp more pronounced now after the exertion of running, her empty home an unappealing destination.

The streets of Porth Gwynn were few, pebbled and lined with stone cottages, and wooden huts each with a fenced vegetable yard, sheltering rows of leek, swede, potato, onion and in the season, parsley, from the harsh coastal winds that whipped the settlement.

The richer yards also held chickens and the occasional pig. The townsfolk lived a life of subsistence farming, fishing and bread. In the season the days were framed by the passage of schools of pilchards through their waters. Announced by the Huer, a young man employed for the task, who perched on the cliff top watching the waves for the telltale silver flash of pilchard scales, or the swarms of gulls that also preyed upon them. With his cry of "Hevva" the town would empty to the shores, women and older men in the shallows hefting the smaller seine nets. The younger men in groups of four filled the row boats and ventured deep into the bay, setting the massive seines. All the nets were provided by their town benefactor Mr Symons who lived in Wadebridge, but sometimes entertained guests at the large castle that overlooked the Port. The men would deploy the seines in a circle to trap the migrating fish as they moved north following the smaller fish on which they fed. A natural curve in the coast line, the bay provided shelter to the townsfolk when the storms off the Atlantic coast ravaged the cliffs. It also provided a natural trap for schools of fish that passed too close, swept into the rocky cove by the currents of the Cornish coast.

Fish caught, the preparation began: scaling, gutting, barreling in salt. The streets running with fish blood and guts, the gulls hovering in wait to poach from the unwary fishermen. After a good haul the processing could last for days, the townsfolk working late into the night, storing the catch in the large wooden sheds that lined the foreshore, or in dark stone cellars, waiting for the trade ships that came with the easterly winds to collect the packed barrels and carry them away to Cork, Liverpool and even across the ocean to Newfoundland. A way of life that had sustained them for generations, in the small years of Kerensa's life, the town was thriving.

The months of August to December earned the town their livelihood, stocking fish for trade and for their own winter sustenance. A good season was critical to their survival.

It meant months of hard work, long hours, exhausted sleep, early rising. And absolute freedom for the children deemed too young yet to work the nets. Children like Kerensa and her friends.   They   were meant to go to school, to walk the hour to St Endellion together through the dawn dew, sit on the hard wooden benches in the white washed school house and practice their letters on slabs of board, white chalk in hand, before walking home as the sea winds of the coast picked up for evening.

They were meant to.

And they did - in the off season. But when the fish were running, their parents too distracted by their work to care, they rarely did. Besides, what was the point of the school? They were the children of fishing folk, and fishing folk they too would be.

Kerensa passed the last row of stone cottages, following a long narrow dirt track through the wild grasses and blackberry bushes that surrounded the Port. Heading for her own home, on the far edge of the settlement. The winds of the coast had fallen off. The lull between noon and later afternoon, when the air rested, still and heavy over the land. Before the setting sun would again summon the winds to whip the salt spray up from the cove and over their dwellings.

Kerensa entered her mother's small stone cottage, shutting the door softly, some part of her unwilling to break the still silence of the house. Inside was dim, the shutters still closed from the night before. From the low beam that held the roof aloft hung bundles of drying herbs, the scent of rosemary and thyme filling the small space. Kerensa made her way to the bread box and pulled up the lid. The same rock-hard knot of stale bread she'd discovered that morning sat at the bottom. She picked it up, tried to squeeze the ball of dough, hopeful against knowledge, but the crust would not give. She returned it to the box. Opening the flour jar, she ran her fingers through the thin film of rough meal that lined the very bottom. Not enough even for flat bread. Extracting her hand, she wiped the flour from her fingers down the front of her smock and replaced the lid.   Taking a mug from the cupboard, she walked out the side door into the small fenced vegetable yard and dunked her mug into the bucket of well-water that sat against the outside wall. Sipping slowly she wandered through the vegetables: the green heads of swede and parsley, the purple sprays of silverbeet, the bare soil that hid the seeds of winter onions yet to break the surface. At random she pulled a carrot from the ground. Still too small to harvest, but her growling tummy claimed it nonetheless. Brushing the dirt from the root she chomped down on her snack before discarding the inedible leaves over the fence.

Back inside she dragged a stool to the bench and climbed up to reach the higher cupboards. Stretching on tip-toe she ran her small hands along the cupboard until her fingers brushed the basket of needles and thread she searched for. Pulling down the mending kit she placed it on the table and pulled her dress from her shoulders. Selecting a patch of fabric in the same off-white rough spun cotton of her dress, saved from her baby dresses, Kerensa prepared to patch over the tear in the knee of her skirts. Sitting in only her small clothes, she draped the torn garment over her bony knees and began, her small fingers dexterous and nimble as they passed the tiny needle and slender thread through the fabric, over and back, over and back.

About halfway through her mending a knock came at the door. Kerensa looked up in surprise. People often came up from the village, seeking her mother's advice and skills, but surely they knew she would not be home at this hour? The daylight was for foraging. Quickly biting off the string and pulling her smock back over her head she went to the door and hauled it open.

Rewan stood on the step, a small cloth-wrapped parcel in his hands. He smiled a lopsided grin and held the parcel out to her. The smell of fresh baked pastry wafted from the bundle up into her nose. Her stomach, empty since the night before, groaned to life as her nose caught the scent. Her mouth watered.

"Mother made too many. Misjudged the flour," he explained. "She hates waste, thought you might enjoy it."

Kerensa paused, unsure.

Rewan read her hesitation and understood.

"Take it, as a prize," he announced. "You had me beat today, if Kenver hadn't got in the way. You earned it."

He stepped forward and Kerensa decided.

Reaching out she snatched the parcel from his hands. It was heavier than she expected, still warm from the oven.

"Thank you," Kerensa whispered, eyes cast down.

"Enjoy," Rewan smiled and tousled her hair affectionately. "See you tomorrow."

Kerensa watched him turn and lope down the grassy hill back

towards the town proper. Across the bay the water twinkled in the sunlight, the air heavy and still.

Closing the door she raced to the table and unwrapped the gift. A pasty, fat with root vegetables and salt, mackerel and perhaps even an egg. She leaned down and breathed in the smell of nourishment. Taking hold of the pasty between two fingers still grimy from beach sand, she prepared to tear it open and stuff her famished face. But as her fingers gripped the flaky pastry edge she paused. Mother would be hungry tonight, and tired after foraging, and they were out of flour... But mother didn't know of this gift. Kerensa could eat it all, return the cloth and Meliora would be none the wiser. Kerensa had won it, after all.

Frowning, Kerensa stood back, eyes large with the pasty, stomach growling its opinion, heart knowing what she would do. Carefully she rewrapped the pasty and placed it on the bench by the cloam oven that was built into the side of their hut, pausing only once more to stare at the warm bundle with longing. She returned to her mending.

Tonight they would share it, they would both be fed.

Mushroom Soup

As the sun reached down the sky and the wind picked up the sharp scent of salt and moss and cast it over the land, Kerensa made her way back down into town. The breeze brought relief from the heat of the sun and thinned the thick moisture-laden air. Coming to the foreshore she lowered herself onto a rock overlooking the bay and watched the adults begin to pack away their nets, the row boats returning from the break. Worn-faced, sun-reddened and salt-lined the fishermen trudged up the sand dragging the heavy rope-locked nets. They headed to the sheds to rinse the salt from the fibres, the water spray running in rivulets through the pebbles of the street, before packing them safely in the cellars for the night. Younger men, shirts discarded in the bows of their vessels, leapt from their rowing to drag their boats the last few metres up the shore. Soon the beach was empty but for the resting boats drying in the setting sun, the town silent except for the occasional cry of the gulls circling in the darkening skies above.

The smells of wood fires, bubbling stews and frying fish began to fill the fast cooling air as the townsfolk settled in for their evening meals and family time. At this time of year they would be to bed before the full setting of the sun.

Still Kerensa waited, swinging her feet off the side of the rock, watching the waves lick up the beach lower and lower as the tide itself receded for the night.

As the first flickers of candle light began to shine in the windows of the surrounding houses Kerensa spotted a figure making its way down the far cliff. Climbing to her feet she rushed to meet the figure as fast as her aching foot would allow.

"Mumma, mumma!" she cried, face wide with a delighted smile as the tall woman stepped down into the street. Most nights her mother returned, but sometimes, she was away for a day or two. Kerensa had missed her comforting warmth beside her the night before.

"Kerensa!"

The woman placed her basket and bag down on the road and caught her tiny daughter in her arms as Kerensa leapt up into her embrace.

Laughing Meliora swung her daughter around in a big hug, suitable to Kerensa only because no one was watching, before placing her back on the ground. She was old for a mother to one so young, the soft curves of her youth melted into wiry lines by hard work and malnourishment. But her deep brown hair showed few greys and her blue eyes, though lined with wrinkles, still shone. The great beauty of her youth rested in her smile.

Pushing a strand of knotted hair from Kerensa's eyes, Meliora looked down at her little girl and her heart filled with the same joy it did every time they were reunited. Kerensa turned and picked up the bag her mother had placed on the ground. Taking her daughter's lead, Meliora gathered up her basket in one arm and took Kerensa's hand in the other.

Together they strolled along the foreshore, past the fish sheds and waterside cottages before heading up towards their own dwelling, talking of everything and nothing, sometimes merely silently listening to the sleeping town around them.

Coming home, Kerensa went straight to the candle to light their main room, the soft glow of the cloam oven coals long extinguished.

"How was the foraging, mother?" she asked as she struck the flint and lit the wick of the dining table candle.

"Well my dear one, very well," Meliora replied, setting her basket of herbs on the table. The sweet scent of wild sage and fresh cut thyme, mixed with the tang of fat fennel bulbs filled the little hut. "We have much to prepare tonight."

Kerensa nodded, before fetching a cup and heading outside. Returning swiftly she placed the mug of water by her mother's side.

"You must be thirsty," she stated simply.

Meloria paused and smiled at her daughter, heart clenching. "And you must be hungry!" she laughed, to cover her discomfort. "Guess what else I found out today?"

"What!?"

"Mushrooms! The first of the season change. Big juicy and fat. I thought I would fry them up with some bread and salt. Make us a feast."

Meliora moved towards the bread box and popped the lid. Kerensa waited in silence. Her mother would see soon enough. Meliora pulled the rock hard knob from the box, and paused. The bread was inedible. Blinking in surprise, she moved to the flour, realisation flooding through her. She had not broken her fast the morning she left, nor taken a lunch into the fields, preferring to leave what little they had for her daughter. What she had failed to realise, was that there was nothing for her to take, or leave. There was nothing left…

Glancing back at Kerensa, Meliora's gut clenched. Such a small thing, she thought to herself suppressing the spike of guilt that stabbed at her chest as she took in her child's hollow cheeks and thin arms, her blue eyes too big, her face all angles. A halo of wispy blonde fuzz circled her face, lit by the candlelight.

Kerensa looked nothing like her mother, but she was still beautiful, to Meliora.

Taking a deep breath Meliora rallied, "I've a better idea than bread, a mushroom soup would be much better," she announced bravely. *I can place the bread in the hot liquid, it will soften and we can eat it then*, she planned.

"It's all right mother," Kerensa said then, moving to the oven and collecting up her parcel, "We have this too."

She unwrapped the now cold pasty and held it out to her mother.

Meliora's forehead creased in a frown, "Kerensa, where did you get this? We don't steal from others, daughter, nor do we take charity."

"I didn't mother," Kerensa protested immediately. "I won it."

"Won it?"

"I beat Rewan in capture the flag, well, it was a kerchief, and I didn't exactly beat him because Kenver got in the way and we all fell over, but Rewan knew I would have won and he brought me the pasty to say I won… Meraud made too much and she hates waste and…"

"All right, all right, slow down my child," Meliora said, suppressing a small smile.

"I assume this means there was no school today?" she said, raising an arched eyebrow at her child.

Kerensa looked down at her feet, silent and embarrassed at giving herself away.

Meliora watched her daughter, shoulders slumped, knocked-knees poking out from beneath her skirts, club foot twisted in towards her centre, and sighed. *I have to do better*, she thought.

Determined, Meliora rolled her shoulders and set the pasty on the table.

"A feast then!" she announced.

Kerensa looked up in surprise.

"Fetch an onion from the pantry for the soup and I will get the coals going in the oven to reheat the pasty. Mushroom soup and pasty. What do you think?" She clapped her hands together as if in delight. A smile, bright as the sun, broke out across Kerensa's face.

"Yes mother," she replied and raced out into the night-dark garden.

After supper meant bed for the rest of the village, but not yet for Kerensa and Meliora. By the light of the low burning candles mother and daughter set to work. Kerensa took the sage, its larger leaves easier for her child's fingers to manage. Her mother the thyme and nettle.

In silence they worked, washing the herbs before patting them down with a cloth, then tying the stems together in small bunches. Once all were bundled, Meliora hooked the bunches up in rows along the low wooden beam of the roof.

Asleep on her feet, Kerensa washed her hands and made her way into the side room where they slept and climbed beneath the thin wool blanket of their bed. Head on her pillow she watched her mother through the doorway, as she worked, her practised hands tying up the herbs to dry. Meliora began to hum. Eyes heavy, belly full, limbs weary, the sound of her mother's voice drifting over her, Kerensa drifted into sleep.

She did not wake when her mother rose. Outside still dark, the birds still abed. Meliora splashed her face with water from the outside bucket, dressed and gathered her bag and basket. She did not break her fast, but left the portion of mushroom soup she had foregone the night before on the stove, ready for Kerensa to enjoy.

Outside the sky began to lighten. Kerensa still slept. One by one the birds began to rise, their gentle song trilling through the quiet village. Kerensa still slept. The sunlight strengthened, beams of light peaking into the room, reaching bright fingers across the woollen cover under which the child lay.

Kerensa still slept.

A knock on the door roused her from her slumber. It would be Gerens come to collect her for play. Kerensa threw off her blanket, swinging her legs over the side of the bed. Tearing her nightgown from her body she was reaching for her smock when he spoke.

"Kerensa, hurry up! The others have left. But we can still catch them up."

Kerensa paused, what did he mean 'left'?

The answer came soon enough. "Father was angry with us last night. Rewan told him about the... crash. Couldn't avoid it, his leg was all scuffed up. Father ordered us to school today. So we are going, but just for a few days, until he forgets. Come on Kerensa, hurry up."

But Kerensa was no longer hurrying. And she was not going to school. Slowly and silently she slipped back into bed, rolling away from the door.

"Kerensa?" Gerens tried one more time. Then, deciding his friend was not at home, raced away down the path to catch the others on their walk to St Endellion.

Bundled in bed Kerensa pulled the blanket up over her head and closed her eyes. Her tummy, full enough as she fell asleep that it felt it could burst, had emptied already, as that of a growing child is want to do. The hollow felt even deeper after the feast of last night. Tucking her arms about her middle, Kerensa snuggled into the blankets. She would get up to play, she loved to play. But when the offer was school, Kerensa preferred a day to herself.

That evening, as always, she awaited her mother. Delight lit through her like a lightning flash when she saw Meliora's lanky figure moving down the cliff.

No night away tonight.

Hand in hand they walked home along the foreshore. Meliora had traded a moss and thyme tincture for potatoes in the neighbouring town of Port Isaac and so cooked up a rich pot of potato and leek soup for dinner, saving two potatoes for another purpose. After her mid-morning mushroom broth, the thick soup was welcome to Kerensa's grumbling belly. After, Meliora showed Kerensa how to split sprouting onions to plant and grow outside, and explained why she had selected two potatoes from her basket to place in the sun to shoot. "Then we can split them too, and plant our own crop."

Vegetables planned, Kerensa worked to clean and bundle the new batch of herbs, while her mother tested the others, selecting those that were ready to be potted or cooked into elixirs and remedies.

"Come here my child," Meliora said. "Sit."

Putting down a handful of rosemary, Kerensa did as her mother bid. Taking off her right shoe and sock, Meliora poured a tincture onto her hands and began rubbing the liquid into Kerensa's swollen foot and ankle.

The liquid smelled like wild grass and seaweed, and tingled on her skin.

"This is a mix of sorrel, thyme and fennel. It will help the pain," her mother said.

"It doesn't bother me," Kerensa lied.

Meliora nodded, her daughter's bravado did not fool her. From the first moment she had held her baby girl in her arms she knew the life her child would have, she knew the pain. Her right foot, shrivelled and curved inward, the ankle bone prone to press downwards and under Kerensa's weight, sometimes striking on the ground. The bones were malformed, for her daughter to walk they ground together, bone on bone. It could be excruciatingly painful. It would only get worse.

Kerensa had never let it stop her. That made Meliora proud.

"There," she said, "now, to bed. I can finish up here."

"But I haven't finished the rosemary…"

"To bed, you are dead on your feet. I see the bags under your eyes. Time for sleep. You have school tomorrow."

Kerensa frowned. Did her mother know she hadn't been going all season?

Surely not.

Unsure and not wishing to risk further discussion on the topic of school, Kerensa complied, shuffling into their room, donning her nightgown and snuggling down under the covers. Her foot felt warm, like it was wrapped in a thick woollen swaddle. The ache that travelled along the bones was still there, but lighter. Or perhaps she was just imagining it.

In the kitchen Meliora began to hum, shuffling about the kitchen. Then a new sound, the gentle scraping of a spoon on a bowl, wood on wood. Kerensa sat up and looked into the kitchen, squinting against the dark. Meliora held a mixing bowl in the crook of her arm, beside her on the table sat an open bag of meal. Kerensa smiled. Meliora was mixing up bread. Tomorrow they would break their fast together.

Perhaps, after that, she might go to school after all.

Cornish Daisies

The season was ending, the cooler winds washing away the summer's heat. Bundled in her winter coat, Kerensa sat on the rocky foreshore watching the waves. Shortly, she heard a bustle of noise emanate from the fish sheds. Glancing over she watched as the women of the town made their way from the sheds, hauling baskets full to the brim with salted fish. One by one they helped each other to swing the hefty baskets onto their backs, strapping them down across their shoulders.

It was market day.

While most of the fish of Porth Gwynn was destined for the large trade vessels that combed the coast throughout the season, collecting wares to transport across their fair isle and further on to the lands beyond, the fish that remained as the season wound down was destined for trade at the markets of St Endellion.

Gerens appeared from the shadows of the boat sheds and skipped across the pebbled streets to her side.

"I'm going to market with mother today," he announced excitedly, "Rewan is working on the boat with father. They... don't need my help..." A shadow crossed his face briefly, before he brightened again, smiling, "Wanna come along?"

Kerensa's eyes flicked from her friend's open face to study the cliff face on the other side of town. Meliora had not been home that morning. Kerensa had expected her mother would be heading to the markets too, to sell her herbs and fusions. Casting her eyes back and forth over the cliff, Kerensa saw nothing but grass and rock. No Meliora.

Kerensa paused. She knew her mother would want her home, preparing the herbs they had left from the night before. But the thought of the markets, the tables of food giving off their mouth-watering scents, the colours and energy of the place… and the promise of time with her most fun friend, won.

Without a word Kerensa stood up. Gerens clapped for joy and seeing his mother Meraud emerge from the sheds, back already laden with fish, made a beeline for her side. Meraud's tired eyes watched her skipping son fondly before coming to rest on Kerensa.

"Joining us then?" she asked warmly. "Here…" she reached into her ample skirts and produced a sweet bun, which she pressed into Kerensa's hands. It was still warm from the oven. "You'll need your strength to keep up with that one," she laughed as she nodded at Gerens, who was already making his way along the road out of town. Gerens loved market day. Almost as much as Kerensa.

Kerensa paused, the warmth of the bun seeping into her cold hands, the scent filling her nostrils with desire, making her mouth salivate.

Meraud smiled down at her kindly, understanding shaping her heavy features into something gentle and light. "Eat up small one," she said softly. "And run along before we lose my son!"

Without another thought, Kerensa stuffed the sweet bun into her mouth, its soft texture melting along her tongue. Chewing furiously, she turned to run after Gerens.

Meraud watched as Kerensa caught up to her son, her tiny frame dwarfed by his well fed limbs. The smile slipped from her lips. Emblyn came up to her side.

"You do what you can," she said firmly. "We all do. But Meliora…"

"I know," Meraud said, shaking her head and beginning her trek to the markets.

The women all fell in together, laughing and sharing stories of frustration with husbands and sons, irritation with proud daughters. Meraud felt lost herself to the familiar rhythm of town gossip as she made her way to market. But in the back of her mind her concern for the tiny girl keeping pace with her second born continued to spin.

Free to run on the buoyant legs of the young, unhindered by the weight of trade, Gerens and Kerensa made it to St Endellion well ahead of the women, despite Kerensa's limp. Gerens plunged into the mill of people and traders, heading straight for the tables of fish from nearby ports and cuts of meat from the neighbouring farms. Kerensa paused. Standing on the periphery she watched, eyes scanning the scene, taking it in.

Soon the smell of roasting meat caught her attention and she made her way slowly towards its source. She was standing to the side of the spit, indulging in the warmth of the roasting pit and savouring the smell of cooking pork, when Gerens found her.

"The prices are down," he said, without preamble.

Kerensa turned to him and frowned. "What prices?"

"The fish," he looked at her expectantly. Seeing the blank stare she returned he sighed heavily. "You are just like my brother," he chided in frustration. Dipping his hand into his pocket he produced a coin. Stepping forward he passed the coin to the trader who manned the spit and purchased a chunk of warm flesh in a paper bag.

"Here," he said, handing the pork to Kerensa. "We can share it."

Kerensa smiled and snatched up the bag. First a sweet bun and now meat, she hadn't eaten this well in days!

The two friends walked in companionable silence together through the markets chewing on the rich meat. Kerensa filled her eyes with the sights, imagining how it would feel to have coin of her own to spend here.

Beside, Gerens swallowed his last mouthful of pork and took up his conversation from before. "I think the problem is oversupply. Too many towns around here trying to sell the same fish… so the prices drop."

Kerensa continued chewing thoughtfully before asking around her mouthful, "But I thought we were low on stocks? So, less fish?"

Gerens nodded thoughtfully, "That's true, the runs have been getting shorter, and the hauls smaller. But there is still ample fish for us locals. The real money is on the Continent."

"The Continent?"

"Where the trade ships take the fish. It's rarer over there, so better priced."

"How do you know this?" Kerensa demanded.

Startled, Gerens turned to his friend, "Pastor Henry was talking about it at school last week. Surely you remember?"

Kerensa shrugged, no longer interested now that school had been mentioned.

"Look," she pointed before them, "I see your mother and the other women, we should help them set up."

She quickened her pace and Gerens followed. Trade and fish prices were something Kerensa didn't understand. But working hard to prepare your wares, that she fully understood.

* * *

As the sun was setting over the Cornish coast the two friends made their way slowly down the hill into Porth Gwynn. It had been a long and tiring day, helping Meraud to set up her stall and sell her fish. Kerensa had delighted in being useful, calling out the available fish and prices, helping to pack the sold produce for the customers. It was the side of work she understood, and she was good at it. Organised and efficient. And customers always smiled at her. She was careful to keep her foot well hidden.

Gerens had helped too, though he'd disappeared for a few hours after lunch. Kerensa had barely noticed.

Now, as their little town nestled in the curve of the bay came into view, he disappeared again, running off to the side of the road.

"Gerens!" Kerensa stopped and planted her fists on her hips. "What are you doing?"

Grinning, her friend came racing back from behind a length of blackberry bush. Coming to a stop before her, he pushed a bunch of Cornish daisies up to her face.

"For you!" he announced happily.

Kerensa eyed the delicate white flowers, their yellow centres glowing in the dawn light.

Frowning she looked at her friend. "Why are you giving me daisies? You can't do anything with daisies."

Now it was Gerens turn to frown, "Do anything with them?" he repeated, "Kez, they aren't for potions or treatments. They just look pretty."

"What's the point of that?" she asked, taking the proffered posey from him.

"It's something people like. Especially women. Father often brings pretty flowers home for mother."

"And what does she do with them?"

Gerens shrugged, "Puts them in a pot on the table usually. Trust me Kez," he smiled, "people like flowers on the table."

"I don't know… I think my mother would prefer a useful flower."

They continued making their way down to the town through the fading light.

"What's a useful flower then?"

Kerensa paused, thinking. "Lavender," she finally announced. "It can be used to cover bad smells and it's good for calming an unsettled baby, or mother for that matter."

The two grinned at each other, enjoying her small joke. Both had known their mothers to be rather distressed from time to time.

"Put the daisies on the table, Kez. They might not smell as strong as lavender, but they will make you feel happy."

"All right," Kerensa agreed, but was unconvinced.

"Oh Kez! Look!" Suddenly Gerens darted forward, pointing at the bay.

There bobbing in the gentle currents sat a huge wooden vessel. Above its decks rose two tall masts, sheets of canvas sail wrapped up against wooden struts for the night.

A trader had come.

It was late in the season for such an event, but that only made it more exciting.

"Come on!" Gerens called.

Kerensa grinned and raced down the hill after her friend. The traders always brought excitement to the town. Kerensa might even be able to sneak a few pies at the trolys that Braneh was bound to throw to welcome the sailors. A shame Meliora was not home to see it. She so often missed the trade boats.

Kerensa pushed the thought aside and made her way to the foreshore.

The posey of daisies fell to the dirt behind her.

Red Ribbon

The days shortened, the shadows lengthened, the fish barrels filled, the potatoes grew to harvest. Some days Kerensa went to school with the other children, some days she did not. Some nights she slept alone, some nights the scent of fresh herbs and the song of her mother's voice carried her to rest. As the winds turned chilly and the rain to sleet, the ground froze and the fish run dwindled, the people of Porth Gwynn turned away from the sea that shared its bounty and focused on the land that would warm them for the winter.

Crops were harvested, root vegetables stored in buckets, wood cut and stored, pigs slaughtered, their meat preserved with salt, heavy woollen coats pulled from cupboards, thick woollen socks mended and the sparkling promise of Christmas whispered through the children.

Not a time for fancy gifts, but a time of rest and family, filling food and celebration. A time together as a community before hunkering down to wait out the winter freeze. As the last week of December neared, the buzz of Christmas filled the homes of Porth Gwynn, puddings baked, chickens fattened for roasting, small gifts, a new scarf or cooking pot, an extra pouch of salt or sugar, were secreted away on market days ready for the morning of the Lord's birth.

Finally the day came and the town gathered in their Sunday best, dresses and trousers worn only for Church and walked as one along the path to St Endellion and the morning service of Pastor Henry. Dressed in her same smock, clad in last year's coat, wrists now poking well out of the sleeves, Kerensa hobbled beside her mother.

Meliora had been absent the night before, as Kerensa took to bed. She'd tossed and turned unable to sleep, but in time the chill of night dragged her down to rest. She'd awoken to the soft light of a candle shining on the table and her chest filling with joy knowing her mother was home. "Come Kerensa," Meliora had said, "Let's get you ready for church."

She'd produced a bright red ribbon, shining and new from within the folds of her apron and held it to Kerensa's face. "Perfect," she'd announced and, drawing Kerensa down onto the stool before her, proceeded to brush, smooth and curtail Kerensa's wild blonde curls into a long braid down her back, tipped with the new ribbon.

"It's beautiful mother," Kerensa breathed, stroking the silky ribbon that held her braid. It was more beautiful than anything she'd ever owned.

"As are you," Meliora patted her child's head. "Now, let's go."

Gerens ran up beside Kerensa as the town made its way as one to the Church. His coat was new, the buttons shiny, but Kerensa didn't notice. All she saw was her bright red ribbon bouncing on her chest.

"Will you be at the troyls after church Kerensa?" Gerens asked, face intent.

Kerensa looked over at her sometime playmate, then up at her mother, hope blooming on her face. In her seven Christmases, Kerensa and her mother had never joined the town in the emptying fish cellars to share food and good cheer, to celebrate a season well done, and fill their bellies before the winter rationing began.

"Not this year, Gerens," Meliora answered gently, "we've far too much preparation to do."

The disappointment on his face mirrored that in Kerensa's heart. But, determined not to let anything sour the joy of her ribbon, Kerensa pulled herself up tall and beamed at Gerens. "No matter, I will see you other times and at school."

Gerens bobbed his head. He looked as though he might speak, but changed his mind. Waving, he ran ahead to catch up to his brothers. No one else came to walk beside them.

After church, as they returned home, Kerensa watched her friends running down the hill to the town streets, voices high with excitement, legs energised to play, and despite her best intentions, longing pulled at her heart. Soon the sounds of laughter, voices raised in song and cheer would fill the streets, the town cast in the warm glow of lamps and fires, the smells of roast vegetables and chicken, of cinnamon and raisin pudding encouraging all to a second helping.

But Kerensa would remain apart. Separated, sitting in her mother's little hut just up the hill, able only to watch from afar as the bubble of kinship and shared experience bloomed up from the town, and was carried away on the sea breeze. Meliora saw her daughter's regretful stare. Shame blushing her cheeks with red, she took her daughter's hand and squeezed, "I've another surprise for you my child, come!"

She led Kerensa through their home and into the backyard. There sat a slatted wooden box that Kerensa did not recognise. She looked at her mother in question.

Meliora smiled and pushed her daughter forward. A bubble of excitement began to form in Kerensa's belly. She placed a hand on the lid of the box and paused, taking a deep breath, then opened it.

Inside, in a circle like a cushion, sat a fat mound of brown feathers. Confused, Kerensa cocked her head. Then the mound moved, a crop topped head and beak appearing from the mass. Kerensa clapped with delight.

Her mother had bought them a chicken!

"She is young yet, but soon will start to produce eggs," her mother said, coming up to Kerensa's side. "We should get many seasons from her before she is past laying and ready for the pot. Until then it will be up to you to take care of her. She can feed herself mostly from the scraps in the yard, but we must be generous and save some of our grain for her also. At night she must be in this box, to keep her safe from foxes. And when the snows come we shall bring her inside. Well, Kerensa, what do you think?"

"She is beautiful mother!" Kerensa grinned, throwing her arms about her mother. "Can we bring her inside now? To share Christmas lunch with us?"

Meliora looked down at her child. Kerensa was practically bubbling over with excitement. She had turned back to the chicken and was gently stroking the soft brown feathers. *It was worth it*, Meliora thought and swallowed, *it's always worth it.*

"All right, Kerensa," she conceded, caught up in her daughter's joy. "But only for lunch, she sleeps outside unless there is snow, understood?"

"Yes, mother," Kerensa nodded and reached for the chicken, carefully lifting her from the box and folding her into the crook of her arm. She beamed up at her mother.

My beautiful child, Meliora thought, eyes filling with bitter tears as she took in her daughter's tiny frame, twisted foot, and joyous face. *It's not fair.* Anger and frustration began to bubble in her gut. She turned away.

"Come, we must begin the stew or Christmas lunch will be more like dinner!" she announced bravely to cover her momentary distress.

Kerensa let out a delighted squeak. Meliora turned. The chicken was plucking gently at the curls that had escaped Kerensa's braid and now framed her angelic face. Kerensa giggled and pressed a kiss to the chicken's head.

This time Meliora could not stop the tears and made her way quickly back inside.

They peeled swede and potato from their garden and set it to stew in a large pot over the cloam coals. Kerensa sliced bread while Meliora fried salted pilchards in butter, then wilted silverbeet over the top. They sat at the table, a candle lit between them, for atmosphere, not for light, and feasted. Kerensa stuffed mushed pilchard's on bread into her mouth, grease dripping down her chin as she chewed, then scooped spoonfuls of swede and stew in after to wash it down. Subtly, she fed her silverbeet to the chicken sitting at her feet. Meliora pretended not to notice.

After lunch they played games of spillikins and marbles and took the chicken - "her name is Eia," Kerensa declared - outside to explore the yard. Later, well after the sun had set, they ate reheated stew and Meliora told fairytales of witches and goblins and fairies and Kerensa pretended not to be too old for such stories!

As bedtime neared Kerensa was filled with an emotion she rarely enjoyed, and could not keep her lips from curving. Suddenly she stood up. Taking the red ribbon from her braid, she fingered out her hair, letting her curls drop. Then, without a word to her mother, she dragged her stool over to the high cupboard and reached for the sewing kit.

"Kerensa?" Meliora asked, watching her child, a small line creasing between her brows.

Kerensa said nothing, just pulled down the basket, fingers searching inside. Eventually she produced the scissors and, measuring out the ribbon, carefully cut its beautiful red length in half.

Meliora watched in silence as her daughter cut the ribbon she had saved all season to buy for her, packed away the sewing kit and crossed the room to her side. Gently Kerensa pulled her mother's thick dark locks back into a tail at her nape and clumsily wound the ribbon about her hair, securing it in place.

Job done, she returned to her stool and sat across from her mother, a smile of love on her face.

"Thank you," Meliora breathed, voice shaking. Reaching across the table she took her daughter's hand in hers and squeezed. On the floor Eia clucked and pecked at the small stones the wind blew under the door jamb.

Eyes drooping from fatigue, bellies sore from laughter, mother and daughter wished Eia a good night and climbed into bed. Kerensa fell to sleep in her mother's arms, warm and full and safe and content.

"Mother?" Kerensa sat up in the dark bedroom, eyes wide seeking any light to see. The night was pitch black. "Mother?" She didn't know what had awoken her, but the bed beside her was cold and empty and the house silent, the only sound the whistle of the winter winds that whipped around the hut outside.

In spite of the cold, Kerensa slid out of bed and hobbled into the main room. Lighting a candle she confirmed what she already knew, her mother was not at home.

Kerensa was used to waking to an empty home in the mornings, her mother having already left for foraging, and to nights alone when Meliora stayed out on her search for herbs. But never did her mother leave her in the middle of the night like this. Kerensa paused. She knew she should blow out the candle, climb back under the covers and go back to sleep, but something felt wrong. Glancing at the front door, at her coat hanging alone on the wall rack, Kerensa decided.

She blew out the candle.

The moon was merely a sliver in the black sky, its fragile light barely touching the ice hard earth at her feet, but Kerensa moved with confidence. She knew the path to the village. As she rounded the cottages at the edge of the town she saw the warm glow of lamp light still spilling along the pebbled foreshore. She followed the light. Hovering in the shadows of the homes that lined the beach, Kerensa watched. Some of the fishermen had yet to return home from the afternoon festivities, instead they sat in a tight circle lit by lamp light. Huddled in thick coats, mugs of ale in hand, their voices laughed and sighed, conversation ebbing and flowing with the tide at their back, breath misty in the cold night air. Kerensa recognised Braneh, Rewan and Gerens' father, his broad back hunched forward, streaks of white in his beard catching the lamp light. To his left and right sat Peren and Jago, his crew, laughing heartily and smiling. Kerensa liked Braneh and his crew, they sometimes gave her a fish or two from their catch when the season was new and the promise of plenty still buoyed the townsfolk. It wasn't charity, she always told her mother, it was a thank you, for all the herbal knowledge Meliora brought to the town. Meliora had argued once or twice, but only ever halfheartedly.

One man was missing though. Carworan. Kerensa didn't like Carworan, he called her names, like 'cripple' and 'by-blow'. Cripple she understood well enough, and heard regularly on market days in St Endellion when she shopped with her mother for flour and, occasionally, pork. But 'by-blow' meant nothing to her. She didn't need to know to understand. Coming from Carworan it would only be cruel.

Inching quietly along the houses she passed the men and headed towards the fish sheds, happy for Braneh that Carworan had found his bed early and left the good men without his company. No conscious direction steered her footing, no planned search filtered through her mind, she was led solely by instinct and the need to look, to find her mother. Gloomy shadows surrounded the sheds, the pale moonlight distorting the familiar wooden structures, making them seem to shift and move in the darkness. A coil of fear ran down Kerensa's spine as the cold night air found every sliver of her exposed skin to wrap itself around, sucking the little remaining warmth from her limbs. Kerensa shivered, but walked on.

That was when she heard it, a low moan coming from behind the last shed. She froze, ears peeled. A voice, pitched low but clearly angry cut through the winds, then a thud, muffled but audible, followed swiftly by the clap of running feet coming her way.

Kerensa pressed herself into the darkness of the shed, its rough wooden slats digging into her back and legs. A man, broad but short, head low, white breath misting before him, rushed past. Kerensa held her breath. He did not look up, but his gait was unmistakable. Carworan had not yet found his bed after all.

Releasing her pent breath in a rush, Kerensa felt her limbs go weak. A low whimper sounded from behind the shed Carworan had come from. Kerensa turned, her shuffling gait slow and careful as she made her way towards the sound. With each step her heart beat louder and louder, until its drumming filled her ears, blocking out the sound of the sea, the faint laugher of the men at the foreshore, of her own breathing. There was just the beat of her heart and the soft scuffling sounds from the alley ahead. At the corner of the shed she paused, breathing heavily, hands shaking. Forcing bravery to activate her limbs Kerensa swung herself around the shed to face whatever had been making those strange sounds and saw… nothing. The lane was empty, the moonlight illuminating nothing but black dirt and cliff rock. She shook her head, confused, sure she had heard a second voice drifting from the dark. Two shuffling steps into the alley stole what little light the moon could provide as it hid behind the shed roof. But it didn't matter, there was nothing to see. Kerensa turned and began the walk back to the main street, but something caught on her foot. Glancing down she saw something wrapped around her shoe. Reaching for the ground she pulled up a silky ribbon. It was bright red. She wiped the mud from the smooth material, caressing it gently with her thumb until its length was clean, then folded it into a neat square. With a single glance back into the murky alley she placed the folded ribbon down and started forward, heading for home as fast as her clubbed foot would take her.

Kerensa slept the rest of the night caught in a fitful dream. Starting awake she sat bolt upright in bed. Slowly, her eyes adjusted to the dim light of the oven fire glowing from the adjacent room. She breathed with purpose, taking her time to dismiss the night terrors from her mind before slipping from her bed and shuffling to the table.

The smell of baking bread filled the hut and Kerensa's tummy rumbled. Usually, that scent meant her mother's singing, meant food to break her fast, meant safety and security. But not that morning.

At the table Meliora sat motionless, illuminated by the glow of the coals, eyes cast down, a bowl of water at her elbow. In her hand she gripped a bright red ribbon.

Cautiously Kerensa pulled her stool to the table and sat across from her mother. Meliora didn't move. Kerensa shifted in her seat and Meliora looked up. Her eyes wide and unfocused, then suddenly sharp. Her pupils narrowed in the dim light, locking on her daughter's face. She reached out and gripped Kerensa's hands in hers, the silk of the ribbon rubbing between them.

"Trust it always, Kerensa. Trust the feeling in your gut, in your core."

She drew away, placing a hand upon her belly. "It knows more than your head knows. Always listen, Kerensa. Promise me you will always listen!"

She gripped her child's hand again, eyes staring straight and wild.

Kerensa swallowed and nodded in silence.

As if by magic her mother's face transformed, the hagged lines, the red-rimmed eyes, the twisted mouth, melted into her usual settled and calm facade, and she stood. Walking to the stove her light and bouncy morning voice rang out, "Freshly baked is always best. With oven warm bread you don't need any toppings!" She pulled the golden brown loaf from the oven and brought it to the table. Knife in hand she began to slice the loaf as though it were any other winter morn.

But Kerensa saw the shake that trembled along her mother's fingers, and the long, angry mark that graced her left temple and cheek, still dappled in port side mud.

Carefully, she reached out and slid her finger through the butter waiting to be spread. Rising on to her tiptoes she gently palmed the butter over the bruise forming on her mother's face.

"All better," she smiled as she took a slice of bread for herself.

Meliora stared at her in wonder, tears threatening to fall.

"Yes, all better," she agreed.

Goose Fat and Brown Paper Bags

Doctor Mayard shook his head.

"I'm sorry," he said, voice firm but kind as he stood from the cot by the window.

Meraud's hand flew to her mouth, covering her lips, holding in the wail of pain that threatened to break free. Swiftly she turned from the room and strode for her kitchen, shoulders quaking.

Silently Kerensa watched the young doctor as he made his way from the hut.

Braneh had sent Rewan to St Endellion to fetch him. Meraud had sent Gerens for Meliora. The people of Porth Gwynn might shun Kerensa's mother, but they were also a superstitious bunch; doctors didn't know all the ways of healing that were valued on the coast.

Not like Meliora.

A cough rang through the four rooms of the port side cottage. Moist, thick, fat.

"Fetch me a fresh cloth, Kerensa," Meliora said, passing the now warm cloth into her waiting hands. Kerensa nodded, dropping the cloth into the bucket of water, sage floating on its surface, that sat at her side and fishing out a fresh soaked one. Folding it carefully she passed it back to her mother.

Gently Meliora laid the dripping cloth over the forehead of the small boy. Treeve lay on a makeshift cot in the main room of Braneh and Meraud's home, the soft light of autumn morning casting his face in pale shades.

Meraud returned, a fresh bowl of fish broth in her hands.

"Will he take some?" she asked Meliora, her eyes scanning the body of her youngest son. His small body slick with sweat, his lips chapped with the cry for water. The words hovered between them. It wasn't the real question Meraud held within her. Meliora answered the one in a mother's heart.

"We must try."

Meloria stood and gently lifted Treeve's head, sitting herself behind him to brace him in an upright position, making room for Treeve's mother to perch upon the cot. Carefully, Meraud filled a spoon with broth and brought it to her child's mouth. Treeve's lips opened, accepting the salty fluid, his throat bobbed as he swallowed. Meliora nodded and Meraud served another spoon and another. Treeve's throat hitched, a small sound like a hiccup straining from his neck. Then the cough returned, his chest heaved, his boney ribs almost flattening against themselves as he fought to suck in air, fought to clear the green sludge from his chest.

The cough flattened and Treeve leaned over, mouth open, gaping. Meraud looked up at Meliora in horror.

Treeve was not breathing.

Meliora's face was a mask of calm, what she felt inside even Kerensa could not tell. Calmly, she began to rub Treeve's skinny back in large sweeping motions. Then she brought her hand back and smacked the centre of his back, once, twice, hard. A rush of air left Treeve's chest and a glob of green flew from his mouth to splat on the floor. Treeve wobbled in Meloria's arms, too weak to hold himself up. Suddenly his stomach clenched, his face a rictus of pain, and with another flurry of coughing, the broth his mother had just fed him and the water from earlier vomited to the floor.

Meliora calmly resumed rubbing his back until the boy had emptied himself, his body now only retching air. Gently she laid him back. His skin was burning, hot to the touch, but now his body began to shiver.

"Blankets, all you have spare," she ordered Meraud.

The mother looked up, startled. "But he is burning up!"

"And yet he shivers. We must warm him up until the shaking stops, burn the fever out. The cold cloths only help when he feels hot himself."

Nodding, Meraud rushed from the room leaving Kerensa alone with her mother and Treeve. Meliora reached into her basket and produced a jar of goose fat. Carefully she began to smooth the fat over the sleeping boy's chest, before laying a brown paper bag over the grease, to hold in the warmth of his body, trapped and sealed to his skin. Kerensa looked down at the small boy. He was longer than last summer, but much leaner, his cheeky grin gone, his eyes hollow.

"Dr Mayard said…"

"I know."

"Will he?" she couldn't finish the question.

'Not without a fight," Meliora answered.

They stayed the night, sleeping on the floor in the main room, her mother at constant vigil, watching, pouring water into the sleeping child's mouth, then broth, then teas of nettle and moss and sage. Meraud stayed with them, cradling her boy, singing to him, wrapping him in her own warmth as he shivered.

Kerensa watched on the periphery, mind blank, acting only when ordered by her mother.

Time became meaningless, was it today or tomorrow, dusk or dawn? At some hour Braneh looked in but soon left. Later Rewan, then Gerens and Cardor.

Gerens stayed the longest, standing by Kerensa's side. He took her hand. It shocked her, but she didn't pull away. She understood. She was scared too.

The night was dark, darker than before, or at least it seemed. Outside thick storm clouds blocked the moon and rain lashed the Port. Treeve's cough still sounded, but weaker now, his tiny body exhausted. Meliora tended the fire, stoking the flames, Meraud stroked the sweat drenched hair from Treeve's forehead and sang a lullaby. Kerensa drifted to sleep.

She woke. Light, bright and white shone in her eyes. The window shutters were open. A blue day had broken, a truly spring day. Seeing the blue skies Kerensa's heart filled with hope. Sitting up she looked over to Treeve's cot. Meraud was hunched over her boy, as if in sleep. Kerensa rose, moving to take the bucket from her side and freshen the water, but a hand on her shoulder stopped her. Meloria shook her head gently and gestured her to follow.

Her cheeks were wet with tears.

St Endellion, named for St Endelienta, the dying saint who ordered herself taken up the hill and died where the church now stood, served the people of Porth Gwynn in life and today, death. The whole town attended the funeral, walking the hour to St Endellion as one to watch as Treeve's father and brothers lowered him into the fresh dug earth.

His lifeless body encompassed by a wooden box Braneh crafted himself. Treeve was only three. The box felt too large for his body, as though he had shrivelled in death.

Pastor Henry read a sermon, but nobody heard. Treeve was not the only soul taken by the late autumn illness that swept the village, but he was the youngest. In a small village such a loss touches every heart. Kerensa watched as Braneh, his normally imposing figure now diminished, walked back to his wife and wrapped an arm about her shoulders. Meraud did not react. She had not made a sound at all during the walk to the church yard, nor during the service. She simply stood in silence, her eyes fixed ahead unseeing.

It wasn't until the first shovel of soil hit the coffin that she moved, launching into action, screaming at her sons to stop. Startled and terrified Rewan, Geren and Cardor froze. Kerensa watched on through a veil of her own tears of grief as Braneh wrapped his powerful arms about his wife and held her, whispering gently in her ear, holding her upright as her legs gave way and her cries turned to howls of loss. Tears streaking down their faces, the boys resumed their morbid task, filling the hole to lay their brother to eternal rest.

As they made their way slowly back to town Kerensa was sure she heard curses on the wind, "Witch", "Child-killer". Then clearly heard over them all, Carworan's voice, "bastard cripple. It was a sign, I told you all. She's an ill omen."

Behind them Braneh cleared his throat loudly. The whispers stopped. But Kerensa's face still burned with shame. She didn't fully understand the meanings being breathed into the air on hushed but angry voices, but she knew it was about her, and the meaning was clear. She was 'wrong'. Pulling her shoulders in tight, shrinking herself down, she continued on.

When Kerensa and her mother arrived home, Meliora flew into a rage. Kerensa had seen her mother angry before, when the children at the market threw stones at 'the cripple', when Carworan called her 'whore', her eyes had burned with fire. But those times were nothing on that evening after laying Treeve into the ground.

"How dare he!" she exclaimed, pacing their tiny hut in a fury.

Kerensa stood silently at the door, unconsciously giving her mother as much space as possible to stomp and shout.

"He was just a boy! A little boy!"

Oh, Kerensa realised, her mother was angry with God for taking Treeve. That was an anger she well understood. Sister Pierce and

Pastor Henry always said she should trust in the Lord's ways. But when Kerensa's foot ached so badly she had to remain in bed, or when her belly went empty days in a row or her mother came home with more bruises on her arms, she too wanted to shout at heaven.

"It's all right mother," she ventured.

Meliora whirled around to her daughter bringing her face right up to Kerensa's.

"It is not!" she spat, face flashing red, eyes wide and watering. "A child is an innocent! God will always take them straight to Heaven. How dare he suggest otherwise because the boy was unshriven! Or that honest prayer may have held his soul with us for longer. Where were we to get a Priest that night? I've never seen him come to our town. How could he say that! Put that onto Meraud in her grief? Pastor indeed." She spun away from Kerensa and commenced her fruitless pacing once more.

Now Kerensa stood in frozen silence. Mother was angry with Pastor Henry? What was 'unshriven'?

Meliora stopped in the middle of the room and took a gulping breath. Brushing tears of hate from her eyes she turned and smiled at Kerensa.

"I'm sorry little one," she said, extending her arms for a hug, "come."

Kerensa, overwhelmed by the emotions of the day, the tears of the town, the screams of Meraud and now, this outburst from her mother, ran into Meliora's arms and promptly began to cry.

Meliora gathered her daughter into her arms, rocking her side to side, gentling caressing her hair until she calmed.

"It's all right my little one, it's all right. I'm sorry. I was just so... it doesn't matter. All is well."

Once Kerensa's breathing returned to normal, Meliora gently lifted her daughter's face to hers. Where fury had twisted her features into something Kerensa did not recognise, now the familiar calm kindness of her mother had returned.

"You are all right now mother?" Kerensa asked tentatively.

"I am," Meliora replied, "But Kerensa there is something you must know, something very, very important. Are you listening?"

Still bewildered by everything the day had shown her, Kerensa nodded warily.

Meliora sniffed and flicked a lock of her hair out of her eyes with a shake of her head.

"No matter what anyone says, anyone, remember this truth. God sees you," she tapped Kerensa's chest right above the place where she felt her heart pound when she ran or when she was afraid. "He sees the real you and that is all that matters. Not the words of some Priest or the rules of men. God does not follow those rules. He follows the light. True goodness, in here, inside us all. You are a good person Kerensa, God sees that, nothing anyone else ever says can take that away from you. Do you hear me?"

Confused, but seeing the desperate glow in her mother's eyes, Kerensa nodded her small head and wrapped her arms around her mother's neck. Meliora returned the embrace, allowing her daughter to snuggle close. Determination flared within her gut once more, she would protect her child from this world, whatever the cost to herself.

A week later a knock sounded on Kerensa's mother's hut. Meliora went to the door, but where a visitor should have stood sat a jar of stewed apples and pears. Curious, Kerensa joined her mother, looking out across the bay to the little village they were part of, and also not.

"Pick it up Kerensa," Meliora said, moving back into their home.

Kerensa did as bid, bending down and plucking the jar from the dirt. The slices swam in water thick with sugar and cinnamon, cloves floating at the rim.

"What is this for?" she asked her mother.

"It is a thank you," Meliora replied.

"For what?"

"For trying."

Interlude

City folk think of winter as the tough time, the lean time. But you and I know better daughter. Winter is cold, and harsh and dark and filled with the threat of sickness, but there is food for our bellies, stored roots, winter leaves, salted fish; there is wood for fires, and stoves, there is wool for blankets, clocks and shawls. Huddled in our homes we pass the times of snow and ice, door closed to the winds that whip the jagged coastline we call home. Perched in our hut we make our tinctures, feed Eia, tend the vegetables, mend our summer clothes in preparation for the spring. For then the days begin to lengthen and the earth begins to thaw, still months until the fish will run, the Huer's post unmanned, the lean time begins.

March, the hunger gap, the month of little, the month of lent, the time between seasons for the edible plants of the land. Weak from the long cold time inside, the dark days and smoky air, we venture outside, called by the pale sun that shines upon the tender green shoots of new growth peeking out from beneath the icy earth. It is cold still, but the air that cuts the lungs has mellowed, growing heavier with water and warmth. And with the strengthening sun comes the western winds, bringing warmer air from the south, and rain. So much rain. We have no choice but to plant our crops as the clouds dump upon the land. We are forced inside again. But the air is different now, it is moist and heavy, it lays thick inside the chest.

As our stored roots begin to wither and shrink, our reserves of salted fish run low, our flour moulds in the humid temperatures, our bodies crave the fresh bite of spinach, the crunch of apple from a tree, the juice of a blackberry. And if the sickness of winter returns… fevers not fully burnt out before the seasons change, the call of renewal, the call of spring planting, the drive to restock and restore our supplies, weakens us as the sunlight lifts and our lungs fill with rot.

Treeve taught us that. The image of his tiny body contorted with pain haunted my mind and every season since, I have met the changing winds with trepidation. Fearing to see you wither as he had done. I prayed and fretted until the first chipples burst their bright green heads from the soil, begging to be made into pie.

And you did not wither. Despite it all, my child, you grew stronger and stronger. You were becoming a woman.

PART 2

The Huer's Cry

The soft earth felt good in Kerensa's hands. Using the small trowel as her mother showed her when she was but a child, she turned the earth and placed the seeds for turnips, lettuce, parsley and pumpkin, saved and dried from last year's harvest, covering them gently ready to sprout and grow. At her side Eia clucked and scratched and searched for bugs. She had grown thin these last months, nearing the end of her life. The past seven years her egg laying had been exceptional, keeping Kerensa and her mother happily fed each morning. But this year as the autumn sun faded into winter, Kerensa stopped collecting her eggs to give her a rest from laying. A chicken won't lay if she has a batch to nest. She was too old now to produce eggs so frequently. Meliora lamented that they'd let her live too long, she'd be nothing but gristle and bone by now. But Kerensa didn't care. Since Eia came to stay, she'd decided she didn't even like chicken.

Overhead the sun shone bright and strong in the clear blue sky. Sitting back on her heels she wiped the sweat from her eyes and watched as a gull rode the winds that whipped up from the shore, ducking and weaving, hovering. It was almost as if it were playing. Spring was giving way to summer, soon the men who worked the local farms in the off season would return for the fish run and her town, so quiet in these in-between months, would once again come to life with the sound of fishermen yelling, saws cutting wood and nails sealing barrels, the scent of fresh paint over last year's peeling bows, of fish guts and slime, of salt and sweat.

But there would be a few more weeks of the quiet yet.

Kerensa finished her last row of vegetables. Standing she placed her hands on the small of her back and leaned back, stretching the aching muscles here. It was a nice ache though, the ache of a job completed, unlike the ache from her ankle. Pushing the thought aside, Kerensa washed her hands and trowel in the bucket drying both on her skirts. Reaching down to give Eia a quick pat she headed inside, blocking the back door open with a stone so the old chook could follow at her leisure. She slept on one of Kerensa's old smocks by the oven everyday now, not just when it snowed, the warmth of the fire soothing her old bones.

The light from outside cut a bright swathe through the home, Kerensa walked about the main room, reaching up to gently squeeze the bundles of drying herbs that lined the ceiling to check their progress. The thyme was done, the sage not far off. Tonight she could start the bottling for sale.

A knock came at the door. Smiling to herself Kerensa opened the door. Derwa stood in the entranceway, practically bouncing out of her skin.

She didn't wait for an invite, but barrelled into Meliora's hut. "He's coming back! Jory ran ahead to tell mother and me. The men are returning. Today!"

She spun on her heel heading back out the doorway where Kerensa still stood. Stopping on the step she turned to her friend. "Well, aren't you coming? You haven't seen him since December. Surely you are as eager as I am to see how much stronger his shoulders have become! Come on!"

A wicked light glinted in her eyes as Derwa gripped her friend's hand and pulled. Kerensa paused, the herbs needed grinding, the meal sifting and the roots were as yet unprepared... Derwa looked back at Kerensa, eyes shining with mischief and enthusiasm.

The roots could wait.

The two girls walked arm in arm down the gently sloping hill into the town. The sun shone bright on their hair, glossy with youth and promise, accenting the red highlights that hid among Derwa's brown mop. The scarcity of winter laid their bodies thin, but could not deny the budding curves of womanhood that refused to be denied. Not yet old enough for marriage, but it would not be long, and their thoughts and dreams had certainly turned to plans for such a future.

In Derwa's case such plans were also constantly on her tongue. Kerensa, keeping pace beside her friend despite her limp, held such hopes close and private, her secret fear that her malformed foot would keep any would-be suitor at bay. Even Rewan.

She had come to understand the taunts some folk threw her way.

45

She was born deformed. It was a bad sign. And the fish-runs were dwindling. But where the girl had shrunk from the words, trying to hide from the superstitious talk, the young woman stood tall and faced the jeers in the full light of the sun. She remained on the edge of town, but her friendship with the wild-hearted friend now at her side brought her within the fold more and more. And Kerensa was determined to embrace that.

Coming into the main street of town, Kerensa felt her lips curve in a joyous smile. The news had travelled, the men were returning. Along the street wives and daughters and toddling boys waited at their doors in the sun. Pots of flowers kept in the shade of huts were placed now along the pebbled foreshore, a vivid splash of colour to welcome them home. The air was electric with anticipation and joy.

It had been a hard winter and spring, the fish yield from the previous season had been low, yet the rent on the nets and catch still increased. Even Braneh, who owned his own fishing boat, had had to take up his hoe and shovel and, Rewan and Gerens by his side, take to the neighbouring farms that spread out from the coast in search of extra work.

But now, with the rising heat proclaiming summer's height, they returned.

Tonight there would be a celebration. A feast. The abundance of spring produce saved carefully over the past season, now prepared with abandon. Mouths watering at the possibility that a man may bring back a lamb or even beef leg to roast and share.

The girls took up a spot on the foreshore, bay at their backs. The waters were peaceful today, only a gentle breeze ruffling their skirts, the waves lapping softly on the rocks. High tide.

And they waited.

It was not long before the tell-tale cry started up the street. Beyond where the girls could see, blocked by the natural curve of the town, came the cheer. Derwa squeezed Kerensa's arm, bouncing on the balls of her feet.

"Do you see them? Kerensa? Do you?"

Kerensa laughed at her friend's exuberance and smiled, "Soon, Derwa, soon."

And soon it was. The cheers and laughter rolled down the street, bouncing from the cottage walls, the sound of heavy footfall and patter of little feet. They rounded the curve striding as one into the village centre. Braneh, Meraud on his arm, led the procession. He pressed a kiss to his wife's forehead. Meraud grinned up at her husband, the lines that had marked her face with grief since the winter of sickness years before, temporarily transformed to joy. Behind them strode Gerens and Rewan, little Wenna, Peran's daughter riding Rewan's shoulders, her father's occupied by her twin Eseld. Peran's wife Embyn walked proudly beside them. Jago, arm wrapped about Mabyn's waist, smiled to Derwa, who ran to greet her father and older brother Jory happily. The line stretched on, the whole town emptying onto the streets. As they passed Kerensa fell in with Derwa and her family, all heading for the edge of the fishing sheds, where they would stop and group to hear the stories of the men's spring farming and share the warmth and joy of each other's company.

Gerens moved alongside Kerensa, and she smiled at her oldest friend.

"How was it?" she asked.

"Long," he replied, "it's good to be home."

Kerensa laughed. Gerens hated physical work, but he did what needed to be done.

"It's good to have you."

Gerens smiled, his gentle mouth curving softly. "You…"

"Kerensa! You are looking well. Spring has been good to you I see."

Kerensa looked up. Keeping pace on her other side strode Rewan, shoulders still filled with the giggling Wenna. He flicked a flop of light brown curls from his eyes and gifted her his smile. Still lopsided, still dazzling. His eyes scanned her face, her body, a new light twinkling there.

Kerensa swallowed, suddenly shy. He always called her Kerensa, never Kez like the others. She loved how her name sounded on his lips, it made her knees weak. A strange energy coursed through her body, her tummy a bundle of butterflies fluttering. She felt the heat rising to her cheeks and cursed her fair skin. Derwa saved her.

"And you too are looking fine, Rewan. I swear your shoulders are twice as wide." Derwa said, an unashamed flirt.

Rewan threw back his head and laughed, "Farm work is good training for the sea," he replied. But his eyes never left Kerensa's face.

"Rewan!"

The group looked up. Braneh stood at the front of the first shed, beaming across at his sons. "Come help your mother. We've a feast to prepare!"

"Coming father," Rewan called, and, winking quickly at Kerensa, mouth still twisted in that cheeky grin, lengthened his stride to his father's side.

Noon mellowed to evening and then darkened into night. The town remained collected sharing stories, food and ale, laughter and song. Kerensa and Derwa sat together, Derwa gossiping, Kerensa giggling and feigning shock. Her friend really was the most terrible liar.

"And his hair is the colour of gold, and his eyes, oh Kez, his eyes!"

Kerensa shoved her friend playfully, "Derwa you are the worst!" she exclaimed. "No boy could be so beautiful."

"Not a boy, a man Kez, a man. He works for Mr Symonds. That's why he was at the markets in St Endellion. When our eyes met we just knew."

"How romantic, if it were true."

Derwa frowned at her friend, then her face lit, mischief once again playing over her features.

"What about you... and Rewan? I saw how he looked at you this afternoon."

"There is no 'me and Rewan', he was just being polite."

Derwa rolled her eyes, "*That* look was not polite Kez. He likes you. Has for years. It's obvious."

"You have such an imagination Derwa," Kerensa dismissed her friend's words. But deep inside a tiny flare of hope ignited. She snuck a look over to where Rewan sat with his father and brothers, Meraud had already retired to bed. She found his eyes on her, shining in the candlelight, lips curved in a secret smile. Heat flushed her face again and she quickly looked away.

Weeks passed, shadows lengthened, the town waited, the Huer perched atop the cliff, watching. Meliora returned, Kerensa and her mother prepared herbs and tinctures. Meliora left. Hot days, hot nights, sweat slick over her limbs. The breezes dropped, heavy moisture-laden air weighed down the sky, thick and sticky.

And the town waited, in limbo, poised to strike.

Waiting, waiting to hear the Huer's cry - that the fish run had begun.

The Folly

The knock on the door was soft, but the call for her attention was not. Derwa's voice, urgent and firm, pierced Kerensa's fitful dreams. Rubbing her eyes, Kerensa sat up and swung her legs over the edge of her bed. The air was thick and hot, her skin covered in a thin film of sweat. A poor night for sleep.

Coming to her door she frowned at Derwa. Her friend stood smiling in the dirt, dressed in her Church clothes and shoes. "Derwa?" she asked. "What are you doing out so late? And why are you wearing that?"

Derwa huffed, placing her hands on her hips. "Are you coming with me or not?" she pouted.

"Coming where?"

"Just put on your day dress Kez, I'll explain on the way. I'm already late."

"Already late? Derwa, it's the middle of the night!"

"Exactly!"

Derwa's eyes shone in the pale moonlight, mischief dancing across their dark pools. Kerensa paused, but only for a moment. She rushed inside and donned her dress, running a quick hand through her sleep matted curls before stepping out into the cool of night. Sure this was the wrong decision, she followed her friend down the path to the village anyway.

Derwa turned sharp left and cut along the outside edge of the village, lifting her skirt to free her legs to stride purposefully through the low shrubbery of the hillside. Kerensa rushed to follow. "Derwa," she hissed, "where are we going?"

"You'll see," Derwa replied, smile curving mysteriously.

Forehead furrowed, Kerensa worked to keep pace with her rushing friend.

Soon they cleared the village and started up the steep cliffside that framed the Port. Below, the waters of the bay caressed the rocky shore. All else was silent; the town, the gulls, the pigs and chickens, all asleep. As the two friends climbed the steep path Kerensa realised where they must be going. Tension worked its way across her shoulders and she longed to turn back. But she would not abandon her friend, however foolhardy she may be.

The night air thickened, the land at their feet still giving off the warmth of the long day's hot sun. Beads of sweat collected on Kerensa's brow and nape, a few growing too large and rushing down her spine to pool at the waist of her skirt. Her ankle began to ache. Only yesterday she'd made the long trek into the markets at St Endellion to sell her mother's tinctures, such a walk always meant days of pain. Remembering the busy market, the varied stalls, the heat of the sun and the smiles of her customers, Kerensa felt pride swell in her chest. She was good at market sales. But concern pulled the corners of her mouth down as she thought of her friend striding before her, and the young man, who was indeed very blonde, she'd spied Derwa talking with that day. They'd seemed far too familiar. Recalling the way he'd watched Derwa as she walked away, Kerensa was now certain she knew their destination.

It soon came into sight. Bright candlelight spilled from the tall stone windows, a beacon atop the highest cliff overlooking their portion of the Atlantic.

The Folly Castle of their benefactor, Samuel Symons. Doyden Castle.

He'd come to visit the town when her mother first moved here with her father. Meliora had told her of his confident step, his shining suit and silk cravat in bright purple, his manicured beard and soft hands. Soon after the workers had arrived, demanding a bed in each cottage for the duration of their stay. Then carts filled with pre-cut stone arrived as well as sheets of clear material to cover the window holes. While the folk of the port caught and gutted fish, their young billets toiled on the cliff top erecting a new house, built to represent a castle, overlooking the port and sea, to house Mr Symons and his rich guests on their infrequent escapes to the coast for parties and card games.

Rarely in Kerensa's lifetime had she seen Doyden Castle occupied, but the golden glow of light from within told her Symons was currently in residence. As they neared, the sound of music and laughter drifted to their ears. Kerensa put on a spurt of speed and grabbed her friend's arm.

"What are you doing Derwa? This isn't a place for the likes of us."

"It's all right," Derwa said, "we aren't going inside! Charlie said he would slip out when the men start on the brandy. Says they'll never miss him. He's going to meet us by the servant door. Come on."

Swallowing her protest, Kerensa followed.

They cut a wide berth around the building, hunching down to avoid the light that poured from the windows, across the summer grasses. The darkness hid them, but illuminated the gentlemen within. Ties removed, shirts open to stave off the humid night, mouths wide in laughter, eyes bright with drink, hands holding cards, or cigars, or fancy goblets of amber liquid. Their haircuts were short and styled, their beards neatly trimmed. The type of men Kerensa had only ever seen from a distance and didn't fancy getting any closer to. As they rounded the castle Kerensa gripped Derwa's hand and froze. A shadow moved along the side wall.

Derwa grinned to Kerensa and rushed ahead, one hand waving frantically. The figure stopped and moved to Derwa. They met in the half-light of the leaking windows and kissed. His hands far more liberal with her body than Kerensa thought appropriate. At length Derwa pulled back and waved Kerensa over.

Tentatively, Kerensa stepped forward. Charlie came into focus, a gentle face, kind eyes, misted now with lust, but none-the-less kind. She felt herself relax. He couldn't have been much more than a year their senior, and as green as new spring grass. For all Derwa's proclamations this serving boy was, well, still a boy.

"Hello," Charlie greeted Kerensa. He sounded nervous.

Kerensa nodded to him.

Derwa spoke into the awkward silence, 'Sooo, did you bring it?"

A cheeky grin flashed across Charlie's face. "Of course," he said reaching into his pocket, "I had to be careful, so Master didn't see. But he'll never miss it."

Pulling his hand free Charlie proudly displayed a small, clear bottle. Dark fluid sloshed within.

Derwa let out a muted squeal of delight. "Come on, let's sit over there and have some."

She led the group a few paces from the castle to sit in the dry, windswept grass. Plonking down, her skirts puffed out around her, she snatched the bottle from Charlie, popped the little cork and tossed her head back to drink the glistening liquid.

Coughing and spluttering Derwa almost spat the contents out.

Laughing, Charlie chided, "I told you it was strong. 10 years old that scotch. Have another swig, but slowly."

Eyes glittering, Derwa complied, taking a gentle sip. She still coughed, but held the whiskey down. "Kez?" she offered the bottle to Kerensa. Kerensa paused, she wanted to, but something was tingling down her spine. She paused.

"Come on, it's nice once you get used to it!"

"Ok," she reached forward and took the bottle. Derwa and Charlie watched as she brought it carefully to her lips and drank. A deep, warming burn poured down her throat, like liquid flame. She too coughed, then grinned at her friends as a strange, but welcome warmth spread through her belly and fuzzed her mind.

Laughing, Charlie took the bottle back and took a sip before stretching out to watch the skies move above them. The trio sat in silence, listening to the music emanating from the castle.

Suddenly Charlie sat up, head cocked as if listening.

"Shit," he said, jumping to his feet. "That's my name he's calling."

He turned to race back to the castle, but he was too late. The servant's door swung open casting them all in candle and fire-light.

A tall, well dressed man ambled out, cigar smoke billowing before him.

The friends stood quickly, gripping each other's hands in sudden fear.

"Ah, there you are Charlie! Been looking everywhere for you. Well, well, who are these young ladies then? Eh?"

"Sorry, sir, I, ah, this is…"

The man gave a deep chuckle.

"It's all right Charlie, I was young once too." The man stepped forward. The light behind him cast his features in shadow so Kerensa could not make out his face. But he could see them.

"Pretty girls Charlie, well done lad. Why don't you ladies join us inside? We've whiskey and wine and I'm sure Cook could put together some cheeses if you're hungry. Come on in. I'm feeling generous."

Derwa stepped forward. Kerensa grabbed her hand, shaking her head. She didn't know why but something, something just didn't feel right. "Let's go home Derwa, you can stay at mine. We can bake some shortbread and play with Eia," she whispered urgently.

Derwa frowned at Kerensa, "Are you not listening? We've been invited in! Opportunities like this don't just come along you know.

Come on."

Kerensa stood firm, and did not release her friend's hand.

Derwa let out a heavy sigh, "Suit yourself, but I'm going." She shook her hand free and walked boldly towards the brightly lit doorway.

Kerensa stood frozen in indecision. Then, of its own accord, her foot stepped forward, following her friend as she always did. But Meliora's voice boomed in her head, "If it doesn't feel right, trust your gut." She heard a muted thump and saw a bright red ribbon in the mud.

Breath coming short she stepped back.

"Not coming young lady?" the gentleman asked politely, a hint of mockery lacing his tone. He shrugged elegantly. "No matter, we'll have enough fun for two, won't we dear," he pinched Derwa's cheek and her friend, Charlie, and the silhouetted man stepped inside and closed the door.

She could have gone home, she didn't. She could have knocked on the door and demanded to see her friend. She didn't.

Time passed slowly. Kerensa crept to the large window of light and peered inside. The men still laughed and drank, heads slumping now, some asleep on the lavish lounges that lined the room. But she could not see her friend, or Charlie.

She waited.

As the sky began to lighten and the birds cawed, Kerensa still waited.

Finally, when the first golden rays of the sun were peaking over the sea, Derwa stumbled out of the servant door. Alone.

Kerensa rushed forward to her. "Derwa! Are you all right? You were gone for hours! It's almost day."

Derwa wavered on her feet. Kerensa took her arms to steady her, but her friend lurched away. "Don't touch me!" she cried, "I'm fine."

Her eyes were glazed, her breath reeked of drink, she wobbled on her feet.

"Come on," Kerensa said, "You can sleep it off at mine before you go home."

She wrapped her arm about Derwa's waist to hold her steady on the walk back. Derwa stiffened. "It's all right," Kerensa soothed, "It's me, I'm taking you back to mine, yes?"

Derwa nodded, tears now glistening in her eyes, spilling slowly down her cheeks. Her body quaked, tremors running beneath the skin.

Kerensa held her firm, lending her strength.

One step at a time Kerensa led her friend back down the cliff, behind the town and up to her mother's hut. Inside she lit a candle, gave Derwa water to drink and offered her some bread and cheese. Derwa waved them away then rushed out the back to empty her stomach in the soil by the front door. Coming back in, she apologised sheepishly.

"It's all right, Derwa. You just need some sleep," Kerensa said, stomach cramping at the sight of her friend in the candlelight.

She took Derwa's hands gently and drew her to sit at the table. First, she gently washed her friend's face with water, then Kerensa led her into the bedroom and helped her from her Sunday dress and into Meliora's nightgown. Finally the friends lay down on the bed, Kerensa pulling the blanket up over them both to banish the early morning chill from their bones.

"It will be all right, Derwa. Sleep now." She repeated, fighting back the tears that now filled her eyes too.

She held them back, hummed a lullaby and stroked Derwa's sleek brown hair until her friend's breathing became deep and slow.

Only then did she let her own tears fall. Lying on her back, staring at the ceiling, Kerensa cried. Tears soaking the collar of her dress and the pillow that cupped her head.

She had not missed the yellowing bruise on Derwa's cheek, the scratches along her thighs, the tear in the hem of her Sunday dress, nor the blood on her shift.

She may have only seen 15 summers, but Kerensa knew what those things meant. Looking over at her friend again to check she still slept, Kerensa slipped from the bed and shuffled into the main room. Standing on tiptoe she pulled down Meliora's sewing kit, selected a patch and fibre. She stoked the oven fire, threw Derwa's blood stained shift on the flames and settled down with Derwa's dress across her lap. By the oven Eia cooed, outside the sky brightened and Kerensa mended her friend's best dress.

Carrot Seeds and Raspberry Leaf Tea

"Hevva!"

The Huer called from the cliff top, waving his white bushes high in the air. And the town came alive. The quiet pause between the return of the men from the farms, the time of waiting and preparing, a tension building in the air, suddenly released. Women, girls and older men gathered up the seines and waded into the bay. The boat crews drew their bows into the lapping waves and heaved their oars against the tide, stroking along the long inlet of Porth Gwynn.

Kerensa watched the flurry of activity, eyes scanning until she found who she'd ventured down from her hut to see. Derwa waded in the shallows, dress hitched high, hands full of netting, her mother Mabyn and older sister Gwen at her side. From the shore Kerensa could not make out her features, nor judge her mood. Yet, despite the buzz of excitement and hope that rang around the town with the season's beginning, Derwa's shoulders seemed slumped, her usual springy walk flat.

Kerensa's eyes drifted up from her friend, drawn by the even pacing of the row boats as they cleared the shallows. Even from here she could make him out. Rewan, sitting taller than his brothers beside him, his broad shoulders stretching and pulling. Blushing, Kerensa turned from the bay and put her friend and Rewan from her mind. Both were occupied by their tasks, it was time Kerensa focused on her own.

Meliora had been gone for longer than usual. Kerensa suspected she was trading at one of the farther towns beyond Polzeath. She would come home soon, she always did. In the meantime it was up to Kerensa to maintain their supplies of herbs and tinctures, especially now the fish run had begun. Fish work meant strained limbs, cuts that could fester, sunburn that blistered. In short, work for the town meant

55

work for her and her mother.

Worried for Derwa after the recent events at Doyden Castle, Kerensa had remained home, tending her garden, relaxing in the cool of the house and enjoying the company of Eia. She had hoped her friend would come to visit and talk. So had put off the needed foraging trip she knew was pressing.

But Derwa had not come.

Twice Kerensa had ventured into town to seek her friend, but Derwa was not home, Mabyn unaware of her daughter's whereabouts. Today, Kerensa had come down earlier, skirting the first rays of daylight, hoping to catch her friend before she set off to wherever she was spending her in-between days. But the cry of the Huer had put an end to that plan as the town swung into action. Whatever Derwa had been doing these past few weeks had come to an end. As had Kerensa's excuses to stay at home.

Kerensa tried to set her worries aside and focus on her task. The excitement of the sight of shining silver pilchards and the promise of a full belly tempered by her concern for her friend, she struck out across the cliff, skirting well under Castle Doyden. She'd no desire to see that ugly folly again. She walked until the sun rose high above her head then cut inland to search between the low growing bushes, patches of bright purple heather and wind-stunted trees. Soon, the gentle breezes, the buzz of bees and other insects, the floral scent of sage and comforting weight of a fennel bulb in her hand worked its magic, calming her mind, her body, her soul. As had happened since she'd first come out to forage with Meliora as a small child, Kerensa lost time, drifting around the wild flowers, avoiding the sharp bite of nettle and the tear of thorns, collecting her wares, at one with the world about her. At peace.

The sun sat low in the sky when Kerensa finally straightened from her search and stretched her back, lifting her right foot from the press of the ground to gain a temporary reprieve, before collecting up her basket and trowel and commencing her hobbling walk back to Porth Gwynn and home.

The last pale pink rays of the day danced across the calm waters of the bay as she came into town, the colours of evening and rest. But the streets were buzzing. Candles shone from the fish-sheds, water coursing through the pebbled streets as the nets were cleaned and hung to dry. The sharp stink of pilchard flesh already filled the streets with its ocean tang. Inside the sheds she knew Derwa and the others worked to strip the scales from the silver-bellied fish, before splitting their fat bellies open to purge their entrails. Hopeful gulls hovered in wait in the skies above. Tonight the candles would burn late in her white cove town, a silent companion to her own deep night work: stripping herbs of leaves, bundling them to dry and boiling down nettle and fennel for teas and tinctures.

Kerensa stopped dead in her tracks. The sun was only just peaking its sleepy head over the waters of the bay. The town, exhausted from the first day of the fish-run and the night of processing that followed, was only just beginning to stir, the soft scent of baking bread coating the still, dewy air. Kerensa had risen before the dawn. Keen to travel out further in her foraging, she needed an early start.

She hadn't expected to see him.

Sitting on the rocks that lined the foreshore, watching the tide slowly leeching from the beach, was Charlie.

A hiss escaped Kerensa's lips. The calm of the dawn shattered by the sight of his light blonde hair floating up from his head in the morning breeze. Face set with determination, Kerensa stalked towards him. At the sound of her footfall, Charlie turned, Derwa's name on his lips, hope in his eyes.

Seeing Kerensa he pulled back, surprised, then tried a wary smile. The smile faded.

"What are you doing here?" Kerensa demanded.

"I, I'm here for her, for Derwa," Charlie stammered coming to his feet. "But I don't know which home is hers. Can you show me?"

"How dare you!" Kerensa cried, voice whipping like a stingray tail. "After what you did to her!"

"Did to her? I didn't do anything! It wasn't my fault. I couldn't stop... there was nothing I could do."

"So you watched, huh? As he took her, held her down? Couldn't stop it? What kind of man are you!"

"Please, Kerensa, listen. It wasn't like that. I, I tried, but…"

"Pathetic!" Kerensa spat.

"Look, I can understand your anger,' Charlie continued, voice firming with his purpose. "But I'm here to make it right. I'm here for Derwa, to take care of her." His resolve flagged before Kerensa's withering gaze. He swallowed, then squared his shoulders. "I left Mr Symonds," he said determinedly. "I'm here for Derwa, to marry her."

"Marry her? Ha!" Kerensa scoffed. "After what you did? With no job, no money or prospects!"

"I thought I'd come here, work the fish-run."

"And what crew has a spare place? You think you can just turn up and take another man's seat in a boat?" She shook her head in disbelief. *Fool!*

Charlie's eyes cast around, frantic. "Then I will work the sheds, I'm not too proud to get my hands dirty."

"The truest thing you've said." Kerensa stared into his face, eyes narrowed in anger. "Get out of here you swine. We don't want your kind here. And believe me, once I tell the people what you did, no one will hire you. You'd be lucky if someone so much as spat in your face."

Charlie closed his eyes and took a deep, calming breath, "I know you're angry, I know you blame me... but I'm not here for you Kerensa. I'm here for Derwa."

Rage shot through Kerensa's limbs. How dare this boy come for her friend, after everything Derwa had been through, everything she was suffering. Because of him!

No, Kerensa would not allow it.

"She doesn't want to see you. Why would she? After what you did," she said.

"I want to look after her."

"I'm her closest friend. *I* was there to care for her... after. Where were you?"

Kerensa huffed an exasperated breath and planted fists on her hips. "No, you had your chance, Charlie, and you did nothing. She hates you. Derwa *hates* you. She never wants to see your face again."

Shock stilled his features. His head shook slightly. "She said that?"

Kerensa set her lips with purpose. "Yes," she lied with confidence.

Charlie stopped, his whole being seemed to slump down into itself, hands limp at his sides.

"She doesn't want to see me?" he whispered, eyes dimming, lids welling with tears.

"Never, ever again. The thought of you sickens her," she added for good measure.

Charlie coughed away a sob from deep within his throat. He shuffled his feet as if caught between his choices. Unsure what to do.

Kerensa was happy to help. "Get out of my town," she growled, low and fierce. "Get out and never, ever return."

Tears now escaping to run across his downy cheeks, Charlie turned and fled.

* * *

The shadows lengthened, the breezes cooled, the pumpkins ripened and the landscape browned as the late autumn rains rotted leaves and turned the soil to mud. Meliora was home, mother and daughter working silently in-sync as they prepared a fresh batch of thyme tincture, ready to treat the coughs that would come with the deepening season. Kerensa stirred the fragrant tea as Meliora mashed a fresh paste of sorrel and end of season fennel for easing aches. The fish life was tough, and swollen hands and feet were a common complaint of the townsfolk, even in the off-season. Rain had beat the coast in bands of heavy showers all week, the bitter winds carrying the promise of winter as they whipped about Meliora's hut, reaching their frozen tendrils between the gaps in the wooden slats of the shutters. Eia slept peacefully beside the oven flames, thyme tea bubbled in the potfry nestled in the coals of the stove, the warmth of the steam welcome against the outside chill.

Against the wild Atlantic weather, the knock on their door was unexpected. Using her apron to wipe fennel and sorrel juice from her hands, Meliora made her way to the door. The glance between mother and daughter confirmed what they both were thinking: only one in desperate need would venture out in this storm.

"Derwa!" Meliora exclaimed in surprise. "Come in, come in my child."

She drew Derwa inside, shutting the door firmly behind her. Rivulets of water coursing down her skirts and pooling at her feet, Derwa stood shivering, her face flushed with cold, her lips blue. Her dark eyes, red-rimmed from rain or tears, shifted uneasily about the room, coming to rest on Kerensa.

Kerensa smiled gently.

Derwa quickly looked down.

Coming around Derwa, Meliora took her arm and guided the girl to the circle of the oven's warmth. "Kerensa, fetch a dry shift and blanket," Meliora said. Before calmly but firmly addressing Derwa, "Child, we will dress you in Kerensa's shift and set your dress to dry. You'll catch cold in this wet cloth."

Derwa didn't reply, didn't seem to have even heard Meliora. Something was terribly wrong.

Kerensa rushed from the room to fetch the shift. Returning a moment later she helped her mother to strip the wet dress from Derwa's shaking body and clothe her in the dry shift. After bundling

Derwa in a scratchy but thick woollen blanket, Meliora settled her on a stool by the stove before taking a seat by her daughter to wait. Following her mother's lead, Kerensa remained in silence. Slowly the colour returned to Derwa's cheeks and her quaking body stilled.

Meliora reached forward and took the girl's hands in hers. "When did you last bleed?" she asked gently.

Kerensa looked up at her mother, startled.

"Before the fish returned," Derwa replied, voice flat, eyes downcast.

"May I touch your belly?"

Derwa said nothing, but did not resist as Meliora shifted the blanket and placed her hands on Derwa's stomach. Kerensa watched, realisation slowly dawning as her mother prodded Derwa's middle.

Meliora sat back. "It is early enough. You still have choices."

Finally, Derwa looked up. Something silent was said between her and Meliora.

Meliora nodded, lips firm.

"Kerensa, fetch me the dried carrot seed and raspberry leaf. Start a fresh boil for tea, the sorrel can wait. Derwa, come with me."

Taking Derwa by the arm, Meliora led her into the bedroom.

Kerensa didn't move. Her mother had never spoken to her of those herbs before but, given the circumstances, she suspected their use. She waited, listening to the shuffling from the other room as her mother settled Derwa before returning to the kitchen space.

"Mother, we cannot…" Kerensa began.

"We can. And we must," Meliora interrupted.

"It's a sin! Against God!"

"What is the greater sin? That your friend birth the babe out of wedlock? That she be thrown from the town for her and the infant to starve? Or that she die in childbirth, her womb too small to deliver successfully?"

"There must be another way."

"That way was closed when the father abandoned her. Listen my child, this is the lot of women, the burden we carry. Where we can, we help. That is our job here. Not judgement but understanding. And this, this does not require much understanding. Now, fetch what I asked for and help me prepare the teas. It will be a long night, and we must help her through it."

So Kerensa brewed the two teas to her mother's specification, then fetched a fresh bucket of water and strips of cloth. Coming into the bedroom, she watched as her mother sat Derwa on the floor, a large sheet beneath her. Methodically, Meliora pulled the shift up over an unresponsive Derwa's thighs, exposing her sex, before settling behind her friend, holding her up in a sitting position.

Kerensa handed a cup of tea to Derwa who took it limply. "This is carrot seed," Meliora explained. "It will bring on your bleeding. This may be scary, but we are here with you, and we are not going anywhere. Remember that my child.

"Now, drink the tea Derwa," Meliora said, gently stroking the child's hair. "Drink it all down."

Derwa obeyed. Kerensa took a seat on the bed and watched as her mother gently rocked her friend, humming a lullaby.

Outside, rain lashed the landscape, black clouds blocking out the afternoon sky, winds racing through the valley channels. And Derwa screamed, clutching her belly, eyes wide with fear.

"It's all right my child, it will pass, it will pass. It's all right. Shhhh, shhhh."

Derwa whimpered.

Kerensa breathed deeply.

Then the bleeding began. Gushing from between Derwa's thighs came a thick red river of blood, clotted and dark. "It's all right," Meliora crooned, holding Derwa tight.

"Kerensa, the raspberry leaf."

Kerensa rushed to obey.

"Derwa, drink this. It will help the passing."

The red tea slipped down Derwa's throat.

The blood continued to flow.

"Kerensa, the water."

Kerensa took up the bucket and cloth and knelt by her friend's side. Derwa's eyes were closed, streaks of sweat lined her face and drenched her brow. Gently, Kerensa wiped the sweat from her face, her neck, her chest. The blood slowed, then stopped.

Derwa flopped back into Meliora's arms. "Well done, child, well done," Meliora whispered. "You did so well. All done now, all done."

"Kerensa, clean her up, then we will put her to bed, she will need the rest."

Kerensa rinsed the cloth and carefully wiped the blood from Derwa's legs, thighs, sex, the iron scent of blood filling her nostrils. When she was done Meliora lifted Derwa into her arms as though she were still a little girl and carried her to the bed. Kerensa set about collecting up the cloth from the floor, glancing away from the black masses that dotted the dark red stain. She carried the cloth to the stove and added it to the flames. After rinsing the red water from the bucket and washing her own hands, she walked to the stove top and returned the sorrel to the hob, stirring slowly, rhythmically, calmly.

Soon Meliora entered and took a seat at the table. Kerensa turned to her mother. Meloria's face was ashen, the lines that bracketed her mouth drawn down.

"She sleeps. We will keep her until she wakes, watch over her. Feed her. She did well. She will be fine."

"Will she be able to conceive again? With a husband?"

Meliora looked away, a heavy shadow crossing her face, "Time will tell."

Guilt, a stone sinking deep into the sea, dragged Kerensa's stomach down.

"Mumma," she began, perching on a stool. "There was a boy who wanted to marry her. He asked me where she lived but…"

"Stop," Meliora held up a hand to silence her daughter. "What's done is done, my child. Don't look back, don't question. We move forward."

"Yes mumma," Kerensa nodded.

"Now," Meliora said, "fetch some potatoes and shallots, we will make a stew for the morning, add the mackerel we were saving for winter, Derwa will need her strength."

Interlude

It was a tough lesson for you my child, perhaps one of the toughest. I saw you change afterward. My tough, strong daughter who stared at the world and said 'I am', unfazed by gossip and slurs, the cruelty of the superstitious town, faded. You withdrew, held back. Oh, I am sure you thought you hid it. With anyone else you may have succeeded. But I could see. Doubt seeded inside you, and for the first time, curses rang true deep inside your heart.

I wish I could have softened that night for you, but I didn't have the strength. Derwa's plight I'd seen many a time before in towns along our shores. I'd lived it myself. You didn't know that yet though, and didn't need to know. Derwa was enough for you that day.

Now that we've talked of that night I know of Doyden Castle and the gentleman.

Of the boy named Charlie.

I wish I'd let you speak before, to lift that heavy guilt from your heart. It was never yours to carry.

They don't stay my child, the boys who claim to love us. Not when they know the babe is not theirs.

I know this.

Charlie was not the answer to Derwa's condition. Carrot seed was.

If I'd let you speak, I would have understood your shame. So wrongly placed. Instead I silenced you and focused forward. I was just too tired, my own remembered pain too sharp.

Should I tell you of my own Charlie? The boy I loved at just 16. The sailor who came to Padstow and took my heart. Should I speak of his soft words, his gentle hands, the fire in his eyes that I let consume me? Of the morning I woke and he was gone? Of the bulge that soon pressed my belly to my skirt waist?

Should I share that I learnt of carrot seed and raspberry leaf from my own need, that the pain lasted for weeks afterwards? That it took me five years to conceive my son after I married? That I don't know if my choice was the reason why?

At least Derwa had us, my child. I managed it alone.

No, I don't think I want to tell this story, not now, not yet. There is so much more to see and hear and remember. And this tale is hard, it hurts my soul.

This tale leads to you.

Drift Nets

The oars rubbed against his calloused hands, the sun beat down on his browned forearms, the salt-spray speckled his strengthening beard.

"Aft, Rewan!" Braneh bellowed across the inlet.

"Aft," Rewan repeated to his crew, his own brothers Gerens and Cardor and his friend Kenver.

Their cox Jory called the stroke, "Right and pull."

Rewan swung his right oar in a grand arch, matched by his mates and the boat turned, lining up with his father's craft on the far side. Before them rowed two larger boats, crewed by Braneh, Carowen, Jago, Peren and Madern and his sons. Coming together in a roughly-shaped square, Braneh called the timing.

"Hold, watch the school. Hold," hand raised, eyes scanning the splashing waves, "Drop!" Braneh cried.

The large seine net of woven cotton plunged into the water, the far end weighted down by stones sinking the net to the bay floor.

Rewan waited.

"Drop the stop-net!" Braneh called.

Rewan and Gerens sprang into action, loosing their smaller webbing over the side to seal off the seine.

"Capstans!" Braneh cried, waving his arms above his head, to the men awaiting his signal on the shore, long ropes leading from them to the seine in hand. The men began to pull, the seine tugged together condensing the space inside, herding the pilchards within.

'Tuck-net!"

"Go," Rewan cried. Jory took up the count, "Heave and heave…"

His crew and three other boats made their way inside the waters now cordoned off by the seine and loosed the tuck-net between them. Carefully rowing in closer and closer together the boats formed a circle around the school. The fish, now sensing the trap and feeling the net coming in around them, began to splash and flap along the surface of the water, silver scales catching the sun.

"Let's get 'em lads," Rewan grinned.

Stowing their oars the fishermen took up their baskets and leaned over the side of the boat, slipping the baskets into the water and under the mass of squirming fish, scooping them out and into the boat to flop and gasp at their feet. Again and again they dipped the baskets bringing up mound after mound of slippery pilchards, flapping wildly as they fought for their lives. A few managed to wiggle free, but not for long.

The men worked fast and methodically, collecting up the slippery school. Then, boats full, Rewan waved to his father.

"Release and haul!" Braneh called. The men at the far end pulled up their netting. Rewan and his crew took up oars and began to stroke their way to the shore. The capstans met them to help pull the boats up the beach. The women, holding large baskets between pairs, came ready to collect the fish and carry them up the ramp to the sheds for processing. Off to the side, a few older men and women waded in the shallows with their smaller nets, working in circles to catch the fish that slipped around the seine or were washed to shore by the currents of the bay.

Working as one the town cleared the catch, hauling the baskets of pilchards, now flopping slower, weaker, from the beach. The final fish taken from his boat Rewan looked up towards the cliff top, watching for the huer to see if they would be called to sea again for another round.

The breeze dried the salt of sweat and sea on his brow, and hands on hips he stood, breathing deeply.

Then he saw her.

Coming down the cliff-side, a basket of herbs against her hip as she slowly traversed the decline. She swayed elegantly, sure-footed despite the pronounced limp.

His heart beat faster though he was now at rest, his tummy churning with excitement. He didn't know when the change had come, when she had stopped being a pestering younger child and morphed into a creature that could control his heart. It had crept up on him, and with it a distance had grown between them. The easy company of their days playing chase on the sands replaced with a shy hesitancy.

He didn't care what people said, had heard the talk of a curse: that her birth was an ill-omen, a promise of doom. But he knew that talk for what it was: superstitious fear.

The truth was that Kerensa was beautiful, and skilled. Had always been, even as an annoying slip of a child who'd never let him win a game of capture the flag. The corner of Rewan's mouth hitched up in amusement at the memory; the little girl, eyes fierce and determined, too proud to take the pasty... That light still shone within her. A strength that would not be thwarted.

And he wasn't the only one who saw it, of that he was sure. His was not the only heart that beat for Kerensa Williams.

"... I said, come on sailor! The Huer's waving!"

Rewan looked down at his younger brother. Cardor, slight with youth, the first fuzz of hair shading his upper lip, followed the line of his brother's gaze. Grinning knowingly he elbowed Rewan in the ribs. "Fish won't wait!" he cried running down the beach to their boat waiting patiently on her side.

"But will she?" Rewan whispered to himself. Indulging in one last glance up at Kerensa's soft silhouette, he shook his head. *Focus*, he told himself and hurried down to join his crew.

Later that night the men of his father's crew sat around the family table, ale in hand, an empty pie dish in the centre. Rewan leaned back and rubbed his belly contentedly. His arms ached from the pull of the oar and the weight of the fish nets. But it was a good ache, an ache that meant full bellies and warm winters. His brothers had already found their beds, following soon after their mother. But Rewan was a man now, leader of his own boat. As much as his eyelids drooped and his weary body called for rest, he would stay up with the men. With his father.

The talk over supper had been of the day's yield, smiles and backslaps, confidence in their tone, words bright with the promise of the season. That was, until his younger brothers left. Perhaps it was the fatigue of the long day, the hot sun beating down on ageing flesh. Or maybe it was the dulling effects of the beer they drank, the need for bed their older bodies refused to admit. Rewan didn't know. What he did know though, was that Braneh's crew were worried.

"It's a light start," Peren had said, starting the talk.

Surprised, Rewan had looked up from his mug, his sleepy mind suddenly alert. He'd never heard the men express doubt openly before.

He'd never been a man at the table before.

"Light is putting it mildly," Carworan groused. "Keeps on like this we'll be back in the fields come February. I don't fancy another long winter listening to Lowena grumble about her chilblains. A woman so fat shouldn't suffer from a bit of mild rationing."

"You exaggerate Carworan!" Jago laughed affably, "The start is solid. Today went well. We put in the time, the fish'll come. You'll see."

"They didn't last year, nor the one before. And you know the winds feel the same," Carworan insisted. He eased his broad body back into his chair, rubbing a calloused hand across his bristly cheeks. "More lads left for St Ives last week. Madern's boy's planning to follow. They've started a route direct from Padstow to Newfoundland, so many of our folk are leaving. If the trend holds we won't have a crew to catch the little fish we can find. It's the curse. You all know it. Her birth was a sign…"

"Oh enough Caro!" Jago's voice snapped with tension, his eyes flicking up to Rewan, before nodding firmly. "Lads gotta follow what's right for them. Madern's boy was never a fisherman. Ain't nothing to do with your fancy about fish numbers and make-believe omens."

The words were directed at Carworan, but Rewan knew they were meant for him. He glanced quickly over at his father, a new feeling opening up in his chest. He wanted his father to put Carworan in his place. To tell him he was foolish and wrong. But Braneh sat calmly at the table head, sipping his ale, seemingly unmoved by the talk of his crew.

The men fell silent for a moment. Rewan watched as his father slurped down the last of his beer and placed his mug on the table with a solid thunk. No words were said, but the message was clear; time to head home. Murmuring goodbyes and plans for the 'morrow the crew ambled out of the house to find their beds, the comfort of their wives, if they were lucky, and, more likely, a solid sleep before the dawn.

Braneh didn't move.

Rewan sat across from his father watching his face in the long light of the summer evening. The gold tones softened the hard edges of that face, but the deep lines of age, hard work and grief remained visible across his forehead and down his cheeks. Rewan waited.

Slowly Braneh leaned forward and poured another mug of ale for them both from the pitcher that sat on the table. Settling back into his chair he took his time, savouring the beer as though it were some fine vintage wine and not the swill from the local market hawker. Nervous, Rewan sipped his own. Truth be told his head was spinning from the drink already consumed and his need for sleep. But Braneh had poured him another, he would drink it. He was a man now, after all.

At length his father spoke, his deep voice soft and calm, steady as always, "The men always talk down the fish run. Happens at the start of every season. I think it's become a tradition for them, that if they expect the worst they can be assured everything will work out. Nothing comes of it."

Rewan frowned. Braneh's words comforted the part of him that remained a youth, and he felt the weight of concern begin to lift. Though he longed to accept his father's words and turn for bed assured of their security, he could not. His new role as captain of his own crew and the responsibilities that came with that, as well as his hopes for his future, his desire to wed, meant his mind could not be settled so easily.

"But father, the runs did start later this year. And while it's true our hauls have been good, they have been far between. Gerens was saying…"

"Your brother should spend more time working on his net technique than gossiping like a woman! It's bad luck to count a catch!"

Rewan blinked in shock at the harsh tone. The pull to defend his younger brother was strong. But it was off topic and he had something important to broach with his father.

He tried another tack. "What Carworan said about the mines…"

"Caro likes the sound of his own voice boy, he's the last man you should be listening to in times like this."

Pushing down a flare of indignation at being called 'boy', Rewan firmed his shoulders and faced his father. "I heard talk," he began, voice steady, "of a new net. Some of the men from the South who worked the farms with us last spring were talking about them. They're called drift-nets. They allow you to go out past the bay, into the seas. Rather than waiting for the fish to come to us, we go to them."

"So successful that these men still came north to farm," Braneh said dismissively.

Determined, Rewan ignored his comment and pushed on, "Gerens and I did the sums. If the crews pool our money we can afford our own nets. We won't need to loan them from Mr Symonds, so the profit will all be ours. Then we can be sure we won't have to go to the fields - you know how mother hates to be alone…"

Braneh held up a wide flat hand, bringing Rewan's rush of words to a halt.

"The seas are a treacherous place Rewan. The coast is lined with rocks and death traps. We don't fish outside the bay."

"But in the south…"

"Enough now," Braneh said. Though the words were short, there was no anger in his tone, only calm assurance. "The fish will come. You'll see lad. They always come. Now, we've tarried here long enough, it's time to rest. Sun up waits for no man."

Fat, wet and cold, sleet fell doggedly from the grey February skies. Bundled in his thickest coat Rewan wiped his face, buying himself a momentary reprieve from the icy wet that laced the frozen landscape. At his side their horse huffed, her warm breath billowing white in the cold air. His mother stood in the doorway, shawl pulled tight around her shoulders. Cardor and Gerens were already upon the cart, which sat on the cobbled street loaded with food supplies and ale, ready for their trek inland to find work on the spring farms and market gardens that fed the Cornish coast.

Despite his father's assurances the fish had not come. Even before the season completed four more men had left for the mines. The new year saw two more. Braneh's announcement over lunch the week before, that they would be heading to the farms again this season, surprised no one.

They'd known it was coming, but Rewan's mother's shoulders still pulled tighter, her frown deepening. She'd turned from lunch and walked silently to the room she shared with her husband. Braneh had followed soon after.

The brothers remained at the table. No one said a thing. In silence they ate the loaf of freshly baked herbed bread and salted pilchard their mother had prepared.

Now Meraud stood in Braneh's arms. She was not a small woman, but snugged to her husband in the grey light of winter, she seemed fragile to Rewan. Or maybe that was just his own mind thinking of the long hard months alone that stood before her. His eyes drifted up the incline of the town coming to rest on the small stone hut that sat just outside the village rim, a thin line of smoke rising through the sleet towards the sky.

He swallowed.

The smoke meant she was home. Cooking, sewing, cutting herbs, or maybe just resting, chatting with her mother, passing the winter days like they all did, inside beside the oven coals, warm and cosy. It would be months now before he would see her again. He longed to tell his father to wait, to stride up the hill to her door. He would knock twice, wait patiently. If Meliora answered he would be polite. But if Kerensa answered... he closed his eyes and imagined sweeping Kerensa into his arms and covering her mouth with his. She would be surprised at first, then her warm, soft body would melt into his, aligning with his limbs, fitting tight until there was no space between them, not now, not ever again...

"Rewan, it's time."

Braneh's voice pulled him from his daydream, back into the cold reality before him. He nodded and pulled himself up onto the cart.

This season, he promised himself. *This season I make her mine. Somehow...*

His father flicked the reins prompting the horse into motion, one hand raised in a wave to his wife. His brothers waved to their mother enthusiastically. But Rewan looked up at the hut, at the smoke that curled into the grey skies, and prayed.

As they pulled out of the town Braneh leaned in close to his son and whispered softly, "This season," he said, "we will try those nets of yours."

Shocked, Rewan turned from his vigil and stared at his father in surprise.

His father's eyes were fixed forward on the road, mouth in a grim line. "We go to the fish," he said.

For the first time in Rewan's life he saw doubt on Braneh's face.

A Feast of Fish and Thyme

"Heave, two, three, four. Heave, two, three, four… keep up lads!" Kenver called the stroke as Rewan and his brothers streaked out across the bay, heading for the opening to the ocean beyond. Rewan bent to his task, pulling on his oars with all the pent up enthusiasm of his months away on the farms.

They'd come home early to prepare, after purchasing the new drift nets from a merchant at Padstow and had spent hours practicing with them in the bay. He and his father and crew had been so busy repairing the boats, sanding the hulls and repainting the wood to protect the beams from the whipping waves and rains that Rewan had had barely a moment to himself. Of course, time to himself was not essential when the person you dreamed about walked past your workplace every morning.

And every morning he'd been ready. As Kerensa strolled past, her right foot marking her distinctive shuffle, Rewan had made his way to the cobbled main street to intercept her path. First he brought smiles and good days, then thoughts on the weather and the coming season. Yesterday, confidence buoyed by the progress they were making in their use of the nets, and knowing they would soon launch out beyond the bay, he'd picked a bunch of wild flowers and fashioned them into a simple bouquet.

Kerensa walked past, head facing forward, wry smile touching her lips, she knew to expect him by now. Rewan approached, bouquet secured behind his back.

"Fine day my lady."

"My lady indeed!" Kerensa had almost snorted, flashing him a smile both bewildered and joyous. *She really didn't see it,* he realised, *she didn't see her beauty.*

"You prefer I call you by your name then, Kerensa." He lowered his voice, deep and soft as the sound of her name purred through his lips.

Her face turned scarlet, the smattering of freckles along her nose and cheeks lost in the reddened hue. He grinned.

"We are to sea tomorrow, out beyond the bay."

Kerensa stopped dead in her tracks. "Beyond the bay? Into the sea?"

Surprised, Rewan cocked his head at her. "Why, yes. That's what we've been preparing for all month. Why we came back sooner." His lips quirked into his natural lopsided smile. "Me though, I came back for you."

She didn't laugh or demur, just stared straight at his face.

"Is it safe… beyond the bay? The seas are wild. The trading vessels are far larger than…'

"Hush," Rewan laughed and brought the bouquet from behind his back, "For you."

This time she startled, eyes fixed on the purple and yellow petals he'd spent his evening hours searching for.

Her lips pursed as if holding in a laugh. "They are lovely, Rewan. But… how long did the nettle bite burn? I have salves for that you know."

His bravado dimmed slightly. How did she know he'd grabbed a handful of the infernal stinging herb in his search?

Seeing his discomfort, Kerensa quickly continued, "They are lovely, thank you." And reached out to take them from his hand. As she did so her fingers brushed his. All thoughts of embarrassment vanished and, as if of their own accord, his fingers curled about hers, holding their hands together across the pretty flowers.

His lip quirked up, eyes shining bright and hot he leaned forward, "They are lovely, as are you."

He struggled to contain the surge of desire that raced through his core as he watched her swallow, her throat bob up and down.

She pulled her hand away and placed the flowers within her basket. Tonight, when she returned from her daily forage, that basket would be filled with herbs and wild vegetables. He loved the smells of the land that trailed in her wake.

"To sea then," she said, eyes looking over his shoulder towards the calm waters of the bay. "If I don't see you before you set out tomorrow. Be… careful."

"There is nothing to fear," he announced bravely, almost believing his words. Leaning closer he brought his lips to her ear, "Do you think

I would ever leave? I will always return for you."

Their eyes met, locked for a moment, two. Then Rewan, eyes shining bright, turned and ran down the beach to his crew.

Now that crew were cresting the waves, making fast for the open water.

Rewan pulled hard on the oars, his limbs moving fluidly, his body poised and ready. His muscles worked powerfully but he barely registered the strain on his limbs, he knew only the excitement of the day, of the new adventure before him and his brothers.

They crossed the cliff heads.

Cardor gave a "Whoop!" of excitement and the brothers grinned as one.

"Slow it down boy!" Braneh's cry echoed over the waves.

Kenver looked to Rewan for direction. The men grinned at each other.

"Keep pace boys," Rewan cried, "Let's show those old men what we're made of! Make 'em chase us!"

Eyes bright with mirth, Kenver called the stroke as they glided farther from the protected waters of the bay.

It was a bright clear day, the winds off the coast were moderate and warm, the sun and gulls high overhead. As they stroked farther from the bay the swell grew, but not by much. It was a perfect day to set out, but Rewan knew not all days would be so calm. He would have to talk to his father about the mast and sail designs the drift net merchant had told him of.

Imagine the sea they could cover, the catches they could make if the wind powered them on!

Shaking his head he brought his focus back to the moment.

Braneh and his crew were now in the open waters too. While Rewan loved the idea of continuing to outpace his father, this was not a race. The two boats were needed to stretch the net, moving through the water collecting the fish. He ordered Kenver to slow the stroke and their pace changed. Soon the two boats came into line.

Rewan looked over the water to his father. Braneh's face was stern and focused, but when their eyes met across the water, Rewan saw it, the glow of adventure that matched his own. Nodding to each other they set the net then rowed out, pulling the cords taunt between them, before advancing on the school of pilchards the huer had spotted beyond the break. Rowing as one father and son guided their crews through the school of white-bellied fish, collecting them up and trapping them in their drift net, before hauling the nets up full to bursting with squirming, struggling bodies.

"Haha!" Carawon let out a whooping cry and then the men grinned to each other.

This was going to work.

She was standing on the bayside with the other women of the town as they pulled into the beach. As his mother and the wives of his father's crew ran down to greet them, she waited, watching. Rewan was surrounded by the cry and laugh of the townsfolk as they gazed at the full hulls brimming with fish flesh. All six boats that chanced the new technique had come back, all six bursting with catch.

Rewan made his way through the throng of excited townsfolk, nodding at the cheers. He barely felt the slaps on his back. He just saw her.

In two confident strides he cleared the rocks of the beach and came to her side.

"Not out foraging today?" he asked.

"I heard there was something to see here. A first," she replied, smiling.

"And are you impressed?" grinning he swept his arm out to indicate the beach of folk and fish. "A successful haul."

She sniffed, looking pointedly over the boats below, nodding slowly.

"You smell like fish," she said.

Rewan threw back his head and laughed and laughed. Wiping a tear from his eye he leaned in close and whispered, his breath caressing her neck, "And you carry the scent of sage and thyme. What a feast we would make together."

Red blotched along the slender curve of her neck. He pulled back, but not far.

"I told you I'd return for you."

Something happened between them. Some wall, some hesitation, some block dissipated. He looked down at her nose, her lips, he leaned forward, breath coming in short bursts, heart pounding.

"Hevva!" the cry echoed across the bay. Rewan stopped.

On the cliff top the huer cried out again, waving his bristles high. He had sighted more fish off the coast.

The town behind them got to work. Their joyful milling transitioning into hauling out the fish and lugging them to the sheds.

Rewan hesitated.

"Go," she smiled, eyes full of mirth at his indecision. "I'll see you at the troyls tonight."

His brow furrowed, "The troyls?"

"Yes," she laughed, "your mother has had the wives baking Hevva cake and pie since sun up. The street will be full, once we finish processing the catch. Go. Give us something to truly celebrate."

He held her eyes in his a moment more, then, lopsided grin in place, turned to his boat and his catch.

Troyls

Kerensa watched his broad back move gracefully down the beach. Gracefully? Was that the word? She didn't care, it was to her. He was graceful, and beautiful. She loved him.

Derwa made her way up the beach, arms full of basket and shinning scales.

"It's going to be a big day, Kez. Think you might come help?"

Kerensa looked towards the cliff she knew she should climb, thinking of the herbs she should search for. Then looked back down at the beach and the man she adored as he and his brothers began to push their boat back into the currents of the bay. She should go. But she wanted to be here. Where he would be. With the people of the town.

She smiled at Derwa and nodded. "If you'll have me?"

Derwa grinned, "Come on, I'll show you the ropes. You're a fast learner, you'll catch on quick."

Kerensa followed her friend as a mix of apprehension and eagerness began to roil in her gut. She'd never worked the fish before. 17 summers in this town and she'd never been part of the toil that brought the folk together. Kerensa and Meliora remained on the outside: of the circle of cottages that formed the town, of the income, of the social life. Kerensa had been brought in only by the bonds formed during a childhood of running through the sand and dust, and through the townsfolks' grudging acceptance of her mother's healing talents. Swallowing her nerves she straightened her shoulders and tried to look relaxed, following Derwa as smoothly as her twisted foot would allow. At least this task wouldn't require her to walk long distances as her mother's trade did.

The young women entered the first fish shed. A large cool space opened between the thick stone walls, dim-lit from the little natural light that entered through the open end. The space was lined with heavy wooden tables, knives and other sharp tools scattered along their surfaces, baskets of fish waiting on the floor. Large, grim-faced Beryan looked Kerensa up and down, pausing before handing her an apron of red stained cloth and pointing her and Derwa to a far table. Looping the apron about her neck and tying off the waist, Kerensa made her way to her assigned spot.

"Right," Derwa said. "First you strip the scales, like this." She gripped a knife in one hand, and a fat, lifeless fish in the other and began to scrape along its skin. Tiny flecks of white scale came away with each pass of the knife, forming a mound on the blade. Some flicked off randomly into the air around them.

"Next, gut it. Top to bottom, centre. And get your fingers right in there and pull. The guts go in this basket, the cleaned fish in this one. Then you get the next fish. Got it?"

Kerensa nodded. "And then we salt them?"

"Not us, Wenna and Eseld usually collect the cleaned fish and take them to Meraud and the older women over there," she pointed to the other side of the shed. "They press them for oil and salt the flesh for keeping, the men not fishing collect the processed baskets and take them to be stored in the cellar sheds. We just do the cleaning. Ok, let's get to it now, lots to get through!"

With that Derwa turned to the basket at their feet and selected a large pilchard. With the speed of practice she swiftly descaled and gutted the fish, before moving fluidly on to the next.

Kerensa took up her knife and gripped her own fish. The skin felt wet and slippery. She was thankful it was not moving. How on earth did the men manage to hold on to them out in the water while they still fought for life? Focusing on her task, she began to carefully scrape away the scales. They came away easily, the knife sliding cleanly along the silvery skin. Satisfied, she flipped the fish onto its back and slit its rotund belly in two. Reaching in her fingers slid along fat, juicy organs before finding purchase and pulling the entrails from the body. Discarding the guts, washing the fish, she placed it into the finished basket and released a breath she hadn't realised she'd been holding.

"Good job," Derwa smiled beside her, "Natural fishwife." Her smile turned wicked, teasing and she turned back to her task.

Face flushed hot, Kerensa reached for her next fish.

* * *

Hours passed. Fish blood ran down her fingers and arms staining her apron and sleeves. Red tinged water from the cleaning bucket sloshed at her feet, finding the holes in her soles. Sweat beaded on her brow from the heat of the rising sun and the warmth of the hard working bodies pressed close around her. The scent of fish and blood and body odor filled the shed and her nose. And still she worked. Pick, scale, gut, wash. Pick, scale, gut, wash. Periodically the empty baskets were taken away and replaced with another filled to the brim. The haul was big today, she realised.

At some later time she reached down for her next scaly task and found the bucket empty. Looking up Kerensa saw the women around her standing tall, stretching their backs and rinsing their hands of fish muck and blood. She and Derwa collected up their knives and rinsed them in the water bucket. A group of old men came in. Armed with buckets full to the brim with seawater, they lined up along the end of the shed and threw the water down along the floor, flushing the blood and entrails from the floor and tables. Then, as one, the women made their way out of the processing shed. A sense of weary accomplishment settled into Kerensa's bones. Used to long days foraging her body was not unaccustomed to hard work, but this had been a different labour. She felt decidedly ready to return home to her mother's clean and orderly hut and sleep.

Outside the light was brighter than Kerensa expected. She felt she'd worked to nightfall, but the sun was still long from its bed. On the beach the fishermen were stowing their boats for the night and making their way slowly up the beach, heading home to clean up before returning for the communal supper Meraud had planned for the town. She always threw a celebration on the night of the first catch. Kerensa had never been brave enough to venture down. But tonight she'd told Rewan she would be there... whatever had possessed her to say that?

"Come on," Derwa said, "you can clean up at mine."

Kerensa looked down at her clothes and cringed. Blood splatter and intestine grease covered her skirts and sleeves. Cleaning up at Derwa's could only do so much. And Kerensa only had one dress...

As if sensing her friend's distress, Derwa continued, "I have an old dress I think would fit you too. That'll need a good scrub before you can wear it again. Come on, we don't want to be late."

He was already there when she returned. Sitting on a wooden chair, probably brought from his mother's table, mug of ale in hand, laughing with his brothers. Kerensa hesitated. The whole town was there, sitting in circles of family and friends, laughing voices and loud jests ringing out across the bay. Beside her Derwa linked an arm through Kerensa's and pulled her close.

"You'll sit with us of course," she smiled, leading her to the round of chairs where Mabyn and Jory were already seated.

Noting the women arriving carrying heaped plates of salted fish, bread or thick cut slices of pie Kerensa paled.

"I've brought nothing to share," she said, turning startled to her friend. "I didn't think… I should have known…"

"Not every house can bring food to share, but we feed everyone".

Kerensa frowned in disbelief. "But I'm not really…"

"You are part of this town Kerensa," Derwa interrupted firmly, "whatever some people might say about your mother," her eyes shot a dirty look at Carworan sitting with Braneh and the rest of the crew. "Come, let's get you a cup of ale."

The two friends took a seat with Derwa's mother and brother as Jago struck up a tune on his fiddle. A mug of ale was pressed into her hand, a slice of bread and cheese into the other. Settling in her chair Kerensa tried to relax, but her body simply wouldn't comply. She felt on edge, as if at any moment, something was going to happen, something to embarrass her.

"Drink up, Kez," Derwa grinned conspiratorially beside her. "It's a party."

Dubiously, Kerensa sipped her ale. It wasn't her first ale by any means, every winter her mother bought a keg for the season. It was bitter stuff, but Kerensa drank it dutifully. Her mother seemed to enjoy it. This one was smoother than what Meliora bought, but still held the bitter aftertaste Kerensa had expected. Swallowing a large gulp to please Derwa, she smiled and looked back out at the town before her.

A few children were dancing now, their laughing fathers and uncles clapping their hands and tapping their feet to the rhythm of Jago's fiddle. Jory took up the beat beside his father, keeping time on his crowdys crown. Soon enough some adults swept out to join the jigging youngsters, led by Braneh and Meraud.

To Kerensa's surprise Kenver approached and hauled Derwa up from her chair. Laughing and clinging to his arm her friend joined him on the pebbled road, revelling in the frivolity. *I didn't know they were courting!* Kerensa shook her head. Derwa was always so full of surprises. But it warmed her heart to see her friend smiling, especially after the events of the summer before…

"I see it's no longer just me that smells of fish," a deep voice, right beside Kerensa's ear caused her to jump, nearly spilling her ale.

She turned as he settled down on Derwa's empty seat beside her. "Smells different on you though."

Kerensa stared at Rewan, then subtly tried to sniff her hands. Did she really still smell of pilchard?

Rewan leaned forward, eyes twinkling, "I think it suits you." The humour in his eyes flooded her with relief. He was only teasing.

Feeling the blush begin to heat her cheeks as it always did when he was near, Kerensa turned her head back to the dancing folk before them.

Rewan followed her gaze. "All right then," he announced standing up and holding his hand out before her.

Kerensa regarded him in confusion. "All right what?"

"Time to dance."

"Me?"

"Yes you."

"But I've never…"

"You'd never worked the fish shed before today either, but that didn't stop you. This is no different. I'll show you how. Come on."

Kerensa didn't move. It was as if her body had frozen on the spot. They'd been flirting all season. She knew it, the town knew it. But to dance together, in front of everyone? Did Rewan realise what that was saying?

"I…"

"Come on!" Laughing he reached down and gripped her elbow, gently pulling her to her feet. Then, taking her hand in his he drew her out onto the street. Jago struck up a lively jig.

"I, I don't think I can. My foot."

"Ha!" Rewan scoffed, "Says the girl who scrabbled up the rocks to beat me in capture the flag."

Kerensa flushed red again. He remembered that?

He held her hands and began to bounce, his body movements assured, fluid and relaxed as he hopped about to the tune. Her own felt rigid, unsure, her twisted foot dragging uncomfortably. She wanted to stop, to head home, to retreat where no one could watch her fail.

Rewan pulled her close, "I've got you," he whispered. Their eyes met. Suddenly there was nothing else, only Rewan and herself and the music of the lute. Wrapping an arm about her waist he drew her body into his and began to move her to and fro. She followed. The tune sped up, Rewan increased their pace. She matched. Faster, faster. Her foot couldn't keep up, so she hopped. Faster, faster, faster. Faces flushed with exertion the two continued to jig through the street. Kerensa let out a laugh, Rewan whooped with joy and they pressed the pace again battling to keep up with the music. Kerensa felt she would collapse, but her face was only a picture of joy, her eyes bright with excitement. Jago reached a crescendo strumming at an unbelievable pace.

With a final flourish he brought the dance to an end and Kerensa and Rewan came to a halt. Her legs felt like jelly beneath her and she gripped Rewan's arms to keep steady. His eyes glittered and he smiled, "I told you, I've got you."

Grinning, Rewan led her to his family circle, pulled up a chair for her and poured her an ale.

"Mighty fine jig that," Braneh said, smiling.

Embarrassed and shy Kerensa looked down at her feet.

"Here, love," Meraud said, handing Kerensa a slice of her famous mackerel pie, "You'll need some sustenance after that. I tell you Rewan, Kerensa is a lady and deserves to be treated as such," she scolded her eldest son fondly.

"No doubt about that," Rewan replied, "Kerensa is a lady. And much, much more."

Blushing, Kerensa kept her gaze lowered, unsure how to respond to the compliment.

Braneh saved her, "We're glad to have you love," he said warmly. "Been too long since our families talked."

"Thank you sir," Kerensa said, confusion flashing through her mind. Their families?

Braneh smiled and turned to Gerens at his side. Her old friend was staring at her in open-faced shock. Slapping his second son on the back, Braneh said, "What a day hey boys? Out past the bay. What a haul. It's going to be a boom year. I can feel it."

Vinegar and Lemon Verbena

Well past the setting of the sun, Rewan walked Kerensa up to her hut.

"It's all right, Rewan," she tried, "I walk home late often." She glanced down at the basket in her hands that would usually be filled with herbs, empty tonight but for her fish stained dress.

"And you are capable I know," he agreed. "But it has been a long night, much ale has been consumed. I want to know you are safe."

A red ribbon in the icy mud flashed through Kerensa's memory. Subconsciously patting the cramp that formed in her tummy, Kerensa nodded. They continued up the hill.

"Father is right you know," Rewan said, "with the new nets we can catch much more fish. We will be able to regain our reputation for the finest pilchards on the coast."

"The finest?" Kerensa raised a teasing eyebrow at her beau.

"The finest," Rewan insisted. "We've lost a lot of men to the mines." A shadow crossed his face, Kerensa lowered her head. She knew what this town, this livelihood meant to him, to her, to everyone in Porth Gwynn. It meant everything.

"But not anymore. We will rebuild this town, back to the success of my father's youth. It's our turn now!"

Kerensa laughed happily, captured by his enthusiasm and belief.

"It's true," he continued, mistaking her mirth for doubt. "And once we get the sails we can go even further!"

"Sails?" Kerensa frowned, "Like the trade ships?"

"Yes exactly, but on our smaller vessels. With the wind at our backs we can journey even further for the pilchards and bring in even more with each catch. We'll be even more successful than ever before. The whole ocean is ours to take." He stretched his arms out wide as if gathering the world to his chest.

Kerensa nodded, lips curved. It was a beautiful dream. Sometimes as they worked the herbs, Meliora had told Kerensa of the fish runs of her own youth, when she first moved to the Port with her husband Cubert. She spoke of months of work, long hours in the sun, streets streaked with fish blood, the harbour filled with trade ships come to take the hauls away to sell across the world. A version of that life was still true. But the seasons had grown shorter and more sporadic across Kerensa's short life, the winters leaner, the springs quieter as more men went away to work the fields to supplement their income, and young men took up a pick, to work the mines further south at the end of the horn of Cornwall. They'd all felt the absence of the fish loom up from the waters casting an unseasonal shadow; hollow, empty. Even Kerensa had heard the talk: of folk facing ruin, unable to pay debts; of the extra tax expected by their benefactor.

But Rewan, walking beside her, had found the solution. Their own nets. Drifters. Not bought for them by Mr Symond's of Waybridge, but bought by the folk of the town. Nets they could use out past the bay's edge, bringing the sea to them.

She hadn't realised the fear she'd borne for the people of her town, for their dwindling way of life, until now. In the face of the hope of rejuvenation, she felt the unacknowledged tension slip away.

They came to her door. "Thank you Rewan, I had a wonderful time tonight."

"And I... me too," Rewan looked suddenly awkward and unsure. Where moments before there had been only confidence and passion, now he seemed, worried.

Kerensa cocked her head at him.

"Rewan? Is something wrong?"

"What? No, I just." He looked up at her and her breath caught in her throat.

It was not worry that shone in his eyes, but naked desire, burning bright. She swallowed, remembering the moment between them that morning on the beach. So much had happened since then it seemed a lifetime ago. Like that final symbol of their intensions towards each other was no longer necessary, as though it had already happened.

But it had not. He had not yet kissed her.

Her breathing grew short, her dress suddenly too tight, too hot.

Rewan stepped forward, closing the space between them. He lifted a hand and cupped her cheek. Then... the door to her mother's hut swung open.

Backlit by candlelight Meliora stood in the doorway, Eia curled under her arm.

"Welcome home daughter," she nodded to Kerensa.

What on earth was her mother still doing up? Kerensa often came home late from foraging, so the time was not unusual.

"Thank you for walking her home, Rewan."

Suddenly sheepish, Rewan looked everywhere but at Meliora, "Of course, not a problem Mrs. Williams."

"Safe return home then," Meliora said. "Give your mother my regards. Good night."

"Good night Mrs. Williams. Kerensa."

His eyes lingered on hers, a question and a promise shining in their dark pools. She knew hers answered.

His lips quirked into a grin as he turned and began the walk back down into town.

Kerensa walked through the house into the yard and filled a bucket with water. Meliora took a seat at the table and watched in silence as her daughter began to scrub at her blood stained dress.

"Try a mix of vinegar and lemon verbena," Meliora said, "I've always found that works best for fish blood."

Kerensa looked up at her mother in silence, then collected the herb and vinegar and mixed them through the water. Pressing the dress into the bucket to soak overnight, she placed it by the back door and took a seat opposite her mother.

The two women eyed each other in silence.

Meliora spoke first. "You worked the fish run."

"I did."

"Did you forage too?"

"No."

"And you spent the night in town."

"At the troyls, with Derwa and Gerens and everyone else. I wasn't alone with…"

Meliora held up a hand. "You are a woman Kerensa. Your decisions are your own. But, remember, the word of a man is just that. A word."

"Rewan has promised me nothing."

An eyebrow quirked up Meliora's forehead, "Hasn't he?" She smirked, "Promises are not only made in words."

Kerensa looked away in silence, unsure how to respond.

Meliora set a wiggling Eia down on the table top. The chicken clucked softly and pecked at a few nobs in the table top before settling on the end nearest the open backdoor, savouring the cool breeze.

Eyeing her daughter Meliora sighed, "Work the fish, my child. If that is your wish. But, daughter, look at me." She paused and reaching across the table took Kerensa's hands in hers. "Never give up your independence. You don't need a man…"

Kerensa snatched back her hands. Her eyes lit with flame as she stared at her mother in shock.

"What would you have me do? Live here with you forever? Eia is not long for this earth. And I shall likely outlive you also. What happens after you are gone? Who will I have then if I don't take a husband?"

Nonplussed by Kerensa's uncharacteristic outburst, Meliora shrugged, "I didn't say that. If the boy calls to your loins become a fishwife. Bare his children. Surround yourself with the town that shuns me," she paused, "The town I shun too. But always, always keep something for yourself. A man will not always protect you. Even if he wants to."

Kerensa regarded her mother guardedly, understanding. Marriage, no matter how much she trusted in it, could not ensure her future forever. Even if she made a good match, like Rewan, one day she may find herself alone, as her mother had, regardless of her husband's intentions. The fishing life was a tough one. And it could be dangerous.

"You work herbs and healing to feed us. This I have always known. I thought you taught me so I could be like you but… you want me to have something that is just mine. So I can always feed myself. With or without a man. As you have."

Meliora met her daughter's seeking eyes and smiled sadly. "It was not my plan, not when I first married, but, things change."

"Mother," Kerensa shifted uncomfortably in her seat, working up the courage to ask, "where is my father?"

Her eyes closed slowly, a single tear tracking down her cheek. "I honestly don't know my child," Meliora replied. "I have never lied to you, when you ask."

"But you never explain either. What happened? Where did my father go? Braneh said tonight our families were friends once, but now you stay away. Why mother? What happened?"

"It was a long time ago…"

The old fear of rejection swelled up inside Kerensa, forcing the words from her mouth, "He left because of me, didn't he? Because of my foot. He believed it was a sign, an ill-omen. That's why he left. And why you were shunned."

Meliora closed her eyes and looked away, features going blank.

"That's not the whole truth, my child."

Kerensa waited, eyes fixed on her mother.

"One day I will tell you. One day. But now it's late and we must rest. The sun waits for no man."

The light was not dim enough to hide the breadth of his father's powerful shoulders. Rewan closed the door softly and padded to the table, taking a seat opposite his father. Without waiting for Braneh to speak, he launched into his explanation, "I just walked her home father, nothing more I swear. And anyway, it wouldn't matter what we did, even if... but we didn't. But it wouldn't matter. I love her father. And I am going to make her my wife. Just as soon as I can afford our own cottage, I'm going to ask her. I am going to marry Kerensa."

Braneh chuckled softly to himself, "Slow down son, slow down, you've got me all wrong. I know you're a good and responsible lad. Always respectful to your mother and me. And you've taken to the trade like you were born to it. Not like your brother Gerens, I had a fight on my hands to get him out of that school in St Endellion. And then when he started counting the fish at sea! But well, that's not for now." He shook his head ruefully, refocusing.

"No, you're a good lad and you'll make a solid husband. And whatever folk say, Kerensa is a good girl. She'll make a wonderful wife. I simply wanted to ask about your plans... Ha!" He laughed again to himself, "It seems you've already planned it all. But might a father offer some advice?"

Releasing a heavy breath, Rewan grinned at his father. "I know about, you know... the marriage night. Jago and Carowan..."

"No, no, no!" Braneh exclaimed, "Whatever those two fools told you, put that far from your mind. A woman is a treasure son, treat her as such, always."

"Yes, father," Rewan nodded, but in truth was confused. How else could you ever treat the girl who owned your heart?

Braneh leaned forward, producing a bottle of liquor Rewan had not noticed in the fading light of the stuttering candle. Smoothly he poured them both a large slug.

"Been saving this, drank it with my best friend the day I decided I would marry your mother. Best thing I ever did do. Seems the right time to share some again, don't you think?"

Warmth and love flooded through Rewan. He loved his father. Gruff, abrupt, kind and calm.

"Thank you."

The two men saluted each other.

"Ah, that's a good drop," Braneh sighed. "Takes me back."

A sadness seemed to drift over his face, but was quickly replaced by his usual weary smile.

"Now, like I said, we know Kerensa is a good girl. But there will be talk. Her mother…"

"I don't care what people say about Meliora," Rewan interrupted passionately. "She has always been good to us in the sickness season. You saw how she fought for Treeve even after the doctor gave up. And I don't believe what they say about her and other men…"

"No, you should not!" Braneh said, voice rough with unusual anger. "Those rumours are foul and dirty. And stain the good name of an innocent girl. No, son, I don't believe it either, and neither should you. But Rewan, where rumours swirl there is often a seed that grew them."

Braneh paused, taking another deep drink of his whisky.

"What has Kerensa told you of her father?"

Rewan shook his head, surprised at the change of topic. "Nothing. She has never spoken of him. All I know comes from the town. That he left to work the farms one spring and never returned. I always assumed that was part of why mother hates it when we go."

"Yes, there'd be some truth to that… but it's not the whole story." Braneh sighed. "Son, I hesitate to tell you this… it won't be easy to hear. But I think you need to know the truth about the woman you love."

Anger flared within Rewan's chest, "What are you saying? That Kerensa's father is a bad man? So what? You said it yourself she is a good woman. She is innocent of her parents actions, whatever they are."

Sorrow weighed down the sides of Braneh's face and within a moment he aged years. Wiping a hand across his face to scuttle the traitorous tears that fell from his eyes he took a deep breath.

"No, son, Kerensa is not responsible for her father. Not in any way. And Cubert, Cubert was my best friend. The man I drank this very whisky with. He was a good man, the best of men. No, whatever happened to Cubert and his son Enyon was surely a tragedy."

He leaned back and closed his eyes before continuing, "I still remember the day Cubert brought Meliora to Porth Gwynn. She was so beautiful, still is. I don't mind telling you we were all more than a little envious of Cubert's luck, Carworan most of all." He chuckled at the memory, face lined with wry humour, "I was surprised when he married Lowena. Hoped he would make a proper go of it though. But he never seemed to stop minding Meliora. Still, it is not for me to interfere with the lives of my crew." He paused for a moment, a slight frown marring his brow, before continuing, "Yes, Meliora was beautiful and a good woman too. Skilled at the fish work, good cook. Their son Enyon took a while to come along, but was a healthy, hale lad. They seemed, well, as happy as the fishing life can make you.

"Then Cubert left and never returned. There were rumours… about Kerensa's birth. But I don't put stock in rumours," he paused, thinking how to continue. "Some said her foot was a sign of bad times to come. And when Cubert and Enyon disappeared…"

"They said Kerensa was cursed," Rewan finished for him.

"Superstitious wallop! But…yes. And Meliora didn't help herself. She refused to accept that Cubert had died. She said he was alive, that he had abandoned her and the new child." Braneh's hand formed a fist and anger momentarily lit in his eyes.

Rewan watched in still silence. Rarely did he see such emotion from his gentle father. The surprise took his breath away. He waited.

Eventually, Braneh continued, "Things got bad. You have to understand, lad. Cubert was one of us, born and bred. And when she said he lived… we couldn't mourn him, couldn't savour the memories of a good man. A man of the Port. And Meloria… she lived here yes, but she wasn't from here. Suddenly, that mattered."

Rewan nodded slowly, understanding dawning. "So you rejected her? Chose Cubert over her and Kerensa?"

Braneh sighed, "It wasn't so blunt, but yes. Jago needed a larger house and Meliora only had the babe…"

"You asked her to move?"

"I did. It made sense. Besides, people were already avoiding her. I thought some distance and time, might help."

"You kicked her out."

Regret weighed down his father's heavy brows, "In effect, yes."

Braneh fell silent, watching his son's face as he absorbed the information. Confusion creased his youthful brow.

Slowly he said, "But this was all so long ago. Why does it matter still?"

"The runs have been poor…"

"You can't seriously believe in that cursed nonsense! Kerensa is a person, not an omen!"

"Of course, lad," Braneh held up this hands in a placating gesture and waited for his son to calm."But this is Cornwall, superstition dies hard. And with the questions over her parentage."

Surprise lit Rewan's face, before his eyes narrowed in angry denial.

"What a terrible slur!"

"It could be. It could also be true."

Rewan felt the blood drain from his face and his hands begin to tremor. "You mean she's…"

"No one knows where the rumour first originated, but, like I said, these tales come from somewhere."

Rewan breathed deeply, trying to calm the rising panic within him. "The town believes this of Kerensa, that she is…," he swallowed, unable to say the word.

"No, no they don't. Some suspect…"

"Carowan."

"Is one. But others talk too. Your mother and I have always done our best to turn the gossip. Kerensa never deserved that. Nor did Meliora."

"How can you say that? If what you're suggesting is true then Meliora really is a wh-"

"Stop. Don't say it. Not now, not ever. Not of your wife's mother." Braneh paused, closing his eyes, "Love is a funny thing my son. Rarely simple. What your mother and I have… we are blessed and I thank God daily for giving her to me. Not all couples fare so well."

"That doesn't excuse a cockholds horns!"

"No, it does not."

"And Kerensa, she knows nothing of this, I am sure of it." Determination filled his voice, "She deserves to know the truth."

Braneh nodded thoughtfully, "Perhaps. But ask yourself this, son. This rumour you now know… this anger you now feel towards Meliora at what she *might* have done. What does that mean for your love? Where does that place Kerensa?"

Rewan felt as though his father's gentle words had slapped him cold. He swallowed hard, realisation flooding through him.

"Nothing will stop me marrying her. Nothing."

"I believe it. But it will be best for all won't it, if we let the past rest?"

"But Kerensa… All these years shunned. She's believed it all to be because of her ankle. But it is much, much more. Would knowing the rest help to unburden her? Even a little bit?"

"It's no man's right to tell another how to treat his wife, what secrets to keep and which to reveal. But I will say this, the difference matters."

Rewan paused, mind racing. Slowly he nodded, frowning heavily.

"Will you tell me father?" he asked, "Will you tell me about Cubert and what happened before Kerensa's birth that gave rise to this talk? I fear it will explain much."

"That it will my son, that it will."

And with a heavy sigh Braneh leaned forward and poured them both another drink.

Interlude

Eia passed that winter.

You cried for days, barely ate and slept fitfully as you mourned. The depth of your sorrow shocked me. But it should not have. You were always a sensitive one.

And then, as if your warning had summoned it into being, I felt the first stirrings of my own demise cramp deep within my gut.

I didn't tell you of course. I thought I still had time. I suppose my mother thought that too before she left me, I failed to learn that lesson from her. Hope makes us poor students, I think.

I didn't want to leave you, not ever. But in the end, it was never up to me.

You were right. You needed someone else.

I like that boy. Rewan. I don't remember if I ever told you? If I ever said he was a good choice.

By then I was so weary. Of life, of hope, of men. It hadn't worked for me, love, marriage. But who is to say what life held for you? I should not have made you fear it, I only wanted you to be ready, prepared. In case.

I'm sorry my child.

I hope you found each other's hearts to be true.

I hope you found love.

The Smell of Storm

The wind was bitingly cold, carrying the promise of ice and storm. Kerensa made her way slowly up the cliff face towards the Huer's hut.

She wanted to see them leave.

Down below in the sheltered bay, Rewan and the other fishermen dragged their vessels out into the shallows and began to row for the break as they had all season. But today was different. In addition to the new nets of last season, this year three vessels, including Rewan's, had been fitted with a mast and sail, ready to take advantage of the autumn winds and range even further in their search for pilchard flesh.

Passing the Huer's hut Kerensa waved hello and made her way to the cliff edge. Setting her basket down on the yellowed grasses she stretched her arms up to the cloudy sky above and took in a deep breath of salt spray and air. Looking down below she watched as the boats made their way out of the bay, the white of the furled sails reflecting the pale light, marking Rewan and his father's vessels. The wind whipped up from the cliff edge, forcing her hair back from her face in a stream of golden curls. It smelt of storm.

She'd told Rewan so, as he joined her on her walk from her hut that morning. But he was undeterred. "We fish in all weather," he'd grinned at her, "and the winds mean we can travel faster and be back before the harsher weather arrives. You will see."

He'd passed her a sticky fruit bun and turned their conversation to sail designs and materials, the things he'd been learning at markets down the coast. Such had become his routine. Each day with the rising sun he took two buns, still warm from his mother's oven and made his way out of town and up to Kerensa. There he waited on the low stone fence that marked Meliora's yard, until she appeared. Falling into step beside her, the two would-be-lovers walked down to the town, sharing the buns, laughing, smiling and talking of everything and nothing.

Nothing more than that had passed between them, just time shared. Kerensa wanted more. She believed, hoped, that Rewan did too. So what was holding him back?

Glancing down she saw the figures of the fishermen in miniature as they stowed their oars and prepared the sails. One lone face turned upwards towards the cliff top, a hand raised in a wave. A grin lit Kerensa's face and she returned the wave with both of her hands, shaking them frantically over her head. She'd told him she'd be here, watching. He'd remembered.

Now she knew his boat was the one farthest to the left, closest to her and the rocky coast. The wind lashed against her skin again, tangling her skirts about her legs. Down below the white of the sails began to rise, unfurling as the men hauled them high. Soon the canvas filled with ocean air, the white billowing out like her skirts and pulling the boat and its crew forward. Rewan's boat seemed to soar, cutting smoothly through the chop, heading out into the mass of water that hugged their little coastline. Kerensa wrapped her arms about her to ward away the chill, the smile fading slowly from her face. It really did smell of storm.

The ocean winds filled the canvas. Behind him, Cardor whooped in excitement as their little vessel leapt across the waves. Kenver held the rudder, Rewan tied off the sail and took the main sheet from Gerens' trembling hand. His second brother was not yet a fan of the open waters. Clapping Gerens on the back, Rewan took the rudder from Kenver and pointed their ship straight out from the coast. Their rig was rudimentary, a simple mast added to their row boat with a canvas sail attached. They'd bought the materials and installed the rig themselves. Needs must. For now it was all they could afford. But soon, soon they would be able to invest in a new vessel, one made for sails and distant waters.

"Today we go deep boys!" Rewan cried over the slap of the waves and the howl of the winds. "Out and back and cleaned up for supper before mid-afternoon. I can smell my mother's pasties already!"

Cardor and Kenver grinned, faces turned to the salty winds. Gerens slumped down in the bow frowning deeply, hands clenched over his gut. Rewan's lips twisted in a mischievous grin and he turned the rudder sharply, causing the sail to catch more wind and swiftly lean over, pressing the boat's edge to the waves. Gerens let out a shriek of fear and gripped the boat's side in white-knuckled hands. Openly laughing, Rewan righted the vessel and saluted his brother.

"I've got you Gerens. Trust me!"

Gerens glared back at his brother, red-faced with embarrassment and turned away from the snickering of the rest of the crew.

Rewan shook his head. Gerens would learn, in time. He turned from his crew to look back at the rest of the fleet. Not far behind, his father's boat was also under full sail, Austol's took up the rear. After them came the rowers. They would work the nearer coast today, while the sailboats headed out further. Time to see just how much fish was out there in these waters.

Sturdy legs subtly adjusting his stance as they crested wave after wave, Rewan glanced back at the receding cliffs that marked his white cove home and smiled. Atop the right side stood a tiny white figure. His heart and his future. And should God will it, the mother of his children. He just needed to get the money together for a new home. One built of stone, like his father's. Then he was sure he could make Kerensa his wife and take care of her, for life. Just as his father had done with his mother.

Filled with the excitement of future promise, Rewan turned back to the sea and sailed his crew out into the depths.

The hull was full to the brim, fish slipping and slapping along the decks. Bow pointed for home Rewan eyed the coast, tension strumming through his veins. Beside him, his father's vessel kept pace. Like Rewan, Braneh's focus was solely forward, to home.

They'd found a school of mackerel just as the sun had begun its dip down the western side of the sky. What a haul! Fat and grey and fierce, the mackerel had fought strongly and bravely. Now only a few still wiggled, their mouths gaping. The black, dead eyes of the rest staring at nothing.

Their haul was immense, the success proof of the value of the sails.

But they'd stayed too long.

As deepening autumn sped the sun to its bed, the winds had changed direction, gushing from the north, black clouds in their wake, the waves tipped white by the ocean's fury.

Rain, sharp as needles, pelted down on the little fleet as the raging winds tried to rip the rudder from Rewan's grip. He held fast, eyes fixed on the coast ahead, legs braced to ride the rising waves that slapped the hull. His crew huddled below, eyes down, nestled with the fish below the hull rim. Exhaustion laced his limbs, from catching the fish and bracing against the waves, from the cold that now penetrated his bones, but Rewan kept on.

Suddenly, Gerens lurched to his feet, twisted and then leaned over the edge of the boat and vomited into the sea. Rewan let out a hefty laugh and, leaning over, clapped his brother on his back.

"We'll make a sailor of you yet," Rewan cried encouragingly. "You'll see."

Gerens looked up at his brother, skin tinged with green and tried a smile. Sympathy flooded through Rewan. *He really does try*, Rewan thought to himself, *I need to be more supportive, more understanding*. He resolved to take Gerens out for some individual sailing time, get his brother used to the ways of the sea. He was sure, in time, Gerens would be just as comfortable as he and Cardor already were on the waves.

Just as he turned back to the coast a huge wave launched up from the sea before them. Despite the weight of his fatigue, Rewan moved quickly, angling the boat to take the wave head on. Madern, on his left, was not so lucky. The wave caught his port side and sent the vessel careering towards Rewan and his crew.

"Gerens!" Rewan screamed, "Release the sheet, we have to turn!"

Frozen, Gerens stared out at the oncoming vessel.

"Gerens!" Rewan cried again, turning the rudder hard aft. The sail snapped across the boat dangerously fast, throwing them all to the side. Madern slid past, barely missing their hull. A crash out here in this weather would have been a disaster. Rewan released a grateful breath. But they were not out of trouble yet. The change of angle had overfilled their sail with wind, leaning them over so far the boat edges began to take on water.

Rewan realised Braneh's boat was now ahead of them, and they were closing, fast.

They had to change course.

"Release the main, Gerens!" Rewan bellowed.

Shaking, Gerens looked down at his hands, rope wrapped tightly about his fists.

It all happened at once.

Cardor stood up, pointing out to Braneh's boat. Gerens finally heard his brother's order. And Rewan threw the rudder to the right. The boat lurched over a wave and twisted left, rolling down the side of the water. And the sail snapped back across the hull, right into Cardor's exposed back.

He didn't have a chance. Propelled by the speed of the sail and the lean of the boat Cardor went over and disappeared under the waves.

Braneh's scream of anguish carried across the storm as the father stood at his boat's stern, helpless as his youngest living son went under.

But Rewan didn't hear his cry. Thrusting the rudder into Gerens' hands he tore the woollen jumper from his body and dived in after his brother.

The sky above was black as pitch, only the thin light of the moon lit the gentle waves of the bay. The storm had passed, leaving Porth Gwynn heavy with a moisture that promised ice. The women, old men and rowers lined the cove, only the smallest children were in bed, dreaming peacefully, unaware.

Derwa gripped Kerensa's hand. Kerensa squeezed hers back. Whilst they prayed for all three missing vessels to return, they both waited for the same boat most urgently. Kerensa swallowed the sinking feeling that had dragged down her stomach since the first drops of rain began some five hours before. It now rose as bile in her throat. She squeezed her eyes shut and took a deep breath. She would not vomit.

A cry rang out across the town. As one the folk looked up towards the Huer's hut. A sound like a sob escaped the collective mouths of the wives as they saw the bristles flashing in the moonlight. Boats had been spotted. Meraud didn't wait. Hefting her skirts she ran down onto the dark beach, voice calling out her husband's name, the names of her three sons. The other wives followed, streaming down onto the soaking sands, eyes straining to see in the gloom.

"There!" Meraud cried. "I see them, I see them!"

Now the men moved, racing down to their row boats and dragging them out into the water and stroking powerfully towards the dark shapes that bobbed across the white-lit waters.

Derwa released Kerensa's hand and joined the women in the shallows, wading out to help pull the battered boats in from the sea.

Kerensa didn't move. Eyes forward, she scanned the boats as they came closer, counting the dark figures of the exhausted sailors as they were hauled in by their friends.

Two men missing.

Her hands began to shake, her knees to tremble. The bile surged up in her throat. Again she swallowed. She would not show weakness.

Hitching her skirts she made her way down to the shallows. Men took the arms of sailors, too exhausted from the struggle to take their own body weight and helped them from their vessels. She scanned the faces: Carowan, Jago, Braneh, Madern, Gerens... her heart leapt at the sight of her dear friend.

Derwa gave a cry of joy and wrapped her arms around a soaking figure that had to be Kenver. So where was...

"No!" Meraud's scream cut the night. "No, no!"

Kerensa snapped her eyes to the woman's desperate cries and her heart sank.

Meraud had lost her legs. Too overcome to stand, she and Braneh had slumped into the wet sand. Everyone froze, except Gerens. He moved swiftly, with determination and hooked an arm about his mother's waist. But as he bent to lift her Braneh surged up from the beach and shoved his son away.

"This is your doing!" Braneh screamed. "Useless bloody coward! I saw, I saw it all. If you'd listened. If you'd done as Rewan ordered, they would be here. Get out of my sight. Do you hear me? Get out of my sight! I never, never want to see your white face again!"

Gerens stood frozen, eyes wide and startled in the moonlight. Braneh seemed to shrink, as if his whole core collapsed within him. Face drawn and grey he turned from his son and bent down to Meraud. As though she were a child, he lifted his wife into his arms and slowly carried her back up the beach. How he had the strength, after fighting the storm, no one could fathom, but he did.

Kerensa stood stunned, eyes fixed on Gerens. He turned and saw her. Grief, pure and raw flooded his face. He departed swiftly, walking away down the beach. She watched him disappear into the dark before turning back to the sea.

"Kez?"

A warm hand in hers, a gentle arm about her shoulders, the scent of Derwa filled her nose.

"Cardor went over," a voice said. "Rewan jumped in to save him. We, we searched, and searched and searched, but the waves...."

Kerensa looked up into Kenver's face, his eyes laced with shame.

"We tried," he croaked.

"Come," Derwa pulled on her hand. "Come back to mine."

Kerensa shook her head slowly and untangled her hand from her friend's.

"No," was all she said.

Around them the rest of the town made their way slowly up the beach and back into their homes, full of competing emotions; relief at holding their loved ones close, guilt at their fortune where two young men were lost and deepest sorrow.

Kerensa stayed, eyes fixed on the waters of the bay, feet wet with salt water, body shivering in the night breeze. She waited. Derwa stayed at her side a while, then left. Later she returned with a blanket and wrapped it about Kerensa's shoulders.

Still she waited.

The waters receded, the tide pulling out and away from the coast.

She waited.

The first rays of the sun began to colour the sky overhead. Clear and blue, crisp and cold.

She waited.

Behind her the town began to stir, the scent of wood fires and bread and stew filling the pebbled streets.

She waited.

The Huer slowly climbed the cliff to his hut.

She waited.

And then.

"There," Kerensa raised a finger and pointed, her voice a whisper in her throat, dried out from her all night vigil.

"There."

No one heard.

She turned, frantic, waving her arms at the town. "Help!" She cried but could not make enough sound. "Help!" She stopped and worked her mouth, forcing moisture down her throat, swallowed and then screamed.

"Help me! They are here, they are back! Help me!"

Old Brae looked up from his walk and following Kerensa's frantic pointing, saw.

"By God!" he cried, then raced to the nearest cottage.

There in the middle of the bay floated a lump in the shape of a human.

Kerensa turned and ran into the waters, as deep as she dared. Behind her the town flooded onto the streets and soon Madern led a row boat out into the bay. Kerensa watched, muscles quivering in the icy waters, she didn't notice.

The row boat approached the floating form. Madern reached over and pulled a limp Cardor from the water. Kerensa's breath stopped, her heart stopped, the world stopped.

Madern reached down again and a hand gripped his arm and pulled. Rewan dragged himself into the boat.

"Ah!" An anguished cry escaped her lips as she saw Rewan moving in the dawn-light.

The boat began its passage back to the beach. Slowly, so slowly. Kerensa waded across to intercept it. As the boat came in line with her, Rewan leapt from the vessel splashing into the water beside her.

"Rewan!" she sobbed, her eyes flooding with tears.

She felt his arms go about her waist, pull her to him. She ran her hands across his face, tears flowing freely from her eyes.

He grinned. "Did you think I wouldn't come back for you?"

She let out a low sob of relief and joy and Rewan swept her against his body.

"I will always come back for you," he said and brought his mouth to hers, kissing her openly, passionately. For the first time.

Lavender Cuttings

"I didn't think, I just jumped in. It was so cold. And black as coal. I knew straight away I had no chance of seeing Cardor," Rewan sat in the warming glow of his mother's fire, cup of whiskey in his hand, blanket about his shoulders and Kerensa by his side. Behind them, on a makeshift cot not used since Treeve sickened lay Cardor, sleeping fitfully under a mountain of covers. Meraud was at his side, holding his hand and wiping his fevered brow. He'd caught a chill from his water adventure, his lungs, raw and moist from inhaling seawater. But Meliora, keeping watch from the fireside with her daughter, Rewan and Braneh, was calm. He would make it.

"It was stupid," Rewan continued, "I was stupid. If I hadn't been lucky, if the waves hadn't washed us together, I'd never have found him, and you'd have two more dead sons." He turned to Meraud. "Forgive me mother."

"There's nothing to forgive," Braneh's deep voice answered for his wife. "You both came back, you saved your brother. If it weren't for Gerens none of this would have happened. That bloody coward..."

"It wasn't Gerens' fault either father," Rewan tried.

"You are a good son, a loyal brother. But I saw what happened, watched as he disobeyed you. Look what could have happened? It would have been on his head."

Kerensa was shocked. This illogical anger was so unlike the wise, calm fisherman she'd grown up with.

Braneh stood abruptly and strode from the room, mumbling something about fetching some more whiskey. Kerensa caught the reflection of tears on his cheek. Grief and fear did strange things to a man.

Rewan watched his father's retreating back, hunched and deflated, none of the confident bounce he usually walked with.

"It's as if he aged ten years while we were gone," he whispered softly to Kerensa.

"I think he did."

"So, how did you survive?" Meliora asked, "It was a brutal storm, the rain flooded several of the main street houses as it coursed down the hillside. I can't imagine it was any better over the sea."

"Again, I must give thanks to luck and God. When I first went in I just flailed, reaching my hands about me at random. Then a solid mass thumped into me. I grabbed hold and thank God I did for it was Cardor. I shouted at him, but he was limp. So I pulled him over my chest, with his head up and tried to keep us above the waves.

"We saw the lights," he nodded to the returning Braneh and accepted a top-up of his drink, hands still trembling, the bravado of his return to the Port all gone now, leaving only the naked truth of what he had faced, alone. "I could see the boats, knew they had stopped and were searching. I tried to call out, but the storm…"

"We searched, my son," Braneh confirmed, speaking over his misplaced guilt, "round and round where you went in. But I never heard naught but the wind and rain." He sat down, face drawn down by shame.

Rewan continued, "The currents were pushing us away from the boats. I tried to swim us towards them, but the waves were too strong. I soon gave up and just floated, holding Cardor. Praying.

"I don't know how long we drifted in the water, but the clouds parted and for a time I watched the stars sparkling overhead. Then I saw it, the coast. The black rocks illuminated by the moon. The currents had taken us home. Well, not home, a bit further down the coast, but I was able to get us up out of the water and onto a ledge. And there we stayed, until the sun came up."

He paused, sipping his whiskey and looking back to his mother. "I held him close, mother, I tried to keep him warm."

Meraud nodded silently and smiled at her son.

"When the sun was high enough that I could see the cliff face, I pulled Cardor onto my back, lucky he's always been a scrawny thing, and started to walk along the rocks. I followed the cliff until I found our cove. But I ran out of footing, so I had to swim the last…"

"And that's when Kez saw you!" Braneh announced, placing a warm hand on her shoulder. "I'm thankful to you too girl. You didn't give up. I…"

"You were needed at home," Meraud said firmly from Cardor's bed. "We all did what we did. And it has all turned out well. I'll hear no regrets from you husband."

Her tone brooked no argument, and Kerensa silently hoped it would be enough to still the guilt that had hardened Braneh's calm into accusation. She didn't know where Gerens had gone after Braneh had blamed him in front of the village, didn't know if he even knew his brothers had, miraculously, survived. *He should be here,* she thought, *safe and warm and forgiven with us all.*

As if he heard her thought, Rewan reached over and took her hand in his, squeezing gently.

"Meraud is right," Meliora said, "And Cardor will be fine. His lungs are weak from the salt water and the cold, but the fever is not strong, it will break by sun up. Though I advise bed rest and warm broth for at least four days before he even thinks about going out in this chill."

"I'll keep him indoors," Meraud said firmly. "Lord knows how, but I will." A fond smile lifting her face.

"You have your ways my wife," Braneh said, a hint of mischief dancing over his lips.

Kerensa's belly warmed with hope, that was the Braneh she knew and loved.

"Good," Meliora continued. "Then we will be leaving you. The day is late and you all need time to rest and heal. Come Kerensa."

Reluctantly Kerensa stood to go. Rewan rose with her. "I'll walk you home," he began.

"You'll do no such thing!" Kerensa smiled to take the sting from her words. "You have not slept and have been through an immense ordeal. Mother and I will be fine to get home. You must stay and recover. I will see you tomorrow when I bring the additional thyme and verbena tea mother has advised for Cardor."

Rewan nodded reluctantly then leaned forward and, voice pitched low for just her ears, whispered, "I'll think of nothing but you until that time."

Kerensa blushed and smiled secretly to him, eyes dancing in the firelight.

Braneh coughed uncomfortably.

"Until tomorrow," Meliora announced and led her daughter into the cold autumn afternoon.

The light of dawn was just touching the land when the knock sounded on Kerensa's door. She sat up, swinging her legs over the edge of the bed. Beside her Meliora didn't stir. She was sleeping deeper lately, and longer. Kerensa looked down at her mother's profile, cast in the cool blues of morning. Even rest could not relieve the deepening lines along her brow and mouth. *Still beautiful though*, Kerensa thought.

The knock sounded again, Kerensa got to her feet and shuffled to the hut door. There, as if it were a school morning and they were but seven summers old, stood Gerens, bag slung over a shoulder, cap pulled down about his eyes.

"Gerens!" Kerensa exclaimed, throwing her arms about her friend's neck and squeezing him tight. The words tumbled from her, "They live, Gerens. Your brothers live! They made it home yesterday morning. Tired and wet but very, very much alive. They are well, Gerens. Have you heard? They are well!"

"Yes," he whispered softly, as he gently extracted himself from her embrace. Kerensa stepped back, suddenly embarrassed at her exuberant behaviour. But, they lived! Who cared about proper conduct when Rewan was alive?

"I saw them return," Gerens continued, "saw you waving for help. I spent the night at the Huer's hut, watching for them. Never thought to check the rocks of the cliff face…"

"So you've been home? Heard how they survived? It's quite the story."

"I've been home."

Gerens fell silent, eyes downcast. Kerensa watched him, a bubble of fear beginning to grow in her stomach. She cast her eyes over her friend.

"Gerens, what's in the bag?"

He looked up at her from dark smudged eyes full of pain. "My belongings."

"Why? Gerens…"

"I'm leaving Kez," he stated simply, cutting off her words. "You heard father, I'm no longer welcome."

"But, Gerens," Kerensa said, "Braneh never meant that. He was angry, afraid. He spoke in haste…"

"He spoke the truth. I am a coward. I hate the sea and fishing, and I nearly cost my brothers their lives. It would have killed mother…"

"Rewan doesn't agree with that assessment."

"Rewan is a good brother."

"But they lived Gerens."

"And I must go." He paused, taking a deep breath. Kerensa saw tears beginning to swell in his eyes. "I am not meant to be here, Kez. I can't even stand the taste of pilchards. My father has disowned me. And that's all right. I'm not the fisherman Rewan and Cardor are. And they will continue to be successful, it's in their blood. Like father. I have to find somewhere for me. There's nothing for me here."

"Yes there is, the townsfolk, your friends. Me! You can work the processing sheds, fishing isn't the only task to do here."

"He will marry you soon."

Kerensa stopped, surprised at the sudden change of topic.

Gerens gave a small rueful laugh, "Rewan will ask you to be his wife. We all know what you will say."

Shaking her head Kerensa frowned, "I, I don't understand…"

"There is nothing for me here," Gerens repeated softly. His eyes flicked up to hers, held them for a moment. Understanding flooded through her. She'd never guessed, never even thought.

"Gerens…" she tried, but could not find the words.

"It's all right Kez," he smiled gently. "Nothing makes me happier than knowing you are happy, safe and loved. Rewan will be a good husband, the best in fact. And he will protect you from it all.

"I have to find my place." He stopped, looking up at the lightening sky. "It's time for me to go."

"Gerens," she reached out and took his hand in hers, head shaking. "Please, wait. Come in for a cup of tea and let's talk about this."

He shook his head.

"Here."

He pushed a small pot into her hands. She looked down to see the grey-green leaves of a lavender bush.

"Cuttings from mother's bush, for your garden," Gerens smiled. "Live well Kez," he said and turned away.

Panic seized her chest. This was not how it was supposed to be.

Say something, she chided herself, *there must be something you can do to change his mind. Say something!* But she could not find the words. In her heart she knew he was right.

Gripping the lavender in her hands she watched as he made his way slowly across the hillside and out of sight.

Sorrow heavy across her shoulders, Kerensa walked to the backyard and knelt in the wet earth. Digging her hands deep into the black soil, she shaped a hole to plant the lavender cuttings, right beside Eia's grave. Since the old hen had passed last winter, Kerensa had wondered

how best to mark the spot.
    The lavender was perfect.

The Knockers

The search for work took him far, far south. The need for distance from it all: his guilt and shame, his failure and cowardice, his aching heart, took him to the edge of the land of England.

Stopping at various towns along the way, Gerens turned from fish work, and struggled to adjust to farmhand life. Both too strong a reminder of the only home he had ever known, and love he'd left behind.

January sleet found him on the farthest southern coast in a town called St Just. The work: tin mining, the other great economy of the county of his birth. Many young men from Porth Gwynn had left to try their luck in the mines, but none from Gerens' family. The idea, the work, was foreign. So completely different to fishing the idea freed his clenched heart from the pain of regret and longing.

He found lodgings in a small, dark boarding house and signed on to work the Geever mine. In the dark of a winter morn, lunch bag in hand, he left for his first shift, making his way across the hills and down the beach to the mine shaft that lay beside the sea. Smoke rose from the stone chimney, the grinding of the Trevithick boiler engine pumps that kept the mine from flooding echoing out across the waves. Gerens followed his fellow miners. No one spoke. Tull on his head, pick in hand he mounted the lift that would lower them down into the bowels of the earth, to the heart of the mine. The lift rattled and shook, but they landed gently at the bottom. Lighting his oil lamp, Gerens followed the others down the tunnel, reinforced with wooden planks and nails. The tunnel dug deep beneath the beach, reaching out into the sea. Above him the ocean stirred, rocks scraping along its sandy floor and echoing down the tunnel. Water found tiny cracks overhead and dripped salty droplets that splashed on his face and arms. He walked on.

At the tunnel's end they stopped. Placing their lamps by their sides they began: picking, digging, shovelling dirt to be carted back out and sorted. Gerens applied himself to the task, muscles groaning at the change of demand. They broke for lunch, resting where they stood, downing pasties and tea from flasks. Then they were back to work, grinding away the hours of light above.

When the whistle for the change of shift came Gerens felt he could barely stand. But somehow he hefted his pick across his shoulder and made his way to the shaft and freedom.

Frozen air, thick with salt-spray slapped his face. Its freshness had never seemed so sweet. Gerens breathed deeply of the open air. About him the sky was as dark as it was when he arrived, the daylight having passed as he toiled beneath the waves.

Back at his lodgings, he ate the meal of bread and stew his lady provided. His disloyal heart crying out for home and the flavours his mother cooked into every meal. He buried his longing in a round of ale at the nearby pub with two of the men he lodged with. These two were new. No one stayed long. He never bothered to remember their names.

And so his days were shaped, up before dawn, home after dusk, stew and beer and a cold bed. Alone.

One shift, as he toiled beneath the ocean, a storm raged above, the sound of rock scraping over the sea floor grew, booming along the tunnel walls. The ceiling creaked as if the beams were being pressed down by the angry sea above. Water ran freely down the sides of the tunnel, the stench of sweat and blood and dirt and salt assaulting his nose as the waves crashed above.

It was too much. Unable to ignore the sound of the angry sea above and the fear it stoked deep in his heart, Gerens whistled. Just a simple tune, one from childhood. A gentle ditty to block out the sound of the raging waves above.

Heads snapped towards him as his fellow miners heard his song, their eyes boring into him. His whistle caught in his throat. A large man lumbered up to him grabbing him by the front of his shirt.

"What d'ya think you're doing!" He shouted in Gerens face, his anger a living breathing thing. "You don't whistle in a mine. You'll call the Knockers down on us all. Stupid fool."

Shoving Gerens back against the mine wall, the man turned and stalked away, the others frowned at him a few moments longer before turning back to their toil.

The Knockers; the small, inconsistent folk of the mines. They kept miners safe, and played tricks to harm. A tale for children. A superstition to explain tragedy.

And just like that Gerens knew. He would not return here to this place of darkness and dirt, of soot and pain. Like life as a fisherman, he was equally unsuited to mining. The myths, the fears, the foolish traditions, he could not bear it.

Was there anywhere he would be useful? Any work he would not burden?

As his head broke free of the shaft that night he made his way back to his boarding house as normal, ate his stew, drank his ale.

But the next morn he slept until the sun rose and shone its light, pale and soft, through his window, caressing his worn forehead and cheeks.

He rose and dressed. Packed his few belongings away and left the house.

He didn't look back.

As he walked out across the stretch of his home county he decided. It was time to leave Cornwall. To leave and never come back.

The Caul

"Kerensa, wake up. Come."

Kerensa looked at her mother's face through sleepy eyes. She looked alert despite the dark night hour. But her lips were pinched with worry.

Derwa.

Snapping wide awake, Kerensa sat up and swiftly donned her day clothes, pulling her shawl about her shoulders to ward off the spring night chill. Without instruction, she gathered the herbs they had been stockpiling in preparation. Raspberry leaf, sage and thyme.

"The butter too Kerensa," Meliora said, "I fear we will need it."

Kerensa reached into the butter jar and pulled up their last knob of salty, yellow grease. This was her first birthing, she would not argue anything with her mother this night.

Baskets full, shawls pulled tight, the two women made their way out of their hut into the night. Below their hill the town of Porth Gwynn slept soundly, the still spring air sweet with summer's promise. Only one home glowed with the warmth of fire.

Derwa and Kenver had married barely a week after the boating accident that nearly claimed Rewan and Cardor's lives, the celebration overtaking the town for two days straight. An opportunity to release the pent up tension of the accident and the dwindling fish runs, and focus on something joyful and positive.

Within the month Derwa revealed her pregnancy to Kerensa, excited but also shy. Overwhelming joy had flooded Kerensa's heart, her fears for her friend after the night at Doydan Castle banished by the life that now grew inside Derwa's womb. The happiness in Derwa's smile was enough to cast the tinge of jealousy from Kerensa's heart. Despite his obvious intentions, Rewan had yet to make anything official between them. But how could she be sad when her friend was so joyous? She found she could not.

The two friends had spent many hours together that winter, sitting by the fire in Derwa and Kenver's small hut on the opposite side of town. As was the way, the men of the town had come together to build the new hut. It was of wood, affordable in these leaner seasons. Stone homes cost far more in money and time. The initial hope of the drift net fish hauls had dimmed with the accident. While the season had undoubtedly brought some great days of success, the consistency was still lacking. The truth of empty fish sheds stark in the face of the near tragedy. Rewan remained unfazed, his focus solely towards the next season's success, his thoughts and hopes all centred around the next run. He was so like his father.

Around them the town moved on, adapted to the lower rations and income.

And today, a new life would enter the world, at least so Kerensa prayed.

She knew little of childbirth, save the boasts of overcoming terrible pain from older mothers and whispers of blood and injury from new brides. But Meliora was more than just a mother twice herself. In the years since Kerensa's arrival she had taken on the role of midwife to the town in accompaniment to her healing work. She had safely delivered babes of almost every mother in Porth Gwynn, losing but a few. So Kerensa banished her fears and the seeds of doubt that scratched at her mind and quickened her pace to keep up with Meliora's determined stride.

She heard Derwa first.

A scream of pain split the dark night sky outside her little wooden hut. Outside sat Kenver, head in his hands, Rewan beside him, ale in hand. The men's watch. Kerensa smiled hopefully to Rewan and he gifted her a cocky grin, his face radiating confidence in Meliora and in her. Breathing deeply, she sealed that belief in her heart, straightened her shoulders and followed her mother into the dimly lit hut.

The smell of sweat and fear and blood bit into her nostrils, acid and iron. There on the marriage bed Derwa lay on her side, hair plastered to her head, wet with sweat, hands clutching her belly. Beside her stood Mabyn, her mother, hands clasped before her.

At the sound of their entrance Mabyn looked up sharply, eyes fierce. She softened instantly, a look of relief flooding her features as she moved forward to greet Meliora.

"How long?" Meliora said by way of greeting.

"The first pains started this afternoon, but they were a minor thing. The waters didn't start until after supper. But the blood... I called for you straight away. It's not right, Meliora. It's too soon and I've never seen..."

"Shhh," Meliora placed a gentle finger over Mabyn's mouth and, pitching her voice low so only they could hear, said "She needs our confidence now as much as our knowledge. We show her only strength and purpose. Not a hint of doubt. Am I clear?"

She paused, looking Mabyn and Kerensa firmly in the eye. Both nodded solemnly. Satisfied, Meliora moved to the bed giving orders as she went.

"Mabyn, boil water, Kerensa give her the sage for the kettle and bring me the lamp from the table."

Both women obeyed as Meliora knelt down before Derwa's straining face.

Gently, she pushed the wet hairs from Derwa's face, her expression a mix of pain and fear. Though this was her first birthing, some primal part of Derwa knew something was terribly wrong. Meliora smiled comfortingly to her charge, and took her head between her hands.

"I know you are afraid and in great pain. But together, we are going to bring this baby into the world. Alive. You must believe in me Derwa. You must work with me. You will do that won't you child? You know I will bring your son forth. You believe."

Kerensa watched in silent awe of her mother as her friend's expression changed from one of terror to that of pure determination.

"Good girl," Meliora said firmly. "Now, sit up and drink this, it will help with the pain."

She passed Derwa a small bottle of willow bark tincture from her basket. As Derwa drank Meliora rolled up her sleeves.

"Mabyn, the water?" she called.

Mabyn entered, kettle of sage tea in hand.

"Collect cloths and soak them in the water, we will need them to prevent infection. Kerensa, by me."

Kerensa moved to the side of the bed and took up Derwa's hand, giving it a squeeze and her friend her most confident smile. Derwa looked long at her. Searching, Kerensa realised, for the truth. Kerensa held her head high and projected all her belief down to her friend. She saw Derwa relax momentarily and was thankful she had managed to hide her own desperate fear.

Meliora was a good actress, the best. But Kerensa had worked beside her before, had seen the ones lost. She alone saw the signs of strain across her mother's brow, the pulse of muscle in her temple that foretold failure. Keeping her breathing steady, Kerensa looked to her mother and waited for her instructions.

"Derwa," Meliora began, "I am going to examine you now. I need to find the position of the baby and see how far along you have progressed." She dipped her hands into the pot of sage tea, rinsing them thoroughly then folded Derwa's skirts up over her hips, her movements swift and efficient.

"Knees up child," she said, "Legs wide, that's it. Kerensa, bring the lamp closer."

Kerensa looked away, offering her friend some dignity.

"Kerensa!" Meliora snapped, "focus girl. This is no time for prudishness. We are all women here, this is our sisterhood and we all share it."

Nodding, Kerensa looked down and watched as her mother rubbed butter over her hands then leaned down and reached inside Derwa.

Derwa's face twisted in pain, her body going stiff, but she did not cry out.

Meliora extracted her hand, face impassive and began to press against Derwa's bulging belly. This time Derwa did gasp. Meliora nodded turning to Mabyn.

"Sit by her side and mop her brow, make her comfortable. Kerensa with me, we must prepare some herbs."

Meliora led Kerensa into the kitchen room and began unpacking herbs from her basket, placing them heavily on the wooden table. It took Kerensa a moment to realise her mother was not searching for something, but rather simply making sounds to suggest such a purpose.

Her stomach dropped.

"The babe is wrongly placed," Meliora whispered to her daughter as she shuffled some fresh thyme across the table. "Legs first, twisted so the left knee is stuck in the opening. I have to move the child or she'll have no hope of birthing it. But it is risky. I could injure the child or Derwa and I still may not be able to free up the passage out. The other option is to cut the babe out, but few women can survive that and Derwa's lost a lot of blood already…"

Meliora paused, and for the first time Kerensa saw the shadows of doubt and anxiety pass over her mother's face. Suddenly she looked every one of her 46 years, exhausted, frail, breakable.

Kerensa rallied. "We must do it mother. We must give both a chance to survive. That is the only option."

Meloria looked up into her daughter's face. Kerensa saw her determination solidify. Without another word Meliora strode into the bedroom and sat down beside Derwa. Caressing her face she whispered her intentions to Derwa, "I'm going to move the babe, reposition him so his legs can move through you. It will be painful and the birth will too. You must work hard my child. Can you do that?"

Derwa was exhausted, drawn from pain and blood loss, but in her eyes a fire was stoking. She would fight, for herself and for her child.

"Right," Meliora said. "Kerensa, Mabyn, help her to stand, I need her upright. One under each arm, take her weight on you. She needs you now. All of you."

They rushed to obey, carefully bringing Derwa to her feet and hooking her arms across their shoulders. Derwa trembled against Kerensa's side, her muscles twitching with pain and exhaustion. But her face was set with grim determination.

Meliora positioned herself before Derwa's ample belly, placing a hand on each side.

"This will hurt, my child. Scream as you will," she said. Then, without giving anyone a moment to consider those words, she thrust her hands into the sides of Derwa's stomach and twisted sharply.

Derwa howled, throwing her head back, her screech tearing from her throat. Her legs gave out. Kerensa and Mabyn took her weight, bracing hard. Kerensa felt her weak foot tremble but refused to give in. Derwa was fighting, so would she.

Meliora pressed again and wrenched at Derwa's belly. Derwa screamed again and collapsed.

"Lay her down," Meliora instructed and the three women worked together to get Derwa's limp body back on the bed. She was conscious, barely.

"Butter!" Meliora ordered and Kerensa hurried to pass it to her mother. Hands coated, Meliora knelt between Derwa's legs and pushed both hands into her womb. "Now I need you to push child. Push like the world depends on it. Because it does."

Derwa took a deep breath, her eyes were glazed with pain and fatigue, but she nodded.

"Kerensa, Mabyn, brace her arms, support her head and neck."

Kerensa gripped her friend's back and hand and held firm. Derwa reeked of struggle and blood, her body hot and wet beneath Kerensa's grip. For the first time since her friend's wedding, Kerensa wondered if she wasn't actually the lucky one, not yet wed and pregnant. Shaking the thought aside, she focused on Meliora. Waiting.

Meliora breathed deeply, then fixed her eyes on Derwa. The two women stared at each other. A conversation fierce and passionate swam between them. Then Meliora nodded.

"One, two, three, PUSH!"

And Derwa pushed. She heaved. Gripping Kerensa's hand so tightly her nails cut into the skin, blood slipping between their fingers. Kerensa didn't let go.

"Again, girl, again. PUSH!"

Derwa screamed, Meliora screamed, Kerensa and Mabyn braced, sweat coursing in rivulets down the faces and bodies of all four women.

Then Meliora pulled. Derwa cried out once more, a groan deep with pain and terror, before collapsing back into the pillows.

And Meliora stood up. In her hands she held a shape. Covered in slippery red blood, limp.

Kerensa held her breath. Beside her Derwa gave a new sob of despair. Mabyn wound her arm about her daughter.

Then a cry pierced the night. Shrill and furious.

Kerensa stood up.

Meliora looked down at Derwa. "A boy, as promised. Healthy and whole."

She moved to Derwa's side. The baby had been born still wrapped in his caul. A good sign. Kerensa breathed an unconscious sigh of relief. Her friend had been blessed, the choices she'd been forced to make after The Folly had clearly been forgiven by God.

Peeling the caul from his skin and setting it aside to be given to the fishermen for good luck, Meliora placed the squalling infant in his mother's arms.

The front door slammed shut. The four women looked up as Kenver strode into the room, Rewan close on his heels.

"I tried to stop him," Rewan began but stopped as he took in the scene before him.

On the bed, skirts awry, bed soaked in blood, lay Derwa, around her three women streaked in red and sweat. But on Derwa's chest lay the babe.

"My son?" Kenver croaked to Derwa. She nodded slowly, smile

weary, face beatific and exhausted. Kenver stepped forward.

"Out!" Meliora's voice snapped.

Kenver glared at her, "He's my son…"

"And he is healthy and well. But my job is to care for both child and mother and if you don't get out now and let me finish my job you'll be raising your son alone! Out."

Kenver's face turned ashen. Rewan's arm about his shoulders, the men quickly exited.

"Meliora?" Mabyn queried, voice shaking with fear.

"She will be fine, Mabyn. But she has lost much blood. She needs stitches and broth and water and rest. Not a man blustering all over her. I just needed to ensure some time."

"He is perfect," Derwa murmured.

Meliora's expression softened, "Yes, child, he is. Can we lay him beside you a while? We will watch over him. I just need to check you over once more."

Derwa nodded absently, her eyes never leaving her son. "Breock, we will call him Breock."

"A good Cornish name," Mabyn smiled to her daughter.

Meliora frowned. "Mabyn?" she prompted.

"Oh, right."

Gently, Mabyn took the boy from her daughter's arms and cradled the tiny body against her own chest. Derwa's eyes followed the child, the lids growing heavy.

"Kerensa, the wool padding and sage water."

Kerensa fetched the wool and water and returned to the room. Derwa's head had rolled to the side, asleep. Beside her Mabyn cradled her grandson, eyes wet with wonder-filled tears.

Meliora took the wool from her daughter. "She's a special one your Derwa," she whispered. "She'll make a wonderful mother."

Kerensa nodded and allowed her own tears of relief and exhaustion to fall.

Lavender, Fennel and Sage

Meliora was sick.

Really sick.

In the months since Derwa's son Breock was born, she had barely left their cottage on the hillside, not even to see the babe. Kerensa removed her hand from her mother's forehead, slick with sweat. It was a hot morning, the height of summer punishing the earth. But the sweat on her mother's brow went deeper, into the core of her mother's being.

Thinking back, Kerensa now felt sure Meliora had been ailing for some time. The longer sleeps, the deep smudges under her eyes, the thinning of her face, but Meliora had said nothing, only pressed Kerensa to take more responsibility over their healing tasks.

"You are ready to do more alone now my child. Visit Derwa and check on her son. Old Madern's been complaining of warts since the winter, so take him some nettle paste…"

Feeling pride at her mother's trust, Kerensa had never questioned.

She should have.

But the days supporting the town's sick and the foraging and remedy preparation tasks were tiring, leaving Kerensa in a state of numbed fatigue.

And then there was Rewan. They'd seen little of each other lately. Their morning routine from the previous season interrupted by Kerensa's new responsibilities. Still, he could have made time to court her, yet he hadn't. She'd worried his interest had cooled, that her malformed foot and the ill-omen it promised had finally defeated his passions.

The seasons had been tough lately, and were getting tougher. Kerensa's defiance in the face of the ill-whispers of her fate withered under the weight of fear and prejudice.

Whatever her mother said to dismiss the idea that Kerensa's birth had brought the ill-winds, they still lived separate from the town. A physical distance that spoke volumes.

Standing alone she watched the sail boats set off each morning and prayed for a moment to talk with Rewan. To find out the truth of how he felt. Sadness and longing took up the little time she had left in the day for her own worries, and had overshadowed the more pressing reality that was developing right in front of her.

Moving to the dining table, Kerensa passed a beam of morning sunlight already warming the land. Taking up her mortar and pestle she ground a selection of herbs: lavender for calm, nettle for strength, fennel-fronds for cooling and boiled them on the coals. While the herbs steeped she went out into the yard and fetched fresh water, onion and leek. Propping the back door open to allow in the cool coastal breeze, she returned to the kitchen to chop the aromatic vegetables and place them in the potfry to start a broth. Pouring the herbal tea into a mug she returned to her mother's side. Sitting beside Meliora's head she helped her mother raise her head to drink. Eyes glazed with fever, Meliora's lips moved slowly, liquid running down her chin into the collar of her nightgown. But she got some down. Kerensa gently lay her mother back down and pulled back the covers to allow her body to cool in the breeze from the open back door. As she pulled back the covers she noticed the distinct swelling of Meliora's belly pressing up against the thin cotton of her shift. The arm pits yellowing from old sweat. Surprised, she gently placed her hands upon her mother's stomach and pressed carefully. Meliora groaned in pain, head turning side to side.

A horrid possibility struck Kerensa.

Her mother was well beyond the quickening years, and with the fever…

She reached under the bed and pulled out the bedpan. Unused and perfectly clean. Meliora was always fastidious. She would have to wait to confirm her suspicions, her fear.

She did not wait long. Mere hours later Kerensa was sitting at the table sewing a fresh hem on her winter dress in preparation for the coming season, the scent of bubbling broth filling the little hut, when Meliora cried out, a call of sudden and piercing pain. Quickly, Kerensa rushed to her mother's side. Meliora sat up in bed clutching her bulbous belly, sweat coursing down her face despite the cooling breeze from outside.

Instinctively Kerensa retrieved the bedpan.

"No," Meliora panted, "Help me outside."

"You are not strong enough mother. Use the pan and I will clean it. You must rest."

"No, please."

Kerensa took her mother's face between her hands and held her eyes. "I know mother," she whispered gently. "No more hiding. We must fight this together."

Tears of pain and fear swam in Meliora's eyes, she nodded, defeated. She could hide her condition from her daughter no longer.

Kerensa helped her mother from the bed and stabilised her as she squatted over the pot. Breathing heavily, gasping in pain, Meliora passed her waste. The stench was emphatic, rotten.

Exhausted from the effort, Meliora slumped back against her daughter, taking a moment to recover before they worked together to return her to bed. After settling her mother Kerensa took up the pot to empty it. The heat of the truth flooded her body and her arms trembled. The pot was filled with waste like thick black tar, red at the edges. Kerensa closed her eyes a moment to settle the cry of despair that threatened to escape her throat. Her guess had been correct. Meliora had the bowel-rot disease. And it was advanced. This would be her final summer.

Days passed and Kerensa never left her mother's side. She applied cooling, sage-scented cloths to her mother's brow, wiped her down with rosemary water daily, brought broths and camomile tea, told her stories, held her and cleaned out the chamber pot.

Derwa and baby Breock visited. The giggling pudge of new life brought a brief smile to Meliora's mouth, a light to her eyes.

After that the offerings started.

Derwa told the town of Meliora's condition, triggering an outpouring of support, borne from all Meliora had done for them over the years. Jago's wife brought ale, the twins Wenna and Ella carried up fresh cloth, Madern his wife's bread, Braneh their spare cot for Kerensa to sleep on. Meraud came multiple times each week, bearing pastries and pies and company, staying hours at Meliora's side, tending to her. From the edges of their notice Kerensa watched the two women together, a familiarity and comfort between them Kerensa had never before seen. She left them, allowing herself some moments of respite from her vigil.

The food stacked up, Meliora could not eat and Kerensa didn't care to. But Meraud's care of her mother...

Kerensa never found the words to thank her.

Rewan came too, bearing baskets of herbs.

"I went out with mother and Derwa, we weren't sure what you needed, but these looked familiar from your baskets. I know you've not the time to forage..."

He'd come. His presence sheared the last of her self-control, opening her soul to the flood of pain at her impending loss that she'd held at bay too long. Gratefulness for his thoughtful gift pushed her to an unbearable emotional place that only human contact could soothe.

Kerensa had kissed him, passionately.

Breaking off the kiss she began to weep, then sob. Rewan wrapped his strong arms about her shoulders and held her to his chest as her sobs grew and grew and her knees went weak and she lost time in the release of her grief. When she calmed he led her inside and sat her at the table. He made her tea, spread a thick slice of bread with butter and placed it before her.

"You must eat, Kerensa," he said gently. "You must be strong for the both of you."

Nodding, head light from crying, face sticky from dried tears, Kerensa complied. She didn't taste the soft fresh bread or the salty butter. But she ate. Meraud arrived then and ordered Kerensa to sleep, taking over Meliora's care while Kerensa rested on the small cot Braneh had carried up and placed at the foot of Meliora's bed. She slept until the next morning. It was the last night she would sleep through in her mother's presence.

The night was dark and thick with heat, mid-August bringing the last burst of intolerable heat before the seasons began to shift. Sweat coated Kerensa's face and neck. The stench of sickness and death hung heavy in the air. Gently, Kerensa spooned broth into Meliora's mouth. When her mother shook her head she stopped and, dipping a cloth in her pot of sage water, began to gently wipe her mother's fevered brow.

"Thank you," Meliora croaked, throat dry from the heat and her fever. Her chapped lips split as she spoke, blood running along the seam of her mouth. Carefully, Kerensa sponged it away.

"Of course mother," she whispered, "Now, rest."

She went to stand, to take the bowl of broth, barely touched, out to the kitchen and clean up, but Meliora gripped her arm.

Kerensa paused, sitting back down beside her mother.

"I have to tell you, you must know," Meliora whispered, voice hoarse with fatigue.

Kerensa frowned, "It's late mother, dark outside. You need to rest."

Meliora shook her head, eyes pressed closed, breathing laboured.

"You need to know… about your father."

"There is nothing to tell me mother. I know he left to farm. I know he never returned. It's all right mother," Kerensa breathed, swallowing the lump of sorrow that had formed in her throat.

"I will be safe here. They will take care of me."

As she looked down on Meliora, tears slipped out of Kerensa's eyes, wetting her cheeks. Her mother's skin was ashen, her once lustrous brown hair, limp and breaking, her cheeks hollow.

Meliora took her daughter's hand. "Please my child, sit with me and listen. I need to tell you."

An urgency had entered her mother's voice. Kerensa conceded.

"All right. We can talk a while."

She smiled and climbed onto the bed beside her mother. The two women lay face to face. Kerensa smoothed back the hair from Meliora's face and took her mother's hand. So fragile in her own. *She will sleep soon*, Kerensa thought as she looked at Meliora's drawn face.

Yet a smile touched the corners of her mother's mouth and her eyes sparkled in the candlelight, brighter than Kerensa had seen them shine since she became so ill.

"I loved your father, Kerensa. Deeply. I want you to know that. You were made in love."

Sympathy flooded Kerensa's heart. All these years Meliora had refused to talk of Kerensa's father, though as a child she had begged to know. Now, facing her own end, Meliora wanted to share her past, but Kerensa no longer needed to know. Meliora had given her everything, she had been all Kerensa had ever needed. Her father didn't matter, not to her. But for her mother, she would listen.

Meliora continued, "I don't know if he would have stayed, if he knew about you."

Kerensa frowned, "No, mother, you are forgetting. Father was here when I was born. You told me…"

Sadness flooded Meliora's face. "Cubert, my husband, was here, yes. But…"

She paused and looked into Kerensa's face, eyes full of fear.

Kerensa lay motionless, watching Meliora as she worked to find the words.

Meliora shook her head. "Please, please try to understand." She gripped Kerensa's hand like a vice, as though if she let go her daughter would disappear. Perhaps she thought she would leave, as Cubert had done 20 years ago. Perhaps she held on for her own life.

"I did care for Cubert, and he was good to me. But I was young. I lost my mother well before I was a woman... And now I am leaving you."

Kerensa shook her head and spoke, voice firm, "You are a fighter mother, you always have been. This is no different. And I am strong." Her voice cracked at the end and she squeezed her eyes shut against the tears that threatened to start up again.

Meliora smiled sadly, "I know my child," she said. Her gaze lengthened looking out past Kerensa's shoulder into some memory she could not follow.

"I was so young," she repeated, "I'd been alone so long..."

A mix of confusion and worry swirled inside Kerensa. But looking into her mother's eyes they faded, replaced solely with the desire to know.

"I will listen mother. Tell me everything."

Meliora sighed, her face relaxing. The harsh lines of illness faded in the candlelight and for a moment she looked young again, beautiful as she had in Kerensa's youth.

"He came with the trade winds, on the wooden sail boats that carry our fish to market. But the sea was fierce and the sailors had to seek safe harbour to see out the storm. The crew was large, our town small, so every spare bed was needed..."

"He? He who?"

Meliora smiled, "He came..."

"Came where?"

"Right here. It was the happiest time of my life."

PART 3

The Doom Bar

Porth Gwynn, 1831

Meliora worked the salt into the last leg of pork that lay before her. Around the hut sang the last of the storm that had ravaged the coast for days. The night before, as dusk lay grey and damp over the town, Cubert had returned from the beach frowning.

"The run is over, the season has turned," he'd announced. "Time to slaughter the pig. Salt her up and I can sell the bulk at market next Saturday. Mix up some of your herbs too. With a bit of luck I can trade enough to get us comfortably through the winter.'

"But it's only autumn," Meliora had protested. "The run can last 'til Christmas. It's only one storm."

Not looking at his wife, Cubert had poured himself an ale and drank it down in a few large gulps before refilling his mug. "The run is done. The seasons have changed early. Storms are on the wind. It will be a hard winter, we must prepare."

That morning, despite the lashing winds that scoured the coast, Meliora had bundled Enyon, their son, in his winter coat and taken him foraging with her. Cubert remained home to kill and prepare the pig for salting. Returning home, Cubert had taken Enyon down to the beach with him to help with the boat repairs. The storm had caught the men unawares, so focused on filling their hulls with pilchards they'd ignored the signs. The desperation of the low season evident in such an obvious oversight from experienced fishermen.

Enyon had been thrilled to go with his father. Still a boy to Meliora's eyes, yet she knew sons who'd known less summers were already working the fish. His gentle heart was not ready for the reality of the pig yet though.

Cubert had left the sectioned pig on the table. Meliora rolled up the sleeves of her blouse, poured the salt across the carcass and began the work. Rubbing the coarse granules into the pink flesh before hoisting the sections up and tying them to the rafters to cure. It was tough going. Working the salt into the flesh took time and patience. Finally, as the sun neared the horizon, she hoisted the final leg up and tied it off. In a bucket she washed the brine and blood from her hands, her skin raw and red from the drying salt, then moved to her next task, herbs.

She'd just settled the nettle and thyme to boil on the coals when Enyon burst into the room, face shining with excitement.

"Mother!" he exclaimed, "There's a ship, come see, come see."

A smile tugged at the corners of her mouth as she looked down at Enyon. *Still my boy,* she mused, *for now.*

"Mother, come on!" Enyon insisted.

"All right, all right," Meliora laughed, wiping rosemary and thyme leaves from her hands as she followed her enthusiastic child out the front of their stone walled cottage that sat just back from the bay.

"See it? It's huge!"

Meliora looked out at the bay, the waves choppy from the currents despite the protection of the cove. There anchored in the shallows, the waves retreating fast behind her wooden bulk, sat a sailing vessel. Large and bulbous, she was clearly a trader, probably on a route around the coast from London, collecting copper, tin, stone and pilchards to deliver across the isle.

"She's broken," Enyon said, voice eager. "Father says they weren't due in this port, but the storm forced them."

Meliora placed a hand on her son's shoulder and said a silent prayer for the sailors, hoping none had been hurt in whatever disaster they had faced on this ragged coast.

"There's a large hole on her starboard hull, they hit the Doom Bar on the way out of Padstow, but couldn't turn back," Cubert explained that night as they ate salted mackerel, bread and stew by candlelight. He paused to cut himself another slice of cheese for his bread, before continuing. "Then, taking on water, they lost their second mast in the storm. They're lucky they made it in. If it had been low tide, the currents against them…"

He left the rest unsaid, they all knew the perils of the sea.

"And the men on board?" Meliora asked.

"All well. Braneh arranged beds for them with the townsfolk. I offered Enyon's cot, but they had enough space. Carworan was unusually helpful. Took in three to his single hut. I daresay he wants the company. Must be a hard life alone."

Cubert glanced up at his wife, eyes full of gratitude for her and the son she had borne him.

Meliora offered him a slim smile and turned away. She didn't want to think of Carworan and his roving eyes and hands. He hadn't let up since she arrived in town, already married to Cubert almost 15 years before. Not even her pregnancy had deterred the man. Thankfully, Cubert remained oblivious. That was one confrontation Meliora was determined to avoid.

"They'll stay until the repairs are done," Cubert said, pulling Meliora from her reverie. "Could be weeks, depending on the extent of the damage. Braneh is going to inspect the vessel further in the morning, the light was fading too much tonight. But the men are safe and will stay that way. We look after our own."

Meliora nodded, heart full of love for her town and her people, who cared so much for the others who struggled alongside them in this seafaring life.

"We're lucky you know," Cubert continued, "fishing the bay is rough work at times, and accidents do happen. But out there in the open sea... anything can happen."

"Like pirates!" Enyon piped up, excited. His young face was drawn with fatigue, he needed his bed. But the drama of an injured ship limping into port after a storm had his little body buzzing with anticipation. Getting him to sleep would be a nightmare tonight.

Cubert laughed indulgently and looked over at his son, eyes soft. "Not for many years lad. The Navy has that under control now."

Meliora shivered, remembering the dark days of the pirate raids, the fear along the coast when a ship came in late, the tales of invasions under the cover of darkness, men, women and children too, carried away to be sold at slave ports in a foreign land. It had gone on too long, but England had stood up and protected her coasts. Porth Gwynn had always enjoyed a natural safety from such incursions. Their long channel to the sea a deterrent. It was not the same in Padstow, where Meliora grew up.

She liked it here in her safe white cove.

"But father please! Tell me of the pirates, of the adventures and danger, of Admiral Benbow who drove them back. Please please!" Enyon positively quivered with excitement.

"It's late lad," Cubert eyed his son over his mug of ale.

"Please!"

"All right, one tale, then bed. No complaints. Agreed?"

"Yes father."

Meliora smiled and collected up the dishes for washing as her son leaned forward, hanging on her husband's every word. She liked this time. Full bellies, warm heath, the sound of her family. Life here was tough, but it was safe. Meliora thanked God for her good fortune and turned her mind to her tasks, the sound of her husband's tales of bravery and the sea filling the settled silence of the night.

"Admiral Benbow was the bravest man in the British navy, that's why the King tasked him to save the Cornish coast...."

Later that night as Enyon slept peacefully, Cubert and Meliora enjoyed each other. Their lovemaking was always brief and to the point, but Meliora didn't mind. Cubert was gentle and considerate. He never demanded access to her body as some other husband's did. While perhaps not exciting, afterwards, as she lay beside her sleeping husband, she felt a glow of warmth and security envelop her and drifted off into a contented sleep.

The next morning she saw him.

Enyon had run ahead of her, as he always did, excited to meet up with his friends on the sands. Cubert was in the shallows, working the in-shore seines, the weather still too fierce to head out into the deeper bay on the rowboats. Around her the town bustled, men and women heading to the sheds to continue the fish work, or boat mending. Rising from the far end of the bay stood The Deliverer, the large wooden trading vessel that was seeking respite in their shores. A group of sailors stood in the shallows near the boat inspecting a large gash along her port side. Even from here it looked nasty. Cubert was right, they had been lucky to make it to the safety of Porth Gwynn.

She'd turned, intending to head for the fish sheds, Meraud needed help mending some of the larger nets the men used to haul the fish into baskets, and Meliora had offered her help.

And there he was.

Standing on the rocks that lined the bay, smoking. He looked just as she remembered, tall and lean, blonde hair catching the sun, a quiet strength resting beneath his skin. He blew out a lung full of smoke. Meliora watched as it curled up above his head, saw his brilliant smile flash in her memory as he told her of the sea and promised to come back for her.

She stopped dead, heart pounding. It had been years since she'd had these visions. Seeing another sailor whose shape resembled Ronnie and thinking it was him, finally returned for her. The silly dream of a girl whose heart had been broken, the desperate hope of a woman in trouble. She shook her head and forced herself to walk steadily, heading swiftly for the sheds, eyes cast down as she passed.

"Meliora?"

His deep, rich voice floated across the space between them. Her stomach dropped. Turning around she faced the man and realised, this was no vision. He was really here.

Ronnie gave a laugh and slapped his thigh. Discarding his cigarette, he took one large stumbling step towards her, smile beaming.

Meliora held up a hand as if to hold him back. "I'm married," she stammered. It seemed the most important thing to say.

Ronnie stopped before her, smile smaller now, but no less joyous. He nodded. "Naturally," he said.

They stood before each other in silence. Her body felt suddenly awkward, like it was no longer hers. She wanted to wrap her arms about him, to breathe in his scent, feel his weight above her. She wanted to hit him, slap his face until he bled, until he begged forgiveness.

She did nothing.

"You came on the ship?" She nodded to The Deliverer.

"Yes, we had some trouble in the storm."

"I see Braneh with your captain," Meliora pointed to the short broad man on the beach by the vessel. "He is an outstanding craftsman. Your boat is in good hands."

"I've no doubt," Ronnie replied, eyes never leaving her face.

"Well," Meliora stumbled, "I must… I've work." She pointed to the sheds, flustered.

"Of course."

"Good day," she managed and began to turn.

"I looked for you," Ronnie suddenly said, voice urgent. "The next summer, I returned as promised. But you were gone."

She looked back, eyes bright with fury. "You took too long," she hissed and raced away.

...
* * *

128

"You knew him before?" Kerensa looked at her mother in surprise. "Before father?"

Meliora lay on her back, breathing heavily. Her fever had eased, for now replaced by a chill that brought tremors to her limbs. Kerensa wrapped her in a thick woollen blanket and brought more broth. Meliora sipped at the mug and grimaced. Her stomach rebelling at the very hint of food. Her time was near.

"Yes," she said, "he came to Padstow when I was little more than a girl. He was looking for work, stayed in the local boarding house. I fell in love with him, so deeply. The first love of my life."

"What happened?"

"Promises were made and believed. Then he got work on a trade ship. Left with the tide. I woke up one morning and he was gone."

Kerensa sucked in a deep breath, "He left without a word?"

Meliora shook her head sadly, "I was young. I believed he would return. And he did, though I did not know that until much later. But I was already gone."

"You married father, and moved here?"

"Yes, soon after Ronnie left, Cubert came to town to trade. I left with him."

"Why?"

"I had to get away, too much pain in Padstow," she sighed heavily. "Soon after Ronnie left I found I was with child. But with no way to contact him and being unmarried…"

"Mother! Are you saying Enyon is Ronnie's child?"

"No, no, my daughter," A small smile played across Meliora's lips. "He was Cubert's." Her face relaxed, happiness smoothing her features as she thought of her first born.

"I… ended that pregnancy. As I did for Derwa," she looked into Kerensa's eyes, "I knew the pain I would cause her that night, but I also knew it was necessary."

Kerensa nodded slowly, "You worried she would not conceive again."

"I did. It took me many years to quicken with your brother. Many years. And then after him the same before you… I never knew if it was my body, the herbs or God's wrath. Derwa, it seems, has been forgiven."

She smiled gently. Derwa was already growing with child again, little Breock barely four months old. She and Kenver would have a large family it seemed.

A frown furrowed Kerensa's forehead, "So you knew him before? But he abandoned you. I don't understand mother, why tell me this now? Father is gone, and you did nothing wrong. God forgives all. And you need rest. I will put out the candle and we can get some sleep."

Meliora gripped her daughter's hand, "Wait, please,"she whispered. "I have not finished my story daughter. I should have told you sooner. My own mother didn't live to see me a woman, I should have known... but I hoped... Well, it doesn't matter now. You must listen Kerensa, please."

Seeing the determination shining in Meliora's eyes, she knew she would not win this battle of wills.

Her mother was dying, these remaining moments should be filled with rest and peace, but something in this tale mattered to her.

I will listen, Kerensa resolved, *I will help her to the absolution she needs.*
She settled down under the blankets and listened.

The Mermaid of Hawkers Rock

The weather lifted, bringing the pale light of autumn sun. It lit the browning earth in softly glowing reds and oranges as Meliora made her way home after a day in the fish sheds, Enyon hopping happily by her side. It had been two days since she'd encountered Ronnie at the bay. So far she had managed to avoid him, taking a more direct route to the sheds and keeping with the other women at break times. She'd seen him though, watching her from the bay, cigarette in hand. But she'd kept the distance between them. At least physically.

He haunted her dreams.

Seeing him, hearing his voice, feeling his presence so close had awakened desires long since locked away. Knowing he was here, in her town, sleeping in a cottage only a few doors away drove the peace from her rest, filling her dreams with longing.

Last night, desperate for release, she'd rolled on to her husband and ridden him to satisfaction. Collapsing beside him, Cubert had curled himself around her and whispered into her ear, "I'm not sure where that came from, but I like it." He'd sounded bemused, but content. "My mermaid."

It had been years since he'd used the affectionate nickname; The Mermaid of Hawkers Rock, a tale from her hometown of Padstow. She was his fairytale. The legend said the mermaid created the Doom Bar after being rejected by a lover. The coincidence with the accident that had returned Ronnie to her life sat uncomfortably in Meliora's chest.

Soon the soft sound of Cubert's snoring told her he slept. But that relief would not come for her. She'd slipped from their bed, from their home and walked out into the cold night. Standing barefoot on the cool pebbles of the foreshore, she'd watched the starry sky, gooseflesh breaking out across her limbs. There she'd stood, watching the night until the first rays of light began to break the horizon, ordering her home to bake the bread and begin the day.

Now, as she neared her cottage the exhaustion of a night without sleep and a day in the fish sheds lay heavy on her eyelids. *Tonight I will sleep*, she hoped fervently.

But the world had other plans, for at her door step lay a bushel of flowering kale and sage leaves. Meliora knew, instantly, who had left them there. It wasn't Cubert. Swiftly, she paced to the bundle and fetched it up from the ground. She planned to dispose of them, to throw them out into the nearby vegetation, but the scuff of footsteps stayed her hand.

Turning she saw her husband and son returning from the beach. Behind them loped Ronnie, his limp more pronounced today. Her breath caught in her throat, heat rising to her face. What was he doing here?

Their voices drifted up the path towards her, Enyon chatting excitedly, begging Ronnie to tell him about sea adventures, Ronnie laughing.

"Enough now lad," Cubert said as they came up to Meliora, "you will exhaust our guest."

"But father, he's a sailor!"

"He is also a man who has worked a hard day," Cubert came up beside Meliora and kissed her cheek. "Hello my dear, what have we here?"

He gave her a quizzical look as he noticed the bunch of flowers. "Not like you to collect frivolous things." He grinned at her and winked. No doubt misreading the flush of her face as a sign of their shared memory of last night's bedroom endeavours, rather than the appearance of the tall stranger standing behind him.

Meliora swallowed and nodded towards Ronnie.

"Ah yes. Meliora, this is Ronnie. One of the sailors from The Deliverer. He helped me repair the cart today, so I offered him some hospitality."

"We've not much available…" Meliora started.

"There's bread and ale surely," Cubert interrupted, "We've always spare for those who work the sea as we do."

"Of course," Meliora said, and led the group inside. In truth she could not object, the act of sharing food and warmth was ingrained in the people of her coast. To refuse Ronnie a seat at her table would be inexcusable.

Inside, Ronnie and Cubert slumped down on the stools, closely followed by an eager Enyon. Meliora busied herself assembling some bread and yarg, salted fish and butter, her hands shaking terribly.

"Don't forget the flowers mother," Enyon said, appearing at her elbow. She hadn't heard him approach. "They are beautiful." He passed the bundle to her and she obliged, placing them in a mug of water to keep them fresh.

She caught the small smile on Ronnie's face as Enyon placed the mug of flowers on the end of the table. His eyes danced in the dimming light of the evening, his blonde hair shining almost red with the dying rays of the sun. Meliora placed the food on the table and took a seat. The men were talking of the repairs on The Deliverer.

"That Braneh of yours," Ronnie said, "you weren't wrong about his ability. He's wasted in such a small town. Has he ever thought of heading to the bigger cities in the south? He'd make a pretty penny."

"Braneh's born and bred here. I doubt you'd ever move the man."

"But the repairs are going well," Meliora said, hating the tension in her voice. "So you will be on your way soon then?"

Cubert flashed her a confused look at her bluntness.

Ronnie replied smoothly, "I believe soon yes, within the week, perhaps a little longer. With good winds we may be fortunate and make up the lost time."

"Well don't rush it," Cubert said firmly. "You're all welcome here until she's seaworthy."

"The captain is a sensible man, he won't risk the ship or the cargo."

"Have you ever seen a pirate?" Enyon piped up.

"Enyon, what did I say about hassling our guest?" Cubert reprimanded the youngster gently. "I'm sorry Ronnie, the boy is all about pirates and adventures these days."

"Not a bother," Ronnie smiled. "Seems you have the heart of a sailor lad." He leaned toward the boy, "I've not seen a pirate myself, but years ago, before you were born, there was a story of a crew that went missing off of Padstow. We were called out to search, had to leave port immediately. We never found them." He glanced up at Meliora, briefly. She turned away.

"You think it was pirates?"

"Could've been. Or just a storm. We only recovered one body, the knit of his jumper told us he was a local, but we never found the ship or wreckage."

Meliora stood up swiftly, "More ale?" she asked to cover her unexpected motion.

"Thank you," Ronnie said, eyes dark. She felt them on her back as she moved through the room to collect a fresh jug.

The food was finished, the ale low, the men talked out, night dark and Enyon asleep at the table when Ronnie stood to leave.

"Thank you for this share of your home, Cubert," he said.

"Of course, in appreciation for your help with the wagon today."

Cubert saw him to the door as Meliora coaxed her son from the table and into bed, avoiding the pleasantry of farewell.

Cubert joined her in their chambers, pressing his body against her back, gripping his hips. It was to be expected, she realised, after her behaviour last night and the ale he'd just drunk. Though it was the farthest thing from her own desire. She pressed her eyes closed and gritted her teeth before turning into his embrace. Their coupling was short, efficient. Meliora was sure she caught a look of disappointment flash through her husband's eyes as he rolled over to sleep. It had been nothing like the night before.

Exhausted and filled with shame, Meliora lay in bed watching the black of night about her. Her body longed for rest, but her mind would not allow her the reprieve. Despite the coupling with her husband she could think of nothing other than Ronnie's dark eyes watching her, the offer in his subtle smile. An offer she would refuse. An offer she longed to accept.

"How dare you!" Meliora hissed as she strode across the pebbled street, stopping just in front of Ronnie.

He looked her up and down casually, blowing out the smoke of his cigarette, it caught the wind and blew up and away.

"Good morning Meliora," he said.

"Stay away from my house. Stay away from my family!"

Meliora spun on her heel and went to stalk away.

"It was true you know," he said. "The story of the missing boat. I had to leave, there was no time."

Meliora whirled around to face him. "You think that matters now? After all these years?"

"Perhaps not," Ronnie looked down, shuffled his feet. "But it's the truth."

Meliora opened her mouth to admonish him, to rail at him for being so inconsiderate, so rude and disrespectful, but no words came out.

Ronnie looked up at her, his eyes rich with desire. "I think it does matter. I think you know it does."

"I..." Meliora swallowed, suddenly frozen, unable to work through the flood of emotion that threatened to drown her.

"Meliora? Is everything all right?" Meraud's firm voice echoed out over the bay.

Thankful for the interruption, Meliora turned to her friend. "Yes, coming," she called.

"Stay away from me!" she hissed back at Ronnie and walked purposefully away, up to the sheds and the women waiting to start the day's work.

Standing on the beach Carworan watched her progress, jealousy swirling deep in his gut. Oh how he wanted her. Had done so since Cubert first brought her to town. But no amount of hinting or suggestion had ever got him anywhere. He hadn't missed Meliora's exchange with the sailor the day before. Like a needle pressing against his heart, the memory had replayed in his mind all night, keeping him awake. He hadn't known what to make of the interaction between the sailor and Cubert's wife. But now he was sure. Despite all his gestures and offers of affection, this out-of-towner, this sailor had arrived and she couldn't stay away. Whore.

Cubert was packing the cart. "Please, husband, I should come with you. Padstow is a long journey. You will need my help."

"The town needs your hands, Meliora, you know that. If more fish come in, or nets need repair. Besides, Enyon is almost a man now," he glanced over at his son who was struggling to lift a pork leg into the cart.

"He is not," Meliora whispered. "And you said it yourself, the run is low. They won't miss us."

"It will look bad if we all go, you know that. Besides, someone needs to feed the chickens." He paused. Seeing his wife's distress, Cubert drew Meliora into an embrace. "We will be back for church next Sunday, it's not so long wife. Some time to yourself might be a nice change."

Pecking her cheek he turned to Enyon. "Grab your bag son, it's time to go."

"Yes father," Enyon ran inside and gathered up his small satchel of extra jumpers and socks.

Meliora hugged her arms about her belly and tried to still the nervous bubbling that threatened to empty her stomach of breakfast.

"Be safe," she said, voice choked.

Cubert nodded and clicked the horse into motion.

"Bye mother!" Enyon cried enthusiastically, eyes full of excitement for the adventure ahead.

Despite herself, Meliora laughed at his joy and, forcing herself to stand tall, waved goodbye to her family.

He came with the rain. A knock on the door, loud enough to be heard over the downpour that flooded from the sky, down the valleys and across the pebbled streets of Porth Gwynn. The rain that forced everyone inside to shelter by their cloam ovens, mend winter coats and bake bread and pie.

Meliora knew it was him the moment the knock sounded. Knew why he came.

She opened the door anyway.

No words passed between them, their eyes said it all; the question and the answer.

He stepped into her hut, stride steady and took her into his arms, pressing his mouth to hers. Pushing her backwards they found the bed. Meliora lay back upon the freshly made sheets, he moved above her.

Hands, mouths, tongues, clothing strewn across the floor. Gasps, sighs and groans of pleasure. Hot and slick and desperate. And done.

Afterwards they lay together, naked, limbs entangled, Meliora's fingers curled in the blonde hair of his chest. He smoked a cigarette, the smoke curling up slowly towards the ceiling. Later they ate bread and shared ale. Later still they returned to the bed and the language of their bodies.

"I should never have left you."

"You didn't know."

"Forgive me."

"There is nothing to forgive."

"I love you."

"I love you."

The day became night, became day, became night. The rain continued to fall, the wind to howl, the town to hunker down in shelter. And they stayed entwined, in passion and at rest, clinging to one another as though afraid to let go. Perhaps they were. They talked of meaningless things. Of the moment: "Would you like more ale?"; "Bread or pie?". Not the future. And Meliora slept, deep and calm and long, her lover wrapped about her like a cocoon, protecting her from the rain and cold and from the years to come.

Meliora awoke. Something was different. Opening her eyes she lay still, reflecting. Outside a bird trilled its morning call. The rain. The rain had stopped. It did not matter, Cubert would not be home for days yet. Languidly she rolled over, hands reaching for the warm body that had shared her bed these past nights. The space beside her was empty. Cold.

She sat up.

No candle glowed in the kitchen, no smell of cigarette wafted from the doorway.

Coming to her feet she padded quickly to the front door and stepped out into the budding dawn. Before her Porth Gwynn slept on, the golden sunlight catching the morning dew and reflecting a brilliant orange glow across the grasses. The water of the bay murmured softly, the tide flushed full against the cove.

It was empty.

A knot locked in her throat. The Deliverer was gone.

"No," she whispered, "no."

She raced inside and threw on her day dress and shoes, hastily wrapping her shawl about her shoulders as she ran out the door. Walking swiftly, careful not to slip in the water-logged mud she hurried to the bayside, eyes scanning the waters. Gone.

"Left before dawn," Meraud came up beside her. "Wanted to catch the tide."

Meliora nodded, swallowing hard. She smiled, praying that her features remained neutral despite the turmoil that churned within her breast.

"Men'll be out again today. You'll be down for the fish run?"

"I... yes, yes of course."

"Good. Braneh says we are due a late windfall. He can be overly optimistic, but this time, I think he might be right. We're due some good fortune. See you at the sheds."

Meliora waved to her friend absently, her eyes stuck fast to the gentle currents of the bay.

"He left," she whispered, "without a word. Again."

Tears welled up in her eyes. She let them fall in silence.

Burning Sage

"A month later when I realised I had quickened, I knew."

"Do you mean? Are you saying…"

Kerensa had sat up straight in bed. Mind reeling.

"Yes, my child. Cubert was not your father. Ronnie was."

"But, how can you be sure?"

"Your foot for one. Ronnie could hide it better than you, but he had the same twist in his ankle. But I knew before that, though. I felt it. A mother knows."

"And father?"

Meliora sighed, "When he saw you, he knew too. And he left."

"You say he left. But Braneh says he went to farm. Like the men often do in the spring."

"He never returned."

"An accident?"

"No. My daughter, he chose to stay away."

"How do you know?"

"I know," Meliora said in a tone which brooked no argument, before closing her eyes and leaning back into the pillows. "As you grew so did the rumours. Carworan saw to that. His jealousy knew no bounds. I learned that the hard way." She broke off, eyes distant. Kerensa felt the tremor that quaked through her mother's body at the memory of a cold, dark Christmas night.

"What happened with Carworan, mother? That Christmas when you gave me the ribbon? What did he do?"

Meloria frowned deeply. "Sometimes a man wants something so much he can't take it, even when it's offered freely."

Kerensa shook her head, confused. Meliora sighed. "It's no secret Carworan wanted me, right from when I first arrived at Porth Gwynn.

I thought his desire would wane with his own marriage to Lowena, but I was wrong... Over the years it turned into something else, something dark."

Kerensa cocked her head in consideration. "You went to meet him that night. To be with him, despite Lowena?"

Meliora looked into her daughter's eyes. "I did."

"Why?"

Meliora paused, seeking the right words to explain. "I was lonely. I had you, but I wanted... needed a man. It had been so long. I thought he would be willing... and he was, at first. But, then he couldn't perform and he became enraged. Blamed me for his own inadequacy. You saw the result of that."

Kerensa blinked, trying to understand what her mother was saying. She really knew so little of the fires that burned between men and women.

Taking a deep breath she drew the conversation back to the story of Meliora's husband.

"What happened after Cubert left?" she asked.

"I stayed in our home for a while, but soon the town came knocking. There was only the two of us you see, and Jago needed the larger space. Carworan saw me off, spat at my feet... But I didn't mind. After your father left, no one wanted me here. This little hut,"she smiled affectionately, "this was perfect. A place just for us.

"No one visited, except Meraud, once or twice. But she with Gerens at her breast and Rewan just learning to run, ha, she didn't have the time for me. I made do. I made my way. As my mother taught me. For us both."

"Your mother taught you the herbs?"

Meliora nodded, "It was as if she knew her time on earth would be short, that I would need to care for myself. It is a security. And I have passed it to you. When I am gone, whatever happens, you will have a trade."

Whatever happens, rang in Kerensa's mind. Her birth was not just ill-fated by her malformed foot, but by her very existence. A bastard child, marked by sin. A bringer of sorrow and pain.

"Did he ever return again? Ronnie, I mean."

"No, he did not. News came some months later that The Deliverer had floundered. No survivors." She looked away, closing her eyes to fight the pain Ronnie's death still caused her heart, despite it all, "I doubt he'd have come back anyway. There was nothing for him here."

"You kept me."

"Yes."

"But you knew. You knew what I would mean, for you, for your family. Why didn't you end me?"

"Because I loved you."

Meliora looked up into her daughter's face, her eyes limned with tears. "Because I knew you would be special, so, so special."

"But I brought loss and pain. And my ankle... the promise of hardship it signified... the curse."

"My daughter," Meliora interrupted, voice dry but firm, "you have not brought the problems of this town. That is down to time and ignorance."

Kerensa swallowed, rubbing her hands down her arms, a chill had come into the air.

"It's nearly light. We are low on nettle and fennel. I'll go fetch some. I won't be long."

Meliora watched as Kerensa rose and rushed to the door.

"Kerensa," she called, "whatever people say or believe. Whatever has befallen me. You have been worth it all."

Kerensa rubbed a hand down her face, as if brushing away the emotions her mother's words placed along her brow and rushed from the hut into the burgeoning dawn.

"It is a lot to take in," Meliora whispered to herself. "I only hope I can hold on long enough for her forgiveness."

Outside the earth was still warm, the night had offered little relief from the oppressive heat and humidity of the day. Kerensa headed up the hill behind her mother's hut, seeking higher ground and solitude. Inside she was a ball of emotion. Anger, fear, shame. Carworan and his predictions of downfall. The insults he threw at her on the streets. It was all true. Her mother was a whore, and she was a bastard. Born deformed, an omen of doom.

Yet it hadn't stopped him seeking Meliora out that Christmas night to slake his lusts. She finally understood what her child's eyes had seen. A secret tryst turned violent. A woman's desperate lunge for protection, slapped away by a man who hated his own desire. Cruel, cruel man.

And now Kerensa knew the truth of who she was.

How she wished her mother had never told her.

She stopped in her tracks, "What will Rewan say?"

Or did he already know? Was that why he had been so distant lately, why they were as yet unwed? Not the ill omen of her foot, but the secret shame of her birth.

Tears burst through her resistance and coursed down her cheeks. She began to run, lunging awkwardly up the hill, her right foot dragging painfully behind her. It caught a root and she fell. Cursing her deformed ankle she screamed to the skies.

"That's how father knew," she sobbed, "That's how they all knew."

Because of her, Cubert had abandoned his wife, gone off to farm and never returned, leaving Meliora to find her own way. Because of her, this town that prided itself on looking after its own had turned from her mother. Forced her to the outskirts, never invited her to feasts or celebrations, shunned her at church.

Maybe they'd never been truly sure, but Kerensa had seen it in their eyes her whole life. Bastard cripple daughter and the witch-whore. It wasn't just the ill omen of her birth, but her parentage that had haunted her life.

Yet Meliora had not given up. She'd used her knowledge and turned her hobby of herbs into her full-time living, eking out an existence from healing in a town that lived for fishing, brought in food for her babe and raised a healthy child.

And she saved lives. When people were sick she helped them to strengthen and heal, when women laboured she eased the pain. And now, as Meliora faced her own death, the town came forward, offerings in hand, bearing food and cloth and support. The very support she was always owed.

Hatred, pure and sharp, pierced Kerensa's chest and she raged at the small town nestled far down below.

"Hypocrites! One and all!! You shame her, shun her, blame her for one mistake, but who of you is without sin! And now, when it's too late, you come for absolution. Shame on you all!"

Her words were choked by her sobs and she flung onto her side. Curling up into a ball she shook with the force of her anger. Soon the heat of her fury cooled, replaced by impenetrable sorrow. Tears wetting her face, neck and chest she faced the real pain that infected her soul. The one she'd pushed down this past week as she cared for her ailing mother. The truth. Meliora would die soon.

Kerensa would be alone.

Meliora's revelation changed nothing. Her mother had raised her, loved her, guided her. She had pushed her to empathy and taught her skills for independence, sheltered her from the worst of the town's gossip. She had loved her.

Who cared what she did almost 20 years ago?

Slowly her tears subsided and a new resolve settled over her body. Sitting up, Kerensa decided. She didn't care who her father was, or what her mother had done all those years ago. Meliora was a good woman, who had helped people, even those who hurt her. And Kerensa loved her mother.

Meliora deserved to pass in peace, in forgiveness. She'd earned that much.

Brushing off her skirts she hastened back down the hill, the brilliant light of the summer sun already prickling the skin of her exposed arms.

Back in the hut she stoked the cloam oven and set the broth to warm in the potfry. Collecting fresh water she limped into the bedroom and settled on the bed beside Meliora.

Her mother's eyes were closed, her mouth slack with sleep. It had been a long night. Gently, Kerensa wiped the sweat from her mother's brow and began to hum a soft lullaby. Meliora's face relaxed, the rictus of pain that twisted her features smoothing with calm.

"You are a good woman, mother," Kerensa whispered, "I love you."

Meliora's eyes fluttered open and fixed on Kerensa's face, pupils wide.

"I love you," Kerensa repeated.

Meliora smiled and closed her eyes again, settling back into the pillows to rest.

Kerensa put the cloth down and climbed onto the bed beside her mother. She was burning with fever again, but Kerensa didn't care. She wrapped her arms about her mother's frail body and held her close, humming the tune of her childhood, the one that promised morning bread, softly in her ear. Soon she too fell asleep, soothed by the heavy breathing of her mother's body, the familiar scent of her skin.

When she awoke, Meliora was dead.

The women of Porth Gwynn arrived, led by Meraud. Gently, they led Kerensa to a stool, placed a mug of ale before her and a heel of bread. Then they went to work.

First they moved the body, carefully lifting the frail remains of a once bold and strong woman and placing her on the table. The sheets of the bed, stained by Meliora's passing, were removed and replaced with fresh linens donated by one of the townsfolk.

Next they removed Meliora's clothes, bundling them with the sheets. The cloam oven was lit, a pot of water placed in the coals to boil. Sage burnt.

Then the ritual washing began. They wiped the body down, cleansing the filth of sickness and death from Meliora's pale skin. They scented the body with lavender oil, working it into the cold skin. Finally, they dressed her in her Sunday dress. Meraud plaited her hair.

Kerensa watched it all, eyes staring without seeing, mind numb.

They buried Meliora at St Endellion, Pastor John spoke. Kerensa didn't listen. Meliora had never liked his sermons.

The whole town came, even pregnant Derwa and baby Breock, who laughed and giggled throughout the ceremony. Meliora would have liked that.

Rewan walked her home, arm firmly about her waist as though he thought she might fall to the ground and never get up. He was right to be concerned. Kerensa felt weak, broken open, laid bare, like the wind could gather her up in its tendrils and scatter the broken pieces to nothing, as dandelion across a field.

At the door he offered to stay. Kerensa shook her head. How could she face him now, with the terrible truth of her parentage fresh in her mind and the impossible weight of her loss pressed against her heart? She would tell him, just not yet. He pressed, then reluctantly left.

Kerensa shut the door and limped to bed. Curling up on her side, she breathed in the new smell of the sheets, cotton and hay, she thought, no hint of Meliora's sage and thyme remained. She heaved a sob and buried her head in the pillows.

Her mother's voice drifted through the empty hut, whispering hope in the silence. "All things pass, my child. This pain will too."

Kerensa sobbed harder as the memory found her ears, and began stroking her back in long soothing passes, helping her to sleep. Somehow, despite the sorrow in her heart, Kerensa fell asleep.

Interlude

You are perfect, tiny and perfect. You are everything to me.

But you are not here yet, this story has not come to you. I must be patient, there is much more to remember, much more to tell.

Painful. Filled with the type of sorrow you don't believe you can overcome, the kind that overwhelms, the kind you die from.

But there is love. Such love! And that memory I will never let go. Never. No matter what came next, there was love. And that is worth it all.

PART 4

Mint Tea

He arrived a week later, on a breeze that smelt of autumn and woodsmoke. He stopped at Jago's, asked directions and was pointed up the hill. The town watched him pass, keeping distant. Whispers swirled, all waited.

He was tall for a Cornishman, dark and broad of shoulder. Grey flecks in his wild beard caught the sun, though his face was smooth, still holding on to its youth.

He knocked

Kerensa opened the door. Expecting Meraud or one of the other women from town, she was surprised to see the man's large frame standing before her. She cocked her head, frowned, watched his face.

He smiled.

Kerensa gasped.

She was there, somewhere in the lines of his mouth, in the dimple of his cheek. Meliora.

Kerensa opened the door wider and bid him in.

Seated at the table, bread and cheese between them, a mug of ale in his hand, Kerensa spoke.

"Enyon."

It wasn't a question, but rather a statement of fact. Enyon breathed out heavily.

"Kerensa," he replied. He frowned, his lips pursing. "I only learnt that a week ago," he smiled shyly, eyes downcast. Kerensa read the sorrow there, the regret.

"She passed here, in my arms, surrounded by love," she said, unsure what else to offer this man. The brother she'd never known. It seemed Meliora had been right, tragedy had not befallen Cubert and Enyon.

"Did you know about us? What did father…what did Cubert tell you?"

"That mother died, complications from your birth. And you, without her milk, followed soon after. That there was nothing for us in Porth Gwynn, no reason to return. I was only 10, I believed my mother dead. I didn't question."

Tears shone in his eyes.

Kerensa reached across the table and took his hand.

"It was not your fault."

He squeezed her hand, "Thank you for saying that. He never remarried, you know. I think, I think he always loved our mother."

"Well, to remarry would have been a sin," Kerensa said sharply, then exhaled and offered him an apologetic smile for her tone. He was grieving too, he had his own loss and betrayal to comprehend.

"Where do you live then?" she sought a safer topic.

"I run a farm near Bodmin. Father got work there when we left Porth Gwynn, worked up the ranks to manager. We lived in the farmhand quarters until I married two summers ago, then I got a rental in town for Mary. She wanted to remain close to her mother."

A softness relaxed his features as he spoke of his wife.

"I kept working on the farm, still do. It's good work. Hard but reliable. Keeps the bread on my table."

"You have children?"

"Three. All boys." He laughed, an indulgent light shining in his eyes. "Mischief makers all. But my wife does good with them."

Kerensa smiled, "It sounds a lovely home. I am pleased for you."

"Thank you."

Silence fell between them, awkward. Kerensa refilled his mug of ale for something to do too.

"So how did you learn of me and mother?"

"Father told me. He died, some years back. He confessed it all then. I, I was newly married, my wife pregnant with our first son, and the farm needed tending. I should have come, but I didn't."

Red blotches broke out on his neck and cheeks. He shifted in his seat.

Kerensa sat in silence, processing this information. She swallowed. Careful of her tone she asked, "What changed your mind? Why did you come now?"

"I heard that mother had passed. I was in St Endellion for market day. I rarely come this far from home, but I heard there was good tin on sale and… well, my trading is of no importance. I heard that the healer of Porth Gwynn had died. I asked questions, and as I suspected, her name was Meliora. So I asked about her daughter, you. I learned your name, Kerensa. Father never knew what mother named you. And I learned you still lived here, unwed.

"I finally told my wife everything. About father and mother, and the lie of her death. About the sister I'd met only as a babe. The sister that now would be alone…

"She was furious with me. Ordered me to come here straight away to find you. Anything could have befallen you, she argued. And she was right. Alone here, without any protector. I had to come and find you."

Kerensa stiffened and sat up straight, "I may be yet to wed but it won't be long. And I know how to take care of myself."

"You are betrothed? That is good news." He sighed as in relief, his face relaxing.

Kerensa fidgeted, picking at her nails, dirt still caked beneath them from her morning in the garden. "Not formally betrothed, but…"

"Not formally? And now you are an orphan, with no man to approve the match? That does not sound acceptable."

"And it is no bother of yours!" Kerensa snapped. "You knew I was here two years ago, that mother was alive, and you never came. Whatever excuse you may place before me is not enough, and you know it. You cannot make up for your poor choices by trying to make decisions for me now! I am a grown woman. This is *my* house and I will not be told what I can and cannot do!"

Enyon looked at her in open shock. Closing her eyes Kerensa brought her breathing back under control.

"Please accept my apologies, I don't mean to be so direct. But there can be no misunderstanding here. Porth Gwynn is my home, and it is where I will stay."

Enyon looked around him at the small but well kept hut. "I know you do not know me, but despite what you may think, I am a good man. My home in Bodmin is spacious, my children lively but well behaved, my wife kind. There is a room there, for you. You would not be alone."

"I am not alone," Kerensa said rising her head defiantly. "I'm a part of Porth Gwynn. We take care of our own."

Enyon nodded slowly, accepting her resolve.

"Then I am happy for it. I'm sorry to have been so… brash. I only meant to help. I feel a responsibility for you. We are family after all."

Though the words bristled, Kerensa read the sincerity in his eyes. She was not used to this side of men. No father ever stood before her and the world, a shield and a cage. There was only Meliora, who had stood beside her, showing her how to make a life in this world.

Life in the cove was harsh, but it was the life Kerensa knew. One where she would work, beside the men, hard and long, but together. It was the life she wanted.

"Porth Gwynn is my home, Enyon. I love this place. To leave the sea…" she looked out her little window wistfully.

Enyon nodded, a sad smile on his lips. "It took me years to sleep well without the sound of the waves."

Their eyes met, understanding, deep from common experience flowed between them.

"I see you are safe and well set up here, Kerensa. I shall tell my Mary there was nothing to fear. But Kerensa, sister, let's not be strangers. I don't know how to be your brother, but I would like to be your friend."

"I'd like that too."

Enyon stayed the night, the two siblings sharing stories of their childhoods, so different in so many ways. Yet in the lessons learnt a common value shone through, one of strength in adversity and respect for hard work. It was hard to reconcile the Cubert that Enyon described with the man who had abandoned her mother.

"When the babe is not his, no man stays," Meliora's words after Derwa's rape swam through her memory. Perhaps such a betrayal really is too much to overcome, she mused.

The moon was high when they finally found their beds. Kerensa in her own, Enyon on a roll on the floor. He left early, taking fresh baked bread and mint for a soothing pregnancy tea. Mary, he'd confided last night, was pregnant yet again. Secretly they hoped for a girl.

Kerensa hugged her brother's solid frame and bid him farewell. Watching him make his way across the hills towards the East she found herself smiling for the first time since Meliora's passing. Her mother was gone, nothing would ever fill that hole. But she'd found her brother to be a good man. And he was happy and well, despite all their parents had put him through.

That was enough.

A week later another man stood at her door.

"Rewan!" she exclaimed happily.

They'd seen little of each other since Meliora's passing, Kerensa's grief and shame too deep for company.

The grief remained, but its heaviness had lifted. For the first time since the hot summer night that Meliora left the earth, Kerensa felt the possibility of life stirring within her once again.

"Kerensa," he replied, but his eyes did not meet hers.

She frowned, "Rewan? Is something wrong?"

"Wrong, no!" he looked up at her sharply, eyes wide with concern. "No, no, not at all, I... um, well, can I come in?"

Confused she stepped aside, "Of course."

"Thank you."

He paced into the main room but didn't take a seat. Kerensa shut the door and moved towards the cupboards. "Can I offer you bread? Tea? Ale?"

"No," he replied shortly, still pacing. "I mean, no thank you. I...oh!"

He let out an exasperated breath, then stilling himself in the centre of the room, looked directly into Kerensa's eyes.

"Kerensa, my flower... I, I should have asked this of you long ago. But I am a fool. And I wanted to have the money for a house in the town and to buy you everything you could ever need. But that was wrong, because none of that matters. But I waited. I should never have waited. And now you're alone, and that should never have been and..."

"Rewan, slow down!" Kerensa laughed moving around the table to the man she loved. "I'm not sure what you are trying to say, but you have nothing to apologise for. You are a good friend to me, you always have been."

"A friend?" he asked, voice breathless. "Only a friend?"

Heat rose to Kerensa's face as she stared into his deep, dark eyes. Her breathing shortened, her limbs felt weak. She opened her mouth to speak but found no words.

Rewan didn't need them. He pulled her into his arms and kissed her. Melting into his embrace Kerensa felt her body relax. All the tension she had been holding on to, all the grief, finally freed.

Rewan pulled away, but did not release her from his grip.

"Kerensa, will you do me the honour of..."

"Oh no!" shock ran through Kerensa's body, stiffening the limbs that had just released.

He couldn't ask that, not yet. He didn't know the truth. That she was an illegitimate bastard. Born of betrayal. The town gossiped and hinted, but no one knew, not for sure. But now Kerensa did. And this, she could not lie to Rewan. He had to know who she was before they could go any further.

"No?" Rewan's face had fallen, his mouth slack with shock. "But, Kerensa, I love you. I thought you loved me too?"

"I," she stepped out of his arms and he let her go, arms falling limp by his sides, shoulders slumped.

"I do love you Rewan, more than anything in the world…"

"Then what? Is it too soon, after Meliora's death? I tried to wait, to be understanding. That's what I was trying to explain before."

"It's not that."

"Have I waited too long? Is there," he gulped, "someone else?"

"Someone else? No!"

Rewan frowned, watching her. "Then, what?"

"There's something you don't know."

Now she was the one pacing, back and forth across the room. She gripped her hands together, wringing them. Her lips trembled. This was it. The moment she had dreaded since Meliora had confided the truth. She'd put it off, allowing herself to dream of a future with this beautiful man, ignoring the possibility of his rejection. But she could not live a lie. Not any longer. She had to tell him.

She faced Rewan.

Throat dry, she spoke. "Cubert was not my father," she announced, pressing her eyes closed. She did not want to see Rewan's face as he digested this new information.

"My father was a sailor who stayed in town. He visited mother while Cubert was away and…"

"Is that what this is about?" Rewan interrupted. He sounded amused.

Kerensa looked up at him in surprise. Anger heated her cheeks.

"'What this is about?'" she stared at him incredulously. "You knew?"

"I knew about the rumour. Cubert was my father's best friend after all. Father told me."

"When?"

"Soon after the accident in the sail boats."

"You never said."

"It was not my place. So it's true then? Ha," he laughed happily, "I thought you had a real reason to reject my offer."

"It's not funny Rewan. You're not understanding. It means, it means everything they jeer, everything they whisper about me, it's, it's true."

Her resolve cracked and she sagged, tears springing to her eyes.

"Kerensa," Rewan whispered as he rounded the table and took her into his arms again. "Don't cry." He placed a finger under her chin and lifted her eyes up to face him. Gently he thumbed away her tears.

"It changes nothing," he said softly, holding her eyes in his. "You are not your parents' choices. You are my flower, there are a few thorns," he teased, twerking her nose gently.

Kerensa let out a half sob, half laugh.

"But to me, my love, you are perfect."

"But the town…"

"Know nothing for certain, and have realised they never cared. You saw the love they brought to you when your mother died. You are a child of this town Kerensa, you always were.

"But more importantly, you are my heart."

"You are mine."

"So, silly," Rewan grinned his lopsided smile. "Can I ask you now?"

"Yes!" Kerensa threw her arms about his neck.

Rewan let out a howl of laughter, "Not yet! You have to let me say it!"

"All right, all right," Kerensa said, practically jumping out of her skin with anticipation.

Rewan steadied himself, eyes locked on hers,"Kerensa, my flower, my heart, will you do me the honour of becoming my wife?"

Trembling, a single tear tracked down Kerensa's cheek. "Yes," she whispered. "Yes."

Some time later, after Rewan had returned home, practically bouncing his way down the hillside, Kerensa began her search. Without her mother there to do it for her, Kerensa would do it for herself.

It didn't take long to locate three candles stored carefully amongst her mother's things. Using the coals of the cloam oven she lit them. Three lights to signify a coming marriage, the union of two families and creation of a third.

A blessing for the bride and, for Kerensa, a true family for the first time.

She hoped.

Pumpkins and Hazelnuts

They married on the day of harvest festival. The town flooded out into the icy air to celebrate, a welcome distraction of the harsh and lean winter that was on their doorstep. The run had failed again. Rewan and Braneh had invested in two new sail boats to push farther out into the ocean, but the risk had not borne fruit. "Soon though Kerensa, soon. We will find those sneaky fish," Rewan insisted, and he believed it.

But today was not about that, today was about them.

The ceremony was held in St Endellion. Pastor Henry kept it short, thankfully. When Rewan said "I do" Kerensa's heart swelled with joy. When Pastor Henry pronounced them wed, tears had flowed down her cheeks.

As they took their first kiss as a married couple, she suppressed a sob. Years of separation, of feeling outside of the town, and now, here she stood before all of Porth Gwynn, and God, marrying her Rewan.

"Those will be the last tears you shed, as long as I live, Kerensa," Rewan murmured into her ear before turning his brilliant smile onto the gathered townsfolk and leading her from the church.

They led the procession of well-wishers down the hill back to Porth Gwynn, laughter and merriment high. Braneh had brought a cart bearing a keg of ale, so mugs of drink could be passed and shared as they journeyed back, leaving the group ready and merry for the celebration now due.

As they came to the main pebbled street of the town, Kerensa drew in a sharp breath. She could not believe her eyes.

Some folk had stayed back from the church. She hadn't cared, never expecting the approval of all the town. But now, she saw the real reason they had remained behind.

Tables and stools had been brought out from all the nearby houses, decked in acorns and fronds of autumn colour. Pumpkins and hazelnuts adorned the ground in splashes of vibrant colour and small fire pits warmed the street. It was simple. It was beautiful. It was all for them.

Before it all stood Emblyn and Mabyn, smiling broadly, clearly pleased with themselves.

"Come, come," Emblyn beamed at the newlyweds. "Come all," she raised her voice to the surrounding townsfolk. "Sit, it is time to celebrate!"

A roar of joy sounded from the townsfolk as they streamed onto the main street taking up seats in family groups. Rewan led Kerensa proudly to their assigned stools, grinning happily, a gleam of mischief in his eye.

"Did you know about this?" she whispered to her new husband.

"Who do you think planned it?" he grinned, nodding over at his mother, Meraud as she appeared bearing a huge fruit cake. She must have used their Christmas pudding supplies, Kerensa realised and felt a blush of embarrassment and joy warm her cheeks.

Smiling, Meraud placed the cake before the couple, "Welcome to the family Kerensa," she said, eyes moist and took her seat beside them.

"Thank you," Kerensa said, fighting back the tears. It was all too much.

It was wonderful.

The night passed in joy and celebration. Food was bountiful, ale flowed freely, Jago struck up his fiddle and everyone danced. Kerensa didn't think she'd ever been so happy in her life as she sat at the table holding Derwa's newest son, Cadan, in her lap. His wriggling pudge warm against her arms she watched the happiness flowing about her and smiled.

Her eyes spotted Rewan standing alone. He had walked to the edge of the dancing and was staring out over the bay. From the slump of his shoulders she could tell he was deep in thought.

Passing the giggling Cadan back to Derwa she made her way over to him. She stood at his side in silence, letting him know she was there with a gentle touch of his arm and then waiting for him to speak. He smiled softly down at her then looked back over the black waters that whispered gently in the dark night.

"I miss him," he said at last, "I wish he were here."

Kerensa didn't need to be told who 'he' was: Gerens.

She wrapped a supportive arm about his waist and squeezed.

"Me too," she said.

"And you must feel it too, your mother? I'm sorry my love."

The only shadow of this perfect day was the missing. Meliora, gone before this joy could come to pass, and Gerens, her childhood friend, who left two years ago now and had not been heard of since. Tiny Treeve, so long in the earth.

"She is looking down on us, I know it. Wherever she is, today she smiles."

Rewan placed a hand on hers and leaned into her warmth. They stood together in silence, as one against the world, together they could surmount it all.

She felt Rewan straighten. He turned to her and took her in his arms. "But today is about us, my love. And you have not yet danced!"

Mischief lit his eyes and his lopsided grin returned as he led her back to the party. A quick nod to Jago and the tune from their first dance together, two seasons before, here, at the start of a new fish run, at the start of their courting, echoed out across the town.

Kerensa threw back her head and laughed as Rewan pulled her close. The town opened up around them, forming a circle, clapping in time with the bouncing tune. And Rewan spun her. Round and round and round the circle they leapt, the music gaining speed, faster, faster, faster. The town clapped and cheered. Cheeks flushed from exertion and laughter Kerensa gripped on to her husband's solid arms, hopping now only on her good foot. The crescendo neared and Rewan lifted her from the ground twirling her around in the air, hands gripping her waist. She raised her arms to the sky in glee and closed her eyes, feeling the cold of night brush against her sweaty face. The music stopped. Rewan put her down, laughing. Jago struck up another tune and the town joined them again in the merriment.

For the first time in Kerensa's life, she felt fully a part of Porth Gwynn.

They walked to what had been Meliora's hut, now their home, hand in hand. At the door, Rewan swept her into his arms and carried her across the threshold. Kerensa laughed at his gesture. This was, after all, her childhood home, but she loved him for it nonetheless.

Inside he set her down, pulling her close.

The energy between them changed, Rewan's face now serious, intent.

Kerensa swallowed as she looked into his dark eyes, filled with desire.

He placed a hand on her cheek and kissed her, slowly, deeply, thoroughly. Gently she took his hand and led him to the bed. Their bed. Together they lay down, bodies aligned, close.

And he hesitated. For the first time in Kerensa's memory she saw doubt flicker across his beautiful features. He was nervous too. She smiled softly.

"I love you," she whispered.

"I love you too."

She leaned in and kissed him gently. His body loosened, melting alongside her own, and they lost themselves in the exploration of each other's bodies, hearts and love.

After, as she squatted over the chamber pot to cleanse herself, Rewan lay on the bed nearby, twirling a lock of her hair between his fingers. Clean she stood up, naked in the firelight before him.

"Beautiful," he breathed, eyes glittering with the flames.

Feeling the blush rise on her cheeks she climbed back onto the bed and curled into his side, head nestled against his chest.

"I will take care of you, Kerensa," Rewan said, voice sleepy, fingers absentmindedly stroking her bare arm. "I promise."

"And I'll take care of you," she replied, snuggling closer.

"I know." Rewan smiled, then lost himself to sleep.

Water and Thyme

The door to Peren's hut swung open. Inside was dimly lit, silent but for the gasps and groans of pain emanating from the centre of the room. Carworan, her arm still gripped in his hand, drew Kerensa inside. He'd come for her. Out of breath, eyes wild, "We need you, there's been an accident."

She'd gathered her supplies quickly and followed him into the chilly early evening air. Gripping her shoulder he'd rushed her down the hill, almost too fast for her shorter and less stable gait to manage. But she didn't complain. This was serious.

Now he released her arm.

She stepped into the room and walked around the row of broad backs that blocked her view of the table. Rewan looked up, caught her eye, his expression strained and tense. He nodded to her. She gave him a little smile and turned her attention to the man lying prone on the table, surrounded by two crews of fishermen.

Peren was wet with sweat and sea, his eyes wide with fear and pain. He was holding himself up on his elbows, panting with the effort of managing his pain, subconsciously pushing down, bracing his injury. She scanned his body and saw what Carworan had explained. The left leg lay flat against the wood of the table, jutting out at an unnatural angle. Blood had seeped through the wool of his trousers.

Rewan stepped up beside her.

"The mast came down on father's boat, about two hours from shore. Peren couldn't get out of its way. It pinned his leg against the side of the hull. We had to help lift it off him, but..." he trailed off.

Kerensa looked about the room for Peren's wife and daughters. Through the passageway she saw the three women sitting in the next room, silent. Wenna looked up. "Do you have scissors?" Kerensa called.

Wenna nodded, squeezed her mother's shoulder and came quickly into the room. Fetching the scissors, she handed them to Kerensa, fear had dilated her pupils.

"Thank you," Kerensa said simply.

She moved closer to the table and took hold of the edge of Peren's trousers. Looking up into his pained face she explained simply, "I need to see the injury, but your trousers are too wet and torn to come away easily. I'm going to cut this material away. Are you ready?"

Peren nodded.

Carefully Kerensa slid the scissors under the material and began to slice, lifting the wool up before her scissors, trying hard not to brush the flesh below. Peren stiffened as some of the wool caught over his injury, but soon she had the trouser leg opened, revealing his limb.

Her arms went limp at her sides. It was worse than she could possibly have imagined, even from the angle of the covered leg.

Above the knee looked sound, but the knee itself and half way down the shin was crushed, splinters of white bone protruding from a mass of pulped flesh. It was not one or two clear breaks but a shattering of the whole lower limb. The leg could not be saved.

Kerensa's mind raced. They needed the doctor from St Endellion to perform surgery. As she watched at the dark blood pooling beneath Peren's crushed limb, Kerensa calculated the time it would take to fetch Doctor Mayard. Hours at best. Too long.

She would have to do it.

Fear gripped her throat and she felt her stomach flip. Peren looked up at her, eyes seeking.

Meliora's words the night they helped Derwa safely deliver her first child, drifted into her mind. "Do not show fear, only confidence. They need your belief to survive."

She took a deep breath, squared her shoulders and gripped Perens's hand. Leaning down she whispered into his ear. He paled even further, but then, as he looked deeply into her eyes he nodded, firming his jaw in determination.

Kerensa nodded back. Chin high she started her directions.

"Wenna, boil water and thyme, you'll find some in my basket. Kenver, Carowan at his shoulders to help support him, Jory at his hip, Rewan by me. Eseld," She called into the opposite room, "I need wool and cloth, as much as you can find." Startled the thin youth stood and rushed deeper into the house.

"Cardor, you are the swiftest, hasten to St Endellion and find Doctor Johns. Hopefully he is in residence. Tell him to come immediately, to bring milk of the poppy and surgical wraps. Fast as you can."

The room went silent, what she intended to do taking shape before them.

Cardor paused, then nodded and raced out the door.

"Braneh?" she scanned the room, searching for Peren's captain. He stood near the back of the room, face cast down. He looked up at her call, features lined with shame. *He blames himself,* she realised, sympathy flooding her heart. She pushed it down, no time.

"Braneh, take Jago, I need whiskey, as much as you have, and a saw. Smaller but sharp and new. Hurry."

The men stared at her in silence, their suspicions confirmed. No one moved.

"Go," Peren cried out, voice rasping over his dry throat. "Bloody hurry up!"

As if slapped by a whip, Braneh lurched into action and raced from the room towards the sheds.

He returned swiftly, Meraud in tow. Kerensa was grateful for his forethought, the older woman's presence would bring a sense of confidence to them all. Meraud nodded quickly to Kerensa and hastened into the side room to sit with the distraught Emblyn. Kerensa arranged everyone around Peren's prone body, pillows stuffed behind his head to allow him to lay back. The comfort would be short-lived.

Braneh handed her the whiskey bottle. She pulled the cork and splashed some over the open wound. Peren hissed and tensed. Focused, Kerensa brought the bottle to his lips.

"Drink. Deeply," she ordered. Peren nodded and started gulping down the brew. As he drank she took a line of rope and wrapped it tightly about his thigh, above the injury, to stem the flow of blood.

"Saw," she said, holding out her hand to Jago. He passed her a short hacksaw blade then took up position by Peren's good leg.

She stood at his wounded leg, placed a cool hand on the burning flesh of his upper thigh.

Quickly, but with intention, she met the eyes of each man standing around their friend. "He will buck and struggle. Hold him down, as much as you can."

She looked down at Peren, "This will hurt. Scream as much as you will."

Peren began to breathe in short gasps and passed the whiskey to Kenver at his head, but he nodded.

Kerensa gripped his upper thigh tightly and aligned the blade, taking a deep breath.

Beside her Rewan took hold of Peren's hips. "You can do this," he whispered to her.

Those words hit her in the heart. He believed in her. It was enough.

She drew back the blade and began.

Peren screamed, blood splattered, the men braced holding him down. At first the flesh resisted, the muscle fighting against the blade, but she did not stop. She drove the saw across the thigh just above the crushed knee, hand slick with hot, sticky blood. Then she hit bone.

Peren went limp. He had passed out.

The doctor arrived with the morning sun, he'd been at a farm some distance from town when Cardor came to find him. It had taken hours to locate him, then wait for the wife he was aiding in childbirth to deliver her healthy babe. But finally he was here.

Peren lay on his marriage bed, slick with fever-sweat and sleeping fitfully. After Kerensa had packed his stump with wool and bandaged it with sheet cloth the men had carried him to bed to rest and, hopefully, recover. Rewan and Kenver had taken the limb, Kerensa didn't know what they had done with it, and hadn't cared to ask.

Emblyn sat beside Peren gently wiping his face with a sage water cloth.

"Dr Mayard," Kerensa said, standing from her place by the oven. She'd refused to leave her patient. Though there would be little she could do if his condition worsened, she would be there.

The doctor's glance swept her from head to toe, taking in her blood stained skirts, blouse sleeves rolled up. The deep fatigue in her eyes.

Kerensa didn't wait on formalities, "He's through here."

She led him to her patient, explained all she had done to cleanse and pack the wound and then retreated to the table once again. Rewan, who had remained with her all night, squeezed her shoulder and offered a smile of support. She tried to smile back, but she knew it did not meet her eyes. Now was the critical time, what would the doctor say? Had she saved a man's life? Or killed him?

What seemed like hours later, but was likely only a ten minutes or so, Doctor Mayard returned to the kitchen. He stood in the doorway and eyed Kerensa.

"You learnt medicine from your mother I take it?" he asked, eyes hard.

Kerensa swallowed, "My mother knew herbs and helped women with their birthing. Yes, I learned from her."

He nodded and stepped forward. "That man in there," he said, "owes you his life."

Relief flooded through Kerensa and she felt herself physically sag over the table. Rewan gripped her hand.

"He's lost much blood, but without your swift and decisive action, he would be dead. I've inspected the cut, untrained but cleanly done. It's re-bandaged now and I gave him milk of the poppy. Emblyn has instructions on dosage to keep him sleeping while he heals. He's not out of the woods yet, but I am hopeful he will make it. Thanks to you."

Tears of relief and bone-deep fatigue flowed down Kerensa's face. Dr Mayard nodded at her and offered a quick smile before looking over her head at Rewan. "Take your wife home, Rewan," he said. "She's done all she can here. It's time for her to rest."

Swiftly Rewan stood and helped Kerensa to her feet. As they made for the door Carworan stepped before them, blocking their path.

Beside her Rewan stiffened. Kerensa blinked up into Carworan's dark face, too tired to care what curses he had prepared to throw in her face.

"Thank you," he breathed. Unable to meet her weary gaze his eyes searched the floor.

Kerensa blinked in surprise. A flare of angry resentment filled her chest as the memories of the shame this man had brought to her and to Meliora flashed through her mind. But the day was new and the flame was short lived. She had saved his crewmate and friend. He knew he had been wrong.

It would do.

She nodded and Rewan led her outside.

They walked up the hill to their home arms wrapped about each other.

"I'm so proud of you my flower," He said, taking more of her weight to get her through the last part of the hill. "You are incredible."

Kerensa smiled, exhausted and patted his cheek.

"I don't think father will sail again," Rewan continued.

Surprised, she looked up at her husband, concern flashing across her drawn face.

"But that's not for now," Rewan said with a shake of his head. "Now, we rest." He pushed open the door to their home and led her to bed and sleep.

A Paste of Black Spider Skins

Rewan was right about Braneh.

Peren's accident had come with the tail end of the season, but Braneh did not emerge from his hut for the last few runs.

The others pressed on regardless. After fixing Braneh's broken mast they sailed out into the rough seas in search of a final haul. It did not come.

Christmas brought a burst of icy winds from the North. Sleet and storms battered the coast. By January snow covered the frozen earth in a thick layer of white beauty. The town retreated indoors, huddling close to wait out the bitter season.

At first, Rewan and Kerensa found joy in those long dark days by the oven fire, time alone to revel in the magic of newly married life.

But soon the sound of coughs, moist and deep, called them out from their joyous isolation.

Breock was the first to suffer. Fearing for Derwa's smaller children, Kerensa brought him up to her hut and cared for him there. He slept between Kerensa and Rewan, sweating, coughing and crying in delirium. Kerensa kept him watered and gently coaxed broth down his throat as often as he allowed. She crushed up a paste of black spiders to rub onto Rewan's back, an old remedy to draw the rot from his lungs before it could take hold. Kerensa doubted the effectiveness of the treatment, but after losing her mother so recently, she was willing to try anything to keep Rewan by her side. Rewan did all he could to help, the memory of his own baby brother lost to sickness haunted his eyes.

But Breock made it. When Kerensa brought him home a week later, weak but hale, Derwa had clutched them both close and sobbed with thanks.

Unfortunately, Breock wasn't the only one to catch the illness.

Peren's wife Emblyn came down with the cough several days later, but refused to be separated from her family. Kerensa left her herbs and instructions and kept her in her prayers. Old Austol and Maderns were also struck down, as well as youthful Cardor. Kerensa did what she could for them all until a tickle at the back of her own throat signalled she too had succumbed. She ignored her symptoms as long as she could, until one morning she collapsed while collecting water for the morning tea.

Hearing the muted thud of Kerensa's limbs as she hit the ground, Rewan rushed to his wife and gathered her frail body in his arms. "You're burning up!" he exclaimed in shock as he rushed her back to their bed.

There he cared for her, mopping her burning brow, feeding her fish broth brought up from his mother's kitchen, holding her steady over the chamber pot. Weak and feverish, Kerensa tossed and turned on their bed. Rewan never left her side.

But her malady brought more than fever. Heavy bleeding at the height of her illness was more than just her monthly courses. Unaware, Rewan simply took the new symptom in hand, the life of a fisherman made him unfazed by the blood.

But Kerensa knew the truth. She'd lost a baby. Early, true, but their child nonetheless.

Dazed by grief she wallowed in her bed, crying out in delirium and sorrow. The evil words of her childhood returned to haunt her. They'd never truly left, hiding always in the depths of her mind. Now her high temperature made them true, dragging her mind into hopelessness, self-loathing and blame as sickness ravaged her body.

She had been born wrong.

She was cursed.

Everything, everything was her fault.

Seeing only her pain and not the cruel thoughts behind her weakening body, Rewan looked on fearing the worst for his wife, and prayed to God to spare her life. "Take anything, anything, even my own life. But spare my wife."

It was as if God heard his plea, for as the snows began to melt into the brighter sun of March, Kerensa awoke clear-headed and bright-eyed. Rewan vowed he would never miss a Sunday service ever again.

Kerensa never told him the truth of their loss. She couldn't bear to see her pain reflected in his eyes. Couldn't face his rejection if he too cast blame at her feet for their dead child. So she carried the burden alone, burning sage in memory when Rewan was out visiting Kenver and Derwa.

Despite it all, she survived.

Sadly, not all the townsfolk were so lucky.

The hunger gap arrived and brought with it the passing of Austol and Carworan's wife Lowena, and the town collected solemnly to send them to God and prayed for those still suffering.

With the spring sun some men left to find farm work to tide them over until the fish season began. Others left more permanently, heading for the mines in the south or trade ports in the larger towns.

Jory was one of them. "It's a tough life here, Rewan," he said. "But so is any trade. I have to feed my family…"

Shame laced his features.

Kerensa knew Rewan was furious, hurt deep in his heart that his childhood friend and crewmate would abandon the port he loved. But he did not show it, not to Jory.

"You must do what you believe is right," he said simply.

Slapping Rewan on the shoulder, Jory promised to send word if he heard anything about Gerens, who had not made contact with anyone from the port since he left in shame some 3 years before, and was on his way.

Time eked on.

By the time the spring potatoes were ready to harvest, Kerensa had been forced to tie extra knots in her skirts to keep them over her hips. Sickness and reduced food had seen her wither.

Rewan had lost size as well. Kerensa tried to keep him well fed, but he refused to take more than what he deemed absolutely necessary.

"You have been unwell," he insisted. "You need your strength to recover. Besides," he gave her his familiar cheeky grin, "you could be growing my son in there!" He lay a gentle hand on her belly, so malnourished it was now concave.

Kerensa grimaced and turned away. Shame burning her face.

"What is it flower?" Rewan asked gently, turning her face to his.

Tears limned her eyes as she watched the concern take shape over his fatigued features.

"It is nothing. I'm just tired, that is all."

He watched her in silence a moment, then brought his lips down to hers. Pulling back, he held her eyes in his, "This hardship is not of your doing. Whatever superstitious talk you hear. It is just the cycle of the seasons. The fish will come, they always do."

Kerensa lost her battle and the tears spilled freely down her face, wetting the front of her dress. He knew. Though she'd never spoken of it, somehow he knew the fears she harboured deep inside. Rewan wrapped her body into his, holding her strong against the pain in her heart. Slowly the tears dried and her body began to relax into the warmth of his strength.

"I will look after you," he whispered, as he had on their first night of marriage.

"And I will look after you," she replied.

As the heat of summer began to shine upon the coast the usual aura of positivity and hope that had invigorated the town in years gone by did not arrive.

Across the hills wild flowers bloomed in pinks and purples, green grasses reached high into the sky and the farming men returned. But no celebration was held. There was no cheer or food left to share.

Every morning Rewan rose with the sun and made his way to the sheds. With his crew he worked the boats, sanding, repairing, painting in preparation for the run. He borrowed money from some men at market to pay for the extra material needed to fit the remaining boats with mast and sails. All the fishermen would sail out from the port this year.

It was their only hope.

But Braneh did not join them.

Kerensa worked with the women in the sheds, repairing the nets and baskets, completing the usual tasks in readiness for the run. At home, she mended Rewan's jumpers and shirts, knitting in the long ridged lines along the sleeves that symbolised his port of origin. Some days she went foraging, collecting herbs and vegetables to supplement their income and food supply.

Whenever she walked past the sheds Rewan would call out to her, his voice pitched high and firm, "Happy collecting my love! Make sure you've extra dill. It's going to be an impressive haul this year. I can feel it."

"It's on the wind!" She'd reply, playing into his little rouse.

Working beside him the other fishermen would call out their own cheers of good fortune, their preferred superstitious signs that foretold bounty: "a cat crossed past the boats and purred", "my right palm's an itch I cannot scratch" , "I saw six magpies on the wind!". Night after night, Rewan invited friends to dine with him and Kerensa. As she dished out generous helpings of salt fish and potato, fretting in silence over their dwindling supplies, Rewan beamed of the riches to come, boasting that their sheds would be too small for this year's catch. He worked endlessly, cultivating an air of positivity and hope and gifting it to the people of Porth Gwynn, working to fill the Braneh-shaped hole that had opened up amongst them.

As Rewan sat by the oven before bed, the warm glow of candlelight accentuated the deep lines of fatigue across his forehead. Yet as he pulled his wife into his lap, wrapping his arms about her waist, his gentle touch remained. Even for her he showed strength and belief, albeit with sleepy eyes and weary smiles. Kerensa wore a smile to match. She would never confess the festering doubt that invaded her heart. The thoughts that wormed their way into her deepest soul: Had Carworan been right all these years? Had she cursed the town to strife?

Rewan's efforts exhausted them both. But it was not in vain.

The town believed him.

Slowly but surely the positive energy of the pending run began to take over the town, as everyone was swept up in Rewan's enthusiasm and belief. Even Kerensa felt a sense of hope begin to sink into her bones. This year, like every year before it, held the promise, the potential, of great success and an end to their leaner times. They would triumph, she was sure. What was the curse of her birth against the iron will of her husband, after all?

In the silence of night, Kerensa nestled safely in his arms, Rewan let down his guard. Eyes open, he watched the shadows pass over the ceiling and prayed to God. This was it. Make or break.

This season had to be a success.

The run failed.

Day after day Rewan and his crew sailed out beyond the bay in search of pilchards, the blistering sun beating down upon their weary heads.

The first Huer's cry didn't come until mid-autumn, and the haul was barely half the boats could hold. As always the women went to work in the sheds, scaling, gutting and cleaning the fish, packing them in salt for sale. This year though no trade vessels would come to collect their stock. The diminishing hauls of the past few years had taught the traders to seek elsewhere for more plentiful supply. Instead, the women strapped baskets of pilchard to their backs and headed to the markets in St Endellion. The prices were low, much below the heyday of yesteryear. But money was made, brought back to Porth Gwynn and distributed amongst the villagers.

Older folk gathered in the shallows, seeking stray fish brought from the currents. Any caught were shared between them, the number too few to be worth processing for sale.

Despite the silent Huer, the men still sailed. Out beyond the break, further and further from the shore, following the gulls that hunted from the skies above and the warm currents that pushed from the south.

Walking up from the beach each evening with bounding step, eyes forward, head held high, Rewan continued projecting confidence. The effort though, was taking its toll. By the light of Kerensa's oven, the façade wobbled. Weighed down by fatigue and the ongoing effort of bolstering the town, Rewan's smile dropped, his shoulders slumped. At night he rarely sought her body, too exhausted from the day to rally. But still he held her close. He slept fitfully, tossing and turning, waking Kerensa from her slumber to join him in his worry over the town and their future.

Without a word to him, she stopped working with the other women of the town and focused solely on her foraging to sure up their position, spending the long days he was away filling her baskets with herbs and wild vegetables, splitting the onions and potatoes left from winter into shoots as her mother had taught her and planting up their yard with seeds and tubers. Soon the hut was filled with the scent of drying thyme, sage, fennel and nettle, the table lined with Meliora's bottles of tinctures, once again filled and ready.

Rewan didn't seem to notice.

When the women went to market with the few fish available to sell, she followed, baskets full of her own offerings. As she limped along the dirt path to St Endellion the wind whispered of her curse, of the despair she would bring to all she loved.

But Kerensa carried on.

Everything she collected and processed she shared with the rest of the town, making special provision for Peren and Emblyn. Of them all Peren's family suffered the most greatly. His leg had healed, but left him unable to fish or farm and a deep sadness had settled into his bones, one Kerensa could not bring him from with herbs. Silently the town brought them bread and cheese and words of support. Peren turned from them all.

Likewise Braneh stayed noticeably distant and silent, refusing to come out and work the runs with his son. Rewan tried repeatedly, "Father, please, we need your experience, your eye for the currents."

"You know all I do and more lad," Braneh had argued softly. "The sea is not for me anymore boy. You have to know when to quit."

His words were laced with heavy meaning. Rewan's eyes had lit with momentary anger at his father's words and he'd turned and stalked from his childhood home, not looking back.

As the icy winds from the north once again marked the passing into winter and the end of another pilchard season, the sheds remained close to empty. Gloom descended over the town.

Only Rewan kept smiling.

"Tomorrow will be the day," he'd say firmly to his fellow fishermen, "I can smell the fish on the wind."

No one argued.

No one believed him anymore.

Kerensa blamed herself.

Where the Gulls Fall Silent

The sky was heavy with gathering clouds, the air thick with the promise of storm. Sleet fell from high, melting onto the earth in pools of icy mud as the town gathered together for the walk to Sunday Service at St Endellion Church. Weather like this, a harbinger of snow, would usually keep some indoors to pray in private. But after the failure of the last two seasons' fish run and the coming winter winds, being on God's good side seemed prudent.

Even Peren had come out, swinging from the wooden crutches Kenver had made him the winter before, finally using them to leave his home with his family.

Kerensa smiled at him and Emblyn as they joined the rest of the town on the bayside ready to leave. Lately they'd taken to walking together, as though their act of unison could hold the town together. Their numbers had dwindled further since last winter.

Braneh and Meraud started towards the town. Cardor behind them talking with Eseld. It would not be long before they wed, Kerensa thought with an all too rare flash of joy. Their mutual adoration was obvious and strong. Next came Derwa, arms full of baby, her fourth, a boy once again. Kenver beside her wrangled their third boy, while Breock dutifully held Bobbie's small hand and guided his brother. Beside her Rewan offered Kerensa his arm and they turned to follow.

A cry, clear and bright pierced the air. As one the town turned back towards the bay. High atop the cliff stood the Huer, bushels raised and swinging in the morning gloom. "Hevva! Hevva!" he cried, pointing his Semaphore bushes out over the sea. Unconsciously, Rewan stepped forward, muscles tense. The bay's curve hid the waters beyond, but the call of the gulls as they flew out over the cliffs echoed back to Kerensa's ears.

Pilchards.

Her breath caught in her throat. It had been weeks since the Huer last cried. The town all but resigned to an early end of a trying and unprofitable run. And now, pilchards.

But it was the Sabbath.

Silence fell like a blanket over the group.

Everyone waited, tense. A silent and collective decision that it was Rewan's call.

She watched the side of Rewan's face as he looked out over the bay. His eyes scanned, the muscle of his jaw pulsing as he fought an inner battle no one could hear, nor fully understand. Only Rewan knew the deal he'd made with God last winter.

The world seemed to stop, as if the waves themselves held back in wait.

"We go," Rewan announced firmly, turning back to the town. "It is a big haul, the gulls prove it. This, this is what we've waited for!"

No one moved.

Kerensa gripped his arm, whispered into his ear. "It smells of snow, of storm."

He looked down into her eyes, "This is it my flower," he said. "The run to bring us through the winter, the run to save our home."

"You are my home," she insisted.

His lopsided grin broke out across his face, a genuine light of mirth shining from his eyes, all too rare these last months. "Do you think I won't come back for you?" he whispered, then winked at her and kissed her quickly on the mouth.

"We go!" he cried again, raising his fist to the sky, "To fill our barrels and our stomachs, to prepare for winter, for ourselves. For Porth Gwynn!"

"For Porth Gwynn," Cardor took up the call and stepped forward.

"For us all," Kenver said, joining his crewmate.

A ripple of energy surged through the crowd as all the men stepped forward at once, eyes eager, bodies tense, ready.

"Pray for us, wives, mothers, daughters," Rewan said solemnly, "and prepare for a long night in the sheds! There will be feasting tonight! Come men, the fish won't wait."

With a cry of hope and determination the men raced forward as one, heading for their boats resting on the beach. The women, children and older men watched as their fishermen pulled woollen jumpers over their Sunday shirts, hefted their vessels from the sand and carried them to the rising tide. Arms straining, they rowed against the heavy currents, the waves in the bay already high with the promise of storm, out towards the open ocean.

Kerensa became aware of a presence beside her. She looked up into Braneh's weathered face, lines deepened by worry. "It smells of storm," she repeated to the old fisherman.

"Yes," he said simply, watching the boat that held his remaining two sons as it streaked for the sea beyond. He said no more, there was nothing to say.

Unable to contain the anxious swirling in her gut, Kerensa rushed for the cliff. Hobbling up the steep incline she climbed until she reached the Huer's hut and walked out to the edge. Down below the waves surged, tipped with white foam. Overhead the gulls flew, circling a spot far out over the waters, on the edge of her vision. She watched as the white canvas of the sailboats bloomed out from the vessels and the boats surged forward, crashing through the heavy swell. Fog was gathering in the north, rolling down the coast across the waves, but the boats sailed on. Hugging herself against the vicious winds that lashed the cliff face and against her own sense of doom, Kerensa watched until the boats disappeared beyond the fog, until the sun tipped over the top of the sky, until the rain began to pelt the earth, until darkness, moonless and deep, fell over the town.

Rewan gripped the rudder, hands white and numb with cold. Rain lashed his face, but he did not turn from his course.

"We should go back," Kenver shouted over the howl of the wind. "The fog, we can't see the way to the fish!"

Rewan shook his head, water streaming from his hair. "We are nearly there, my friend."

"But…"

"We must succeed," he looked at Kenver, eyes ablaze, "We have to feed our people."

Kenver watched his friend's face, saw his resolve and nodded slowly, turning back to the waters to scan for silver pilchards.

"There!" Jago's cry rang across the enraged sea.

Each man's head snapped forward following his pointing hand.

"There!" Rewan cried back in agreement, eyes bright with excitement.

"I told you!" He cried to his crew, "We'll make a season of it yet boys!"

Cardor whooped for joy, Kenver clapped.

The school was huge, spread out across the waters. The three sail boats formed a circle, lowering their nets and whooping around the school, cutting off the pilchards. Fish secured they began to scoop them from the water. So many fish! Rewan could not believe it. Tears of joy and relief streamed down his face as his haul and that of his group's vessels filled to the brim. The winds battered against his boat, but he held the rudder firm, a new energy coursing through his limbs. He thought of Kerensa, of the dress he would buy her with the profits from the haul, of feeding her up, of taking her to bed and making a child, their child, who he would teach to sail and fish as his father had taught him and his brothers. The only trade he'd ever known, passed down family to family, into the future. He'd found the way. To sail out and trust his vessel. To never turn back.

A bolt of lightning split the sky, its eerie white flashing out across the waves highlighting the expressions of joy and excitement of his crew, his friends, in its pale shine. The pilchard bellies flashed silver as they squirmed in their death throes. And Rewan knew peace. He'd done it! Porth Gwynn would live on.

The whipping winds and rain like shards of ice drove Kerensa from the cliff top. Far below, the waves lashed the jagged rocks of the coast with the fury of hell.

Soaked through, she knocked on Derwa's door in the dark and was instantly admitted. Dressed in one of Derwa's spare dresses, she sat by the oven fire warming her hands around a mug of tea. Derwa sat beside her. Neither woman spoke. There was nothing to say. Outside the wind howled, whipping through the township, bent on destruction. In the darkness the waves crested the cove streaming over the pebbled streets of the town, filling the floors of the first row of houses with ice-cold seawater. Mothers lifted children up onto tables, and brought pigs and chickens inside to wait out the rage of the skies.

A blast of artic air caught one of Derwa's shutters, forcing it from its hinges. The clatter of it banging down the street muted by the howl of the storm. Running from the wind and rain that burst into the main room, Derwa and Kerensa joined her boys in the main bedroom, taking up vigil on the floor, a blanket wrapped about their shoulders. Together the two women huddled, waiting for the storm to pass. Waiting for their husbands to return.

The town did not sleep. In each window shone the light of vigil as they all waited for their men to come home to the sound of the beating rains.

Rewan's vessel rode lower in the sea, weighed down by the haul of pilchard flesh. Each of the other boats fared the same. It was a good problem to have, he decided, pushing away the doubt that niggled at the back of his mind as his boat struggled to roll with some of the bigger waves. The storm was fierce, but so far nothing they could not handle.

The sun had long since set and they sailed on instinct alone, following each other by the light of their lamps. Time passed, it felt like they had been heading for port for hours.

"Shouldn't we see the cliffs by now?" Cardor shouted over the winds.

Rewan didn't reply, his brother's words reflecting his own growing fears. He stared ahead, scanning the waters before him. He had to trust in his senses, in the pattern of stars above his head. He had to pray.

Suddenly, a huge wave swept up from the port side. Rewan cried out a warning but the winds muffled his call.

The wave surged over the side of their vessel, pressing them down into the sea. Each man clung to whatever they could, holding their breath. The boat righted, water streaming from her hull.

"Get the fish!" Rewan cried, as he watched his catch slip into the sea.

His crew leapt down grabbing the slippery bodies from the draining water.

"Man over board!" the dreaded call came from behind him. He looked back but could not make out the crew in trouble in the darkness.

"We have to help," Cardor cried.

Rewan paused. To turn around would lose time and this storm was not lessening. He looked down at his earnest brother and knew there was no choice.

"Brace!" he called, "We're going round!"

He pushed the rudder hard to starboard swinging his vessel around. The sail snapped across the stern, the boat shuddered as it strained against the waves. Just then another massive wave surged towards them. "Wave!" Rewan shouted. Water poured down over their heads, filling their vessel, seeping fish from their hull.

Screams and cries echoed from the other boats through the roar of the sea. Rewan held fast to his rudder, eyes pressed shut. His lungs bursting from holding his breath, he waited for the boat to lift, to right itself once more. Just when he thought he could hold on no longer his head broke the surface of the waves. And saw, nothing.

Darkness enveloped him completely, not even the stars shone overhead.

The lamps of all the boats had gone out.

The first rays of morning shone down over a battered town. Seaweed was strewn over the pebbled streets and tracks of sand and mud spread between the houses of the small town. The wind had calmed, but still blew strong and icy along the streets. Dark clouds roiled in the lightening sky above, sleeting rain driving down from their swirling depths. Kerensa dashed through flooded streets to Meraud's home. She found her mother-in-law and Braneh locked in a tight embrace, foreheads pressed together.

Kerensa froze in the doorway

"Please, stay," Meraud whispered.

"I have to go," Braneh replied, "I must find them. It's my fault"

He kissed his wife's cheek and turned and strode for the door, passing Kerensa without a word, face set, eyes forward.

In the main room Meraud collapsed to the floor sobbing. Kerensa rushed to her side and wrapped her in a firm embrace.

"What is he doing?" she breathed.

"He's going for them," she said, voice quavering. "He's going to be with our boys in the sea."

Kerensa looked towards the door, throat tight with dread.

Neither woman believed he would return.

Braneh dragged the small row boat through the rain. The tide was receding now, but the waves in the bay still fought his progress. It did not matter. They would not stop him. Nothing would.

When he first told Meraud he was going, the light of hope in his heart had surged him forward. They'd already lost two sons.

Young Treeve, whose small body could not handle the hunger gap. If Braneh had worked harder, brought in more fish, the lad would have been better fed and perhaps stood a fighting chance when the coughing began. No one can fight hungry. It was a failing he had never forgiven of himself.

Then there was Gerens. He'd let his anger and fear go too far. But he'd never imagined his gentle son would not return. Braneh had thought a few months on his own would right him and he'd come home focused and prepared for the hard work of the sea.

But he never had.

He'd cost Meraud two sons. And the two remaining were now in peril because he had turned his back on the work of the town. After Peren's injury, he'd given up. Left it to the younger men.

His silence had made them desperate. They had floundered.

Pulling on the oars with his massive strength, Braneh rowed out across the bay, into the ocean waves beyond. To find his boys.

With each pull through the vicious surf his hope died a little more. His prayers could not beat the fury of the seas. Striking out through the storm he could barely see before him. It did not matter. He would follow the waves and the cries of the gulls overhead. Until the gulls fall silent, respecting the call of the drowned sailors beneath the waves.

There his sons' souls would stop his boat.

He knew his heart would find the spot.

And they would be together again.

The Knit of a Jumper

The winds died, the sleet turned to fluffy snow, glinting golden and bright in the sunrise.

Kerensa stepped out of Meraud's house into a world pale and white and stumbled to the bay. The tide was fully out now, the waves no more than ripples across the bay. She stood and watched the snowflakes fall from above, settling along the rocky edge of the cove, melting into the sea beyond.

She waited.

As she had before.

She stood alone and waited.

Word was sent to neighbouring Port Isaac. A crew was deployed to search for survivors, the question writ large on every fisherman's face: why were they out there at all in that storm?

Kerensa knew none of that. She kept her silent watch on the freezing beach.

Suddenly she burst forward, racing for the rocky outcrops that lined the cove. Scrambling up the rocks as she had as a child she began to pick her way along the water's edge, making for the open sea. The wet stone was slippery causing her to lose her grip, slicing her knee on the jagged rock.

She'd barely made it a half way to the break when she heard old Austol's call behind her.

Ignoring him she kept going, working her way around the coast. That's where they'd been, she said to herself, last time there was an accident at sea, when Rewan saved Cardor, they'd been on the rocks at the cliff edge. But this time it was colder, snowing, this time they couldn't wait to be saved.

"Come on love," Austol called out, pulling his small row boat up as close to the rocky outcrops as he dared. "You'll not find them this way. The lads from Port Isaac'll check the coast. Come back love, before you catch your death."

Kerensa paused, arms and legs trembling from the severe cold. A sob rose up in her throat and she pressed her head to the cliff face.

Austol waited, patient.

At length Kerensa pulled back from the cliff, nodding and climbed down into the vessel, drenching her skirts in the sloshing waters that buffed the cliff edge.

"Here you are love," Austol said, wrapping a blanket about her shoulders before pulling up his oars and rowing them back to shore. Kerensa sat facing the sea, she couldn't look away. Back on land Austol tried to guide her to his home to warm up and take tea, but Kerensa refused, firmly but kindly.

"My place is here," she said.

He looked sadly into her eyes and nodded. He knew she would not be moved.

And so she continued to wait, watching the waters.

As the sun topped the sky Derwa came out to join her, then Mabyn and Emblyn, Wenna and Eseld, and soon the rest of the women of the town. They stood as one, huddled close, watching the waves. Waiting.

A boat appeared, making its way slowly along the bay. Kerensa stiffened, they all did.

As it neared they saw the colours of Port Issac painted on its hull. The search boat.

Three men jumped from the vessel and dragged it up the beach, then leaned over the vessel's side and lifted, gently, the limp body of a fair-haired man.

Beside her Derwa gave a guttural cry and stumbled down the beach towards them. Splashing through the shallow pools of water that collected in dips in the sand, she collapsed onto the body the men carried between them, screaming to the sky. One man let go of the body and tried to pull her away, but Derwa shoved him off herself, clinging to the body on her knees in the salty pools of sea as snowflakes collected in her dark brown hair.

Kenver's body.

Kerensa closed her eyes.

Two days later the snow stopped. The town now covered in a thick white blanket. Kerensa was sleeping at Meraud's cottage, it was closer to the water after all and her mother-in-law needed her.

Each morning she rose and made bread and tea, leaving it on the table for Meraud. She could barely eat herself. Wrapped in her shawl and an extra blanket, she left and took up her vigil by the water. Watching. When the cold dark of night forced her back inside she made broth and served them both. Neither woman spoke, nor ate much. But the ritual continued, day in day out.

On day four some planks of wood floated into the bay. From their fleet? No one could say. But they were fished out and taken to the sheds to be stored for reuse, the automatic habit of a town used to hardship and making do.

That same day Port Issac officially called off their search. No one could still be alive out there, they said. Any survivors would be in a nearby town. They didn't need to say this was unlikely. Any bodies that washed up further down the coast would make their way home too, the woollen jumpers with ridged knitted lines, lovingly crafted by wives and mothers, would lead them home. No bodies came.

As the cold of new January settled over the town, the women began to leave. First went Beryan, with Madern and Brae, off to stay with family in Padstow. Next Derwa, her boys bundled against the cold, Mabyn walking stiff-backed beside her distraught daughter. Their destination? St Ives to join her brother Jory and try to make a new life.

Slowly but surely the townsfolk moved on until only Kerensa, Meraud and Peren's family remained.

Then, one surprisingly sunny day in February, Emblyn knocked on the door to Meraud's home.

The once proud woman shuffled to the door, head and shoulders bowed beneath her winter shawl and bid Emblyn inside.

Kerensa served tea.

The three women sat in silence together, the weight of loss heavy upon them all. Emblyn, whose husband was spared by his hideous accident barely a year before, somehow now the lucky one, sipped her tea nervously.

"We are leaving," Emblyn said, no preamble, no one had the energy for small talk.

Meraud nodded slowly.

"Peren has family, in Penzance. It's a long way, but, it's something.

We leave tomorrow."

Meraud reached across the table and took her old friend's hand. "God go with you," she said and meant it. Any jealousy Emblyn may have feared from her old friend at her seeming luck, did not raise its head. She was grateful for that.

"Come with us. Both of you." Emblyn fixed them both with long stares.

The silence stretched, achingly.

"Yes," Meraud whispered then rose from the table and walked to her window where she stood and watched the bay.

"No," Kerensa said, turning away.

And so the last family left and Kerensa was alone. She moved back to her hut, stoked her oven, tended her winter crop, made broth, slept, mended Rewan's old jumpers and summer trousers. Her old routine a comfort.

The blood was thick and black, streaming down her legs. Kerensa cried out in pain and sorrow as the child she'd barely known she carried rushed from her body. Spent with the effort and loss of blood she collapsed to the floor. Surging like waves grief smothered her, holding her beneath the surface, drowning her. She fought for the surface, struggled to control the flooding of pain. But could not break free. Sorrow, thick and black and heavy held her down, enveloping her. There was nothing left to fight for. So she gave up. Curled in a ball on the floor, she stared ahead, dry-eyed. There was nothing left to cry for.

In her mind Carworan's words rang, loud and clear. This time, she knew they were true.

Debtors came. She had no money. They took what payment she could offer.

The days eked on, slowly, darkly, covered in ice and solitude. And Kerensa slept and baked and sewed and mended and waited.

Waited.

Waited.

PART 5

Chipple Pie

"Kez?" a voice, distantly familiar, floated into Kerensa's subconscious. She ignored it. She was alone here. There had been people once, she thought. Or no, she was alone. Always alone. Kerensa was alone.

"Kez?" the voice came again, more insistent. "Kerensa, it's me. I'm here."

Slowly Kerensa turned from the bay, instinct obeying the voice's command.

Standing on the pebbled street stood someone she should know. She scanned his face, in its lines a faded recognition tickled her mind bringing the shadow of memories from the time before everything ended. She shoved them away. She had no interest in the time before.

There was only now.

She began to turn away. "Kerensa, please." The voice came again. She paused. "It's me, Gerens."

Gerens.

The word rang deep within her heart, a tiny spark of light and joy igniting within her belly.

She looked up sharply. "Gerens?" she whispered.

"Yes," the word choked in his throat, his eyes filling with tears as he watched her face. "I've come back. I'm here."

"Gerens," she repeated softly. It was a name. She knew that name, from before. No...

"Kez, look at me," the voice pushed itself back into her mind, forcing her to stay in the moment. "I've come back. I'm here, Kez. You aren't alone anymore. I'm here."

That voice, so soft, so kind, it refused, *refused* to be ignored, forcing its way deep, deep into her soul. Bringing out the before.

"Oh," Kerensa sobbed reaching out a hand to her oldest friend.

"Gerens."

He stepped forward and took her hand drawing her to his chest. Nestled there she pressed her head into his warmth.

"Gerens," she sobbed, shoulders quaking, "You came back."

"Yes," he whispered into her hair, "Yes."

"Rewan, Cardor, your father…"

"I know… Let's go inside," Gerens said gently, "I'll make tea."

Kerensa pulled back from him, nodding. That's when she saw the horse and cart waiting patiently behind her friend. The horse snorted and flicked its mane.

"You have a horse," she said, surprised, "and a cart."

"I do. Now come Kerensa," Gerens replied. He held out a hand to her .

She took it then drew back surprised at the soft uncalloused flesh of his palm. Looking at her friend again she frowned.

"Gerens, what are you wearing?" she asked.

She sat at her table, warm nettle tea steeping in the coals. Opposite her, Gerens rolled up the sleeves of his fine shirt. His black jacket hung beside Rewan's rough woollen coat. He had unhitched the horse and led it up with them, securing its harness around a bush outside. Gerens stood and poured them tea, returning to the table to sit with her.

"I came as soon as I heard, but news takes time to make it to London."

"London?"

"Yes," he nodded. "After I left Porth Gwynn I struggled to find work anywhere nearby. I found myself in St Just working the mines, but that wasn't for me." He paused, a shadow crossing his face.

"So I moved on. Eventually I found work on the docks at Plymouth, helping track the cargo in the holding sheds. That's where I met Mr Stevens."

He sipped his tea. "Mr Stevens is a trader out of London, he was looking for a new cargo manager. Impressed with my work on the docks of Plymouth he offered me a job. I took it. I always was better with letters and numbers than fish work."

He smiled softly, though it didn't reach his eyes. The memory of his father's rejection obviously still cut.

"I meant to send word, I planned to. But I was so busy… I kept track of the news out of Cornwall though. The market fluctuations, the stock levels and prices…" he trailed off seeing the lack of comprehension in

Kerensa's eyes.

"Well," he tried again, "I watched for news. When the reports of a storm so large experts called it a 'once-in-a-lifetime-event' came through I just, knew… I asked Mr Stevens for leave and set off across the country. As I got closer to Porth Gwynn the details of the storm took shape, until eventually I learned the full extent of what happened here. That everyone was gone."

"Why didn't you turn back?"

"Isn't that obvious?"

Kerensa shook her head.

"You," he watched her face sadly. "I knew you would not leave the sea. I knew you would be here. I came back for you."

Tears pricked Kerensa's eyes as she watched the solemn honesty of his face.

"It was my fault," she whispered, voice breaking. "The curse…" she gestured at her twisted foot resting against the dirt.

Fury lit in Gerens eyes. "No!" he said firmly, "No, Kez, you cannot think that way."

"They said, they all said. They knew… I was a sign."

"Superstitious fish shit!" Gerens swore, losing his temper. He stopped, breathing deeply to calm himself. It would not do to shout at her. When he'd first seen her standing on the foreshore, staring out to sea, he'd known true fear. She was so thin, so frail. And her eyes, she'd looked right through him. He'd thought he was too late. That the girl he'd grown up with, his dearest friend, was gone. Retreated into some part of her mind that he could not follow.

But the more he talked, the more her eyes cleared. She was fragile, like the slightest breeze could scuttle what little remained of her soul. But he was here now. He would help her back to who she used to be.

"Kez, he said gently, searching for the right words.

Reaching for her he gripped her shoulders tightly, her bones too prominent against his palms. "This was not your doing. It was just time. All things come to an end. All things."

"He went to save us. To save me…"

Gerens swallowed then sighed, "Yes, he did. Rewan went to save all of Porth Gwynn. But also for himself."

Kerensa looked up at him, eyes confused.

Gerens smiled sadly, "My brother was a man of the sea. He couldn't imagine any other life. Just like you, he would never have left. Not by choice. He fought for you Kez, for Porth Gwynn, and for his own heart. That was not your doing. That was his choice."

For a long moment she didn't move, just sat staring into her old friend's eyes. Something in her heart shifted and released. Tears came. Not the raking sobs of loss, but the gentle damp of acceptance.

"Thank you," she breathed.

"Kez," Gerens began dropping his hands from her shoulders and taking her hand. "I'm here to ask you to come away with me. To start a new life. In Newfoundland."

"Newfoundland?" Kerensa looked up at him sharply, withdrawing her hand in surprise.

"Mr Stevens is expanding his operations to a town there called St John's and has asked me to oversee the cargo operations. I have accepted the position. I want you to come with me."

Kerensa stood up and began pacing the small room, head shaking.

"Gerens, I cannot go with you, what would people say?"

"Come as my wife," he blurted.

Kerensa froze, staring at him wild-eyed.

"I don't expect you to break your vows, or to share my bed," Gerens said quickly. "But, as my brother's widow, let me marry you and take care of you. Be your husband. Raise my brother's child with you."

He looked pointedly at the small bulge that pressed against her skirts. Barely there, yet obvious in contrast to her emaciated limbs.

Kerensa looked down at her swelling belly, cupping it protectively with her hands.

"It's not his," she whispered, closing her eyes.

"What?" Gerens frowned, "But…"

"There were debts," she spoke over his objection. "I had no money. They took what payment they could."

"I, I don't understand," Gerens was shaking his head slowly, before realisation bloomed across his features in a storm of fury and horror.

"They…"

"Yes," she interrupted, not wanting to hear the words. They would summon the memory she'd buried deep, deep within herself.

"But," Gerens stammered, "you know the herbs… how to… deal with such a situation."

"No!" Kerensa shouted, eyes blazing. "This is my child. Mine! What those men did was wrong… they hurt me. But the child, my daughter, she is innocent."

Wrapping her arms protectively about her belly she turned away, looking out through the back shutters to the newly green rolling hills of early spring. Meliora's words drifted through her mind, "If it's not theirs, they never stay…" The price her mother paid for her, she too would pay. Gladly.

The soft scrape of a footstep sounded behind her and she felt the warmth of Gerens as he came up close behind her. Slowly, tentatively, he wrapped his arms about her waist, resting his hands over hers. In silence he held her, cupping her belly.

"Then we will protect her," he said. "I will raise her as my own, love her as my own. I will surely love her. She is part of you after all. Come with me Kez."

Tears flowed down her cheeks as she stood staring at the world outside her hut. The only home she had ever known. Porth Gwynn had sheltered her, fed her. She'd found love and joy here. Her heart longed to stay but… that was the past. There was nothing here for her anymore.

The warmth of Gerens' body soaked into her skin, the familiar smell of his body filling her nostrils. Hope and determination rose within her… then shattered.

"No," she breathed, pulling from Gerens' embrace. "I won't leave him."

Gerens watched her face, his heart filling with sadness as the veil of shock came down over her features once again.

"You don't have to decide, not right away."

He smiled softly and turned for the door.

"I think I might stay a few days. Say my goodbyes too. I'll be at my parents' house, if you need me."

Kerensa watched him with wide, distrustful eyes. "I won't change my mind," she said, raising her chin and stepping back from him. "You can't make me leave my home."

Gerens smiled ruefully, "No one could ever make you do anything you didn't want to Kez. I know that. It's been a long time since I have been home," he continued, "I have demons to bury here too."

Taking a deep breath she nodded slowly, shoulders relaxing at the sincerity of his words.

"I hope it helps."

"Me too."

"Damn it!" Gerens exclaimed as he slammed into his parents home. He'd pushed too hard. She needed time. But he'd waited before… and lost. He hadn't wanted to risk that again. Regardless, he'd messed it up.

He shook his head and slumped down at the kitchen table. Closing his eyes he took a deep breath. The scent of the house was both familiar and foreign, the tang of the sea rode the air, but the warm, sweet smell of baking bread and pie was jarringly absent. It took the air from his lungs and all thoughts of Kerensa fled his overwrought mind. Looking around the room it was as if the house were trapped in time. The furniture all in place, even the woollen blankets folded neatly on the footstool, waiting for his father and brothers to return from a day at sea to warm themselves by the fire. But the house was silent, as was the town beyond. The only life to be heard was the call of the gulls, the sound of dead souls crying out their loss.

No men would be returning for supper with the setting sun.

Gerens rose stiffly and wandered through the kitchen to the bedrooms beyond. His parents bed sat cold and dusty by the window facing the sea. In the little room opposite four cots rested, all neatly made up, waiting for his brothers. They would never come.

He was the only one left.

When he heard of the tragedy he had sent word in search of his mother, but after his long absence it seemed he no longer knew where to look. He'd come back in search of her, as well as Kerensa, riding a false hope that maybe, just maybe, his family were spared.

They'd turned him out. Even Rewan hadn't stood up to Braneh when he demanded his second son leave town. But they were still his blood.

Slowly he sank down onto the cot that was once his. Tears sprang into his eyes and a deep, wrenching sob drove up from his very centre. Curling into a ball he lay his head to rest where he had his whole life and let the sorrow flow out from him. Years alone, abandoned by this very house.

Now he was the only one left to return.

The days passed softly, gentle sun warming the earth, blue skies and fluffy clouds. Any other year it would be a perfect spring. The sounds of the town should be bustling about him: the scrape of sanding wood, the thud of stacking barrels, the booming voice of his father calling instructions. Long days of toil bleeding into long nights of companionable chat by the lengthening light of dusk and then to bed with a belly full of mackerel pasty and ale.

Not this year.

Gerens busied himself with the necessary tasks of survival. On his first morning he ventured into his mother's garden. Thankfully the neat rows of vegetables still grew, albeit beneath a generous layer of unwanted weeds. Gerens thrust his hands through the tangles of overgrowth and plucked a selection of potatoes, onions, carrot and parsley from the earth. He didn't bother to tidy the beds. He didn't plan on staying long enough. Back inside he raided the cupboards and found butter and a small jar of salted pilchards from the season before.

A bounty in his childhood, now it seemed slim pickings and he longed to head for the larger town of Padstow and the warm ale and lamb stew he knew would be on offer in the boarding houses. But this would keep him going, while he waited.

As if his thoughts had conjured her, Kerensa passed by his cottage, her blonde hair a golden halo in the midday sun. Silently he watched her from the kitchen window as she made her way slowly to the sandy shore. There she stood silent and still, watching the gentle waves lap at the cove. She remained there for hours, eyes never leaving the far horizon that led out from the safety of the cove, before turning and limping her way back up to the hut she'd shared with his brother.

Over the days that followed he kept his distance, watching her comings and goings. It seemed she kept to her old routine in the mornings, heading out across the cliff top to forage for wild vegetables and herbs. Each afternoon she returned to the beach to wait and watch. A silent vigil of hope and loss. Her fragile body stood with a marked stoop, her limp significantly more pronounced as she made her way about her daily tasks. Gerens' heart cried out to comfort her. To draw her frail limbs into his embrace, to make her safe. But he knew she wasn't ready. Not yet.

He must wait.

The days stretched on. He started to ensure he was out the front of his cottage tending to his horse when he knew she would be passing, to wish her good morning with a wave or a smile. At first she barely acknowledged him, but after a few days he noticed her face looking up in anticipation of his greeting. His heart warmed.

The next day he took his book down to the beach after lunch and sat on the rocks that lined the shore. The bright sun shone down on his shoulders warming along his limbs and easing the fluttering anticipation as he waited. Soon enough the tell-tale scrape of Kerensa's tread sounded on the pebbled path behind him. It stopped abruptly and his breath caught in his throat. Was this too much? Had he pushed too fast? He waited, eyes staring unseeing at his open book, his mind warring with itself. Then the soft shuffle of her passage resumed. He did not raise his eyes as she passed behind him, just listened and left her to herself. Risking a glance over the rim of his novel he watched her make her way to the centre of the beach and take up her daily watch. He returned to his reading, and they passed the afternoon in silence mere feet from each other as the shadows lengthened at their backs.

This became his routine, to greet her in the mornings as she made her way to forage, then to read on the beach near her as she watched the waves. As the week came to a close he snuck a peak at her over his pages once more and smiled gently to himself.

She had brushed and plaited her hair.

She was beautiful.

The knock on the door made him jump. Then, realising it could only be one person, Gerens hurried from the oven where he was making a vegetable stew, badly, to let her in.

Kerensa stood in the doorway framed by the light of the setting sun. In her hands she held a baking dish covered by a kitchen cloth. The evening breeze brought the scent of buttery pastry and onion to his nose. His mouth watered.

"I realised you probably have few supplies. I made chipple pie." She held the bundle before her like a shield, eyes wide and wary.

"That is very thoughtful, thank you Kez." He smiled and ushered her inside.

She strode confidently to the kitchen table and placing the pie at its centre went about collecting plates and cutlery to set the table. Pausing by his stew she sniffed at its contents, frowned, then reached into her basket, plucking out a jar of dried herbs which she then sprinkled over his stew.

"That will make a satisfying breakfast," she said returning to the table. She gestured for Gerens to sit, and he did as he was bid, wanting to follow her lead, to keep her at her ease.

Kerensa removed the cloth from the pie and its scent bloomed up to fill the room. Gerens eyes closed in gratitude. Regret tugged at his heart as he thought of Meraud's proud face and warm smile. He pushed the memories away and watched as Kerensa cut him a thick slice, bacon and onion juices flowing from the knife's incision. What she did to make simple mix of bacon and spring onions so desirable he could not fathom, but his mouth was watering.

Once they were both served Kerensa sat down across with him. Smiling his thanks he reached for his fork. Her words stopped his hand.

"I cannot marry you," she said simply.

Shock hit Gerens in his chest. He opened his mouth to answer but Kerensa cut him off, continuing. "I am already married and that is forever in the eyes of God."

A counter argument welled up inside him, Rewan had passed after all. Many widows remarried. But he kept his mouth clamped shut. Kerensa was leading this discussion. Not him.

"And I would never wish that to change," she said eyes coming up to lock with his. The longing and sorrow he saw reflected there brought a lump to his throat. He swallowed, blinking back tears.

The hope that had been rising in his heart as they came closer and closer over this past week, dimmed. If she would not marry him, then he could not bring her to Newfoundland. It seemed his hope had been in vain. She would never leave Porth Gwynn.

Kerensa turned away, breaking eye contact as she scanned the cottage around them. She gestured out the window at the town beyond. "This is my home, it always will be. Nothing can change that. Nothing." She whispered, eyes seeking his again. There in the shimmering blue depths he saw the truth. A deep longing to explain, for him to understand.

And for the first time, he did. He nodded slowly, then looked down at his pie to hide the tears that threatened to spill, acceptance settling over his heart.

"But I will come with you to Newfoundland."

His eyes snapped up in surprise.

"I can come as your wife. No one need know the truth. After all, I am a Lobb."

"You... I..." Gerens stammered, unable to find words to express the turmoil of emotions that suddenly flooded his mind.

Kerensa smiled softly. "Porth Gwynn will always be my home, Rewan will always be my husband. But there is nothing here anymore, for me, or for her." She placed a loving hand over her burgeoning belly and smiled down at her bump.

"I've known this for many months. But I didn't know what to do. Where to go. Then you arrived and... Gerens, I know it is a lot for me to ask, and it is not what you wished for. It would mean you could never truly marry. And you would have to take on my daughter. But if your offer still stands then…"

He was on his feet and by her side before he knew it. Kneeling before her, Gerens took her hands and held them firmly between his own. "I don't need your hand in marriage Kez. I understand your heart has always belonged to Rewan. And I don't need… the other things that come with marriage," he blushed, looking down to gather his thoughts. "But, I care for you. And I want to protect you and the babe. My offer stands. It always will. I will never leave you."

Kerensa smiled sadly and squeezed his hands, feeling them tremor about her own. She let out a small laugh and wiped a stray tear from her cheek.

"Then we go to Newfoundland," she said. "Together."

"Always."

The Scent of Pine and Ice

They boarded their vessel at Padstow, ticketed as husband and wife. It was a small lie, after all.

The trip across the Atlantic was terrible. Seasickness wracked Kerensa's body, keeping her abed. For someone who had lived her whole life by the sea, Kerensa decided she was glad she was born a girl and had not been expected to fish on the waves. How did Rewan do it?

The thought brought pain, sharp and piercing, cutting her heart. She let the tears flow. After so many months alone suppressing the truth and her grief, the release was welcome.

Gerens brought her broth and bread from the dining room and tended to her every need, teasing her gently for her land-lover's constitution. "Just like me," he smiled kindly.

She didn't hear a single gull during their crossing.

They docked at St John's in Newfoundland a week later.

Rows of towering pine trees reached up to the sky from the surrounding hillside, casting long shadows over the town itself nestled snug against the curve of a sweeping bay. Chunks of ice floated in the salty inlet and lined the banks of the cove leading to the town. The chill wind pushed Kerensa's hair back from her face and reddened her skin as she watched the port come into focus. While not a large settlement by world standards, to Kerensa St John's was impossibly large. Houses of stone and brick lined the shoreline, stretching back towards the gentle hills that cupped the township, and multiple church towers reached up to the pale blue sky. The docks themselves were staggering. Men in thick knitted jumpers scurried along the weathered wooden planks of the dock, rolling barrels, transporting large nets, repairing boats the size of the traders that used to visit Porth Gwynn in the summer.

Gerens stood beside her, a still presence emanating support.

"They are preparing for the cod season. The fish spawn in the coves along the island. People come from far and wide to fish the inlets. They use seines, like we did back home," he explained.

"And the larger vessels?" Kerensa asked, noting the nets and line that rested atop the enormous hulls.

"Seal and salmon mostly. They head out for the Grand Banks, a strip of current just south of here. They'll catch cod too, during the breeding migration. The ships go out on the seas for weeks on end, catching and salting the fish on board to store for their return. It's tough work, but the rewards are great. It allows for a less seasonal trade, more consistent work, more security for their families back in town."

"And the women?"

"More and more stay permanently in town and care for the children. Though some are still needed out on the inlets with their husbands."

Kerensa swallowed the large lump that had formed in her throat, absently placing her hands across her growing belly, and stared at the expanse of enterprise and commerce.

The extent of St John's was astonishing. Having never been further than St Endellion, Kerensa could not believe the size of the port city, the winding streets filled with terraced homes, roofs packed so tightly you could not tell where one house ended and the next began. And the smell! Waste, both human and animal assaulted her nose. Not even the icy sea breeze could freshen the stench.

"They have their own colonial assembly," Gerens explained as he led her past a series of large stone-fronted buildings of commerce and government. "And there is a garrison still stationed here, a leftover from the American Revolutionary War some 50 years ago."

"You know so much," Kerensa said.

Gerens smiled softly. "I make it my duty to know everything before I make a decision. I would never risk you to anything less."

Their eyes met for a moment before Kerensa looked away, the wistful sorrow she saw on his face too much for her broken heart to bear.

They moved into a house not far from the port, so Gerens could easily come and go from work. The building was made of wood and creaked loudly as the air cooled with nightfall. But it was solid and warm and Kerensa felt safe within its walls. She set about preparing for the birth of her child, unpacking the herbs and swaddling she had brought from home and planning the items she wished to knit in preparation. It took up all of her time, keeping her in the house throughout the day and night.

Gerens watched on as she knitted and planned. He'd never known Kerensa to spend so much time indoors. But he kept his peace. *She has been through so much, so quickly*, he reasoned. *She will need time to adjust.* It was a need he understood.

But as the weeks turned into months he began to worry that time would not be enough to help his friend.

The crackling fire drove the chill from the spring air. Nestled in a deep, soft couch Kerensa knitted a fresh blanket for her coming babe, her needles clacking gently. The season was changing, it was sure. Warmer currents swirled about the docks and blossoms scented the air. But summer did not last, and babies always needed swaddling.

The soft scuff of footfall told Kerensa that Gerens had joined her. She smiled and nodded towards his shadow as it moved across her peripheral vision and continued to focus on her work, not looking up. She heard the clink of the whiskey bottle on the edge of Gerens' glass as he poured himself his nightly nip before coming to sit on the couch beside her. Kerensa kept up her knitting, enjoying the silent companionship of her oldest friend. Until he returned from his travels, she hadn't realised just how much she'd missed his quiet reflective presence in her life.

But Gerens shuffled in his seat and took a loud slurp of his whiskey, before shuffling some more.

Alerted, Kerensa stopped her needles and let her work fall into her lap. Looking up she found his eyes trained on her, a frown of concern marring his brow.

Cocking her head to the side she asked, "Gerens? Is something wrong?"

He paused a moment, watching her face in the firelight before shaking his head gently and taking another drink. "No, Kez, nothing is wrong. But…"

"But?" she prompted.

"The season is warming," he ventured carefully. "I thought perhaps you might like to take a walk through the town with me tomorrow. There are some lovely spots along the dock that allow you a view right out to sea and I found a market just down the way…"

Kerensa sucked in a sharp breath and straightened in her chair.

Gerens watched her, eyes missing nothing. "What is it Kez?" he asked gently. "We've been here the better part of two months and you've barely left the house."

"It's my ankle," Kerensa said, eyes sliding away from his face to watch the fire. "My legs are swollen from carrying the babe and it's made the pain unbearable. It is best that I rest, until the child is here."

Gerens regarded her profile, saw the truth mixed with the lie written in the lay of her mouth. It was true that her ankle had swollen immensely, but nothing ever kept his friend from her work. Placing his glass on a side table he rose and pulled his chair over closer to Kerensa. Wordlessly he took hold of her twisted foot and carefully slipped the shoe from it.

"Gerens? What are you doing?"

Without a word he pulled the stocking from the leg and wrapped his hands about the misshapen ankle bones. In silence he moved his fingers, gently massaging the pressure points where the fluid had collected causing the added pain. Slowly, the warmth of his hands, the gentle movement and pressures he exerted began to loosen some of the pain and Kerensa sank back into her chair's embrace, eyes closing. She released a long breath of tension.

Gerens continued carefully moving the joint up and down, from side to side, eyes never leaving Kerensa's face.

"It was hard at first, when I left Porth Gwynn," he began. "It was all I had ever known. Even though it never suited me."

Kerensa opened her eyes and found him staring into the fire, deep shadows cast across his features. She waited. He continued, the rhythm of his massage unbroken.

"I walked for days, stopping in small towns for beer and bread but never a room. I didn't want the people to get to know me. I didn't want them to see the truth."

A sudden lump of sorrow bunched in Kerensa's throat. She swallowed hard. "There was no truth to see Gerens. You've never had anything to hide."

"Nor have you," he replied simply. Looking directly into her eyes.

"I..."

"It took me many years to know it, " he continued, "After my father blamed me for the accident, for the near death of my brothers, I believed, to my core, that I was 'wrong'. I'd never liked to fish, the physical work repulsed me. But my lack of skill put those I loved in grave danger. It was only luck that my mistake did not end their lives.

"But that was still not my fault. I was not born for the sea. In time, I came to understand that and to find my place. Somewhere different. Somewhere other than Porth Gwynn.

"You can too."

They stared at each other in silence, across the flicking light of the fire. Gerens squeezed Kerensa's foot a final time and patted her ankle affectionately. "All finished," he smiled, "I hope that has helped relieve some of the pressure.

He stood smoothly from the stool and took up his glass of whiskey before turning for the doorway and his bed.

"Gerens?" Kerensa's soft voice floated across the room to his ears. "Would you walk me to the market next week?"

Gerens allowed himself a moment to smile to himself before turning back to his friend.

"I'd be delighted."

The Curse

Kerensa gripped Gerens' arm like her life depended on it.

To her mind, it did.

Around her the people of St John's went about their usual routine. The streets positively bustled, in a way Kerensa had never experienced, the warmer weather having brought everyone out to complete their errands and chores. The sun shone warm and bright above, heating the muddy street and releasing the stench of horse manure into the air to mix with that of unwashed bodies, machinery grease, fish and the sea.

Kerensa kept her head down, avoiding the gaze of those they passed. Afraid that they would look into her soul and see the truth. *Cursed, bad omen, bringer of death.*

At length Gerens turned them down a tight side street, leading them away from the dockside. Kerensa pressed closer to her friend as people rushed past, brushing against her side. Suddenly, a young man appeared before them, striding too fast. Kerensa tried to twist away, to allow him space, but the awkward bulk of her unborn babe made her slow and cumbersome. Unable to stop the inevitable, Kerensa braced as the young man slammed into her side. She spun, but Gerens' strength beside her kept her from falling into the muddy lane. The young man stopped, their eyes met and a look of horror bloomed on his face. Kerensa squeezed her eyes closed, fighting to shut out the realisation in the youth's surprise. *He sees me*, she realised. *He knows.*

"My God, I am so sorry," a high, anxious voice cut through the surrounding noise of the town. "I am such a fool. Mother always warns me to slow down. Are you all right?"

Kerensa opened her eyes to find the face of a man barely out of childhood staring at her own. Genuine concern bunched his brow. No trace of suspicion or rejection swam in his eyes.

"We are well," Gerens' familiar voice spoke over her head. "Aren't we Kerensa?" As he spoke he righted his jacket and turned Kerensa back to face the path ahead.

"I am glad for it," the young man said urgently. "With your wife in her condition, I could have…"

Such wretched fear twisted his face that Kerensa's heart almost burst. Unexpectedly, her mouth filled with words. "Do not worry young man. I am well as is the babe within me. No harm done. But thank you for your concern." She offered him her most genuine smile.

Relief flooded his features and his shoulders slumped. "Well, can I escort you on the rest of your journey? The morning is late and I can guess your husband is needed at work. I will ensure you are safely home."

"That is very kind of you," Gerens replied smoothly. "But I have taken the morning off to join my wife at the markets."

"Oh wonderful!" he exclaimed. "I hope you don't mind my intrusion, but you are newly arrived from Cornwall, yes?"

"How can you tell?"

"Your accent," he smiled, "it is my mother's. She is from Cornwall. She and father moved here as newlyweds. Her name is Morwenna. I'm Andrew."

He thrust out his hand in welcome and Gerens took it.

"I am Gerens and this is my beautiful wife, Kerensa." The lie was seamless from his lips. Kerensa swallowed as her nerves swiftly returned.

"Mother always loves to meet someone from the old country. She has a stall at the market. Traditional pasties, she says. She's on the right, with a bright green table cloth, you can't miss it. Stop by and tell her Andrew sent you. I am sure she will give you one of her delicious pasties to welcome you to St John's."

"Very generous, thank you," Gerens said.

Andrew nodded and his face creased with an excited smile. "It seems our meeting was fortuitous after all. Good day."

Gerens nodded his farewell and they resumed their journey to the markets, Kerensa silent at his side.

Misunderstanding her reticence, Gerens tried to reassure her, "There are many people from Cornwall here. As you come to know the town, you will realise just how similar it really can be. It will be as if you never left Porth Gwynn."

Kerensa smiled at him and looked away. How could she explain that was exactly her fear?

The market was enormous. From all sides little laneways like the one they'd traversed opened on to a large open square, packed with tables and carts of wares. It was easily twice the size of St Endellion's. Kerensa scanned the rows of offerings and froze, overwhelmed by the crowd of faces, the tight space. But Gerens steered them on. Banking right, he scanned the stalls until his eyes found the one he sought and drew Kerensa's attention.

There on the right side of the market, standing squat and plump behind a table dressed in bright green cloth stood a woman who would have seemed right at home in Porth Gwynn. Her ruddy, wind-hardened face grinned out at a customer as she handed over a solid parcel, presumably filled with pasty. The familiar scent of baked pasties, vegetables and herbs wafted to Kerensa's nose and despite her anxiety she could feel her mouth was watering. As they came up alongside the stall, Morwenna turned her open and welcoming smile to them. Andrew was there, Kerensa realised, reflected in that smile.

"Lovely day for it," Morwenna greeted her new arrivals. "What were you looking for?"

Her voice was husky with age but flavoured with the lilt of Cornwall.

"We met your son, Andrew, on our way to market," Gerens was saying. "He told us of your pasties…"

"You're from Cornwall!" Morwenna exclaimed, interrupting Gerens' summary of meeting her son.

"We are, yes."

"Well it is wonderful to meet you. And look at you little dove," she exclaimed, "well along with child. What a happy time for you both. Here, you must take one of these."

She turned and selected a large pasty, its sides clearly bulging with vegetables and fish. "It's my mother's recipe from home. Even has some salted pilchard in there. Hard to come by in St John's, but where there's a will. Just the thing for an expecting mother. Keep your energy up to grow the babe."

She wrapped the pasty in paper and thrust it towards Kerensa, who took it slowly, her mind unable to catch up with the surprises coming thick and fast.

"Thank you," Gerens spoke into the silence. "How much do we owe you?"

Morwenna, who was still smiling at an unresponsive Kerensa, glanced up at him and waved a distracted hand. "No, no, first one's always free. Besides, it looks like you might be missing home," she said, looking back at Kerensa with eyes that saw too much.

Panic gripped Kerensa's chest and she took a stumbling step backwards. Ever conscious, Gerens noticed her distress and gripped her upper arm to steady her as shaking began to take over her legs.

"That is very generous," he said to Morwenna as he took more of Kerensa's weight. "We are grateful. But I think this warmer day and long walk has been rather too much for my wife. We will bid you good day."

"It can be a bit close in here," Morwenna agreed readily. "It was nice to meet you. Don't be strangers."

She waved as Gerens turned Kerensa away and started the walk back home. Watching the tall, confident man and the tiny pregnant woman, retreating through the crowded market, a suspicion began to crawl along Morwenna's bones. Her eyes briefly narrowed before she turned to her next customer, ready smile back in place.

The knock on the door jolted Kerensa awake. It was early summer and the heat of the sun was already unbearable. Sweat slicked over her bulbous, swollen body and fatigue rendered her limbs heavy like logs. She hadn't left the house since her trip to the market with Gerens several weeks before, the toil of the later stages of pregnancy on her body the perfect excuse to avoid what she feared. The faces of others. The knowledge in their eyes.

Her curse.

The knock came again. The maid was out on errands and Gerens was at work, leaving only Kerensa at home, dozing away the heat of the day. Kerensa realised she couldn't ignore the summons. Pushing herself up onto her feet she hobbled slowly to the door, one hand pressed into the aching small of her back.

Fully prepared to send the visitor on their way, she swung the door open and froze.

Standing before her stood the pastry seller from the markets, a full basket clutched in her hands, a small boy hiding in the fall of her skirts.

Kerensa opened her mouth to speak but found her throat had gone dry. Fear tracked through her body, a sinking sensation filling her guts.

Why would this woman seek her out?

There was only one reason Kerensa could imagine. She swallowed.

Morwenna watched a flood of emotions course across the face of the young woman before her then took charge. "Good day dear girl," she began. "I hadn't seen you back at the market and thought perhaps your time had come early. Didn't want you to be without some good Cornish sustenance as you breastfeed," she held up her brimming basket and smiled. "But I see now you are just ready to pop! So I'm just in time. You need all the feeding up we can get into you before the babe comes. I should know. I've had five. Ha!" She chuckled to herself comfortably. Then paused, watching Kerensa's face.

"This is Peter," she continued, indicating the elfish child buried in her shirts "he's a bit shy at first, but once he gets something to eat he settles just fine. Why don't you show us to the kitchen?"

Kerensa blinked then opened the door wider, subconsciously following the motherly instruction of the older lady. Morwenna bustled past her and headed directly to the kitchen.

"These houses are all the same," she called over her shoulder by way of explanation. Kerensa closed the front door and followed at a sedate pace, watching little Peter as he toddled after his mother, one thumb pressed into his little mouth.

Coming into the kitchen Morwenna placed her basket on the table and surveyed the room, hands on hips. "Lovely space you have here. Now, you take a seat. Where are the plates?"

Kerensa took a seat, her mind blank with shock as this stranger made herself at home in her kitchen, mumbling to herself and bustling about setting up the lunch table. "Good sized plates, where's a knife? Ah there. All right Peter, you sit here. Thumb out please, there's a good lad. Would you like an iced tea with your lunch Kerensa? Of course you would, now let's get two glasses."

Soon enough the kitchen table was laid out, plates and cutlery, a pasty and iced drink each produced from the deep wicker basket. Peter wasted no time in tucking in, his fat little fingers pulling the pasty apart and stuffing too-large mouthfuls into his open jaws.

"Tuck in," Morwenna ordered, seating herself opposite Kerensa. Obediently Kerensa took up her knife and fork and cut into her steaming pastry. It smelt of home. Warm and buttery with a hint of salty sea from the fish, the pastry melted on her tongue. Tears sprang into her eyes unexpectedly, and she turned her head away to swipe away the tears.

Morwenna missed nothing. "There, there love," she cooed, reaching across the table to place a hand over Kerensa's where it rested on the table. "I remember the longing for home too. Nothing quite like a pilchard pasty is there?"

Tears dried but still threatening, Kerensa looked up at the older woman and sniffed. Morwenna met her wary eyes and sighed.

"I see it love, in your eyes. What is it that haunts you child?"

Kerensa stiffened and withdrew her hand quickly, squaring her shoulders.

"What makes you suggest that?" she said, busying her hands with cutting up her pasty.

Morwenna smiled knowingly. "I know the look. And the habits. I've barely seen you out in the town, and in my line of work, I see all the women. And then there is your limp…"

Kerensa breathed in sharply and glared across the table at Morwenna. "I've had a lifetime of rumour and whispers and I'll tolerate it no longer," she said firmly, "If you've come to say something, say it and leave."

Morwenna chewed on her pasty in silence and regarded the young woman before her. Unperturbed by Kerensa's outburst she reached over to wipe crumbs from Peter's mouth before offering the boy a cookie and patting him on his feather-haired crown.

"Loves a cookie my lad," she said idly, "growing like a weed he is."

Furious Kerensa stared at the woman, "Do you think my words have no meaning? This is my house, and I'll not be treated…"

"Was it the superstitions then?" Morwenna interrupted taking the wind from Kerensa's sails. "Talk of your leg, blame for the seasons? Yes, I see I've hit on the truth of it…" she paused and sighed heavily.

"It was the same in my town, though it was a boy born blind in one eye. Didn't stop him from doing anything mind you. As I suspect your leg never stopped you either."

Kerensa remained silent, mind working overtime trying to understand this woman's angle.

"Girl, surely you can see it means nothing to the likes of me? I don't care what causes you to limp, or what whispers you have heard. It's all just fear-talk. The coast was dying long before you were born my child. But people don't know how to let go, and that breeds desperation. Desperate people seek someone to blame. But the truth of it is, there was no one to blame. It's just life. The tides changed, the fish moved on. It will happen here too one day. Oh, not for a long time yet I suspect, but it will. It's the way of things. They come and they go and we have to adapt. But, you already know that, don't you?"

Kerensa stared at Morwenna's open face and realised she was speaking from her heart. She let the tears fall freely. "They… they all died," she whispered. "All of them, in the storm."

Morwenna shook her head sadly, "A terrible, terrible tragedy. Not the first and not the last. But not of your doing."

"I know that," Kerensa whispered, "Gerens helped me to see… but everyone else." She gestured out towards the town helplessly.

Morwenna nodded her understanding, "Everyone else has their own story behind them child. This is a town of the displaced. Where we come from, people have lived in the same town for generations, we're part of the rocky coast almost." She sighed softly. "But here, this is a traveller's place. Somewhere people have come in search of a new life, of hope. Everyone here, especially from Cornwall, everyone has lost something, or someone. That changes people…"

Kerensa looked up at Morwenna, hope in her eyes.

"This is a new shore child," Morwenna continued. "Who you were, you bring with you, but you can choose to leave some parts behind. I reckon you know which parts."

"Thank you."

"Good, now that's settled, eat up. We have much to do to prepare for your birthing. Have you arranged the swaddling yet…"

A Pink Pouch

Her daughter was born on a hot August morning, the fresh scent of the sea breeze easing Kerensa's pain as she breathed and heaved. Morwenna guided her through, firm and confident after her own multiple births. As the dawn light broke on a night of sweat and pain Kerensa lay back on her bed, baby daughter latched to her breast. Morwenna ordered strict bed rest for at least a week and smiling her motherly joy, left Kerensa in Gerens' capable hands. Though not before treating him to a series of stern instructions for the care of his wife and ordering him up to Kerensa's side.

When Gerens knocked, so softly, Kerensa smiled, "Come," she called.

He entered timidly, as if unsure if he were welcome. She beckoned him over to her side. Perched nervously on the edge of the bed, he watched the tiny bundle that Kerensa cradled against her chest. "Here."

She passed the babe over to him. Carefully, hands trembling, Gerens took hold of her daughter and snuggled her to his chest. As he gazed down at the tiny infant wonder filled his eyes.

"She's…"

"…perfect," Kerensa finished for him.

Their eyes met, a river of emotions flowing freely between them. Love, sorrow, regret, joy and hope.

"Have you named her?"

"Chesten," Kerensa replied.

"Chesten," Gerens repeated, trying the name in his mouth. "A good Cornish name. Hello Chesten. I'm your father and I am in love with you already."

And for the first time since that dreadful winter storm, Kerensa felt peace.

The seasons shifted into autumn and Chesten gained strength, growing plump and rosy on breast milk and love. Well fed, warm and with nothing to do but care for her child Kerensa also blossomed, her gaunt cheeks filled, her hair thickened and her flesh plumped. Slowly, she adjusted to motherhood and to the town around her. As her confidence grew and her body healed from childbirth, Kerensa began to explore more of St John's.

Through Morwenna's introduction Kerensa befriended a group of women much like herself. Bred in the days of working the fish, now running households while their men went to sea. She was invited for tea and scones and found herself absorbed into a community of women, their friendship hastened by common experience. The women cooed over Chesten while a protective Peter watched over his littlest friend. He'd taken an instant shine to Chesten. Even before her birth, he'd been fascinated by Kerensa's growing belly, pressing his sticky hands to her bulge, a look of wonder on his face. Now she was in the world, he'd rather claimed her for his own. The sister he'd never had. Surrounded by smiling faces all lined by the sun, Kerensa realised she had become a part of this buzzing town, accepted in a way she never truly was in Porth Gwynn. Her status as the 'wife' of the port foreman made no difference, the women treated her as one of them. Kerensa would have had it no other way.

Autumn was a bustling time, the port filled to capacity with fishing families. Children ran in packs along the muddy streets and the air vibrated with their laughter and joy. Each week saw tens of boats, hulls high and solid against the violence of the open sea, dock at Gerens' port to unload their hauls before moving out again with the next tide. Gerens overlooked the processing and ensured the catches were all properly stored for export across to Europe, the proceeds sent to Mr Stevens back in London.

As the winds cooled, however, the men returned from the inlets. In a matter of weeks the docks filled with vessels and burly sailors, faces red and split from the cold. The boats were hauled from the sea, cleaned and packed into sheds to wait out the winter. Women and children were gathered up in tired loving arms, carts were laden with belongings and, as the first whispery snow began to whiten the frozen paths, the town of St John's emptied; the fish season was done. Kerensa watched, waving to the children who rode high on the horse-drawn carts and set about preparing for the winter months.

It was a harsh season.

Kerensa was used to the cold, to storms and winds and hacking rain and snow. But not like this.

Delayed compared to the winters of Porth Gwynn, the season came on strong and sudden, pummelling St John's with vicious winds and storms and covering the streets and grooves in a thick blanket of snow.

There was a beauty to it though, when the skies opened and the soft flakes of snow fell gently, sparkling in the pale sun.

Gerens had enjoyed a successful summer, and in the new year he moved them to a townhouse of their own in the centre of the seasonal town, two storeys high. There was even a room for a live-in maid, so Gerens hired a local lass named Mary. All bones, but with a bonny smile, Mary settled in nicely and helped with the daily work of running the home and caring for the new baby.

Despite the whistling winds, the heavy cold, the ice and sleet, Kerensa and her child were safe. Warm and bundled in a home with carpets and multiple fireplaces. Bellies full. It was the most comfortable winter of Kerensa's life.

Yet she fretted.

She'd known comfort before, had it torn from her grasp.

Restricted by the heavy winter raging outside, she planned.

As the sun of spring illuminated the new green shoots on the birch trees, Kerensa packed some sandwiches in a basket, wrapped a wriggling Chesten to her chest in a shawl and trundled from the muddy town streets out into the surrounding hillside. It was time to forage.

"I can't calm her," Mary said, panicking. "I don't understand."

Gerens, just returned from work, surveyed the scene from the kitchen door.

Kerensa stood in the middle of the room, hair awry, eyes wild, sleeves rolled to her elbows, various leafy cuttings sprawled before her, water boiling at the stove. In the corner stood the maid, face pale, shoulders hunched. She shot over to him the moment he stepped into the room.

Gerens made a soothing gesture with his hands, "Where's the babe?"

"Safe asleep."

Nodding Gerens dismissed Mary for the night and turned to his frantic friend.

"Kez?" he questioned gently, "What is the matter my dear?"

Kerensa's eyes snapped up to his, then her face crumpled into tears. "Oh Gerens!" she cried, "What am I to do? I don't know them… any of them. They're all different."

Though confused Gerens stepped forward and pulled Kerensa into a gentle embrace. "Breathe Kez," he whispered, "I don't yet understand, but I will. And whatever it is, I will fix it."

Kerensa sobbed against his chest, allowing the warmth of his arms to soothe her rattled nerves. Finally her breathing slowed and she stepped back. Gesturing to the various greens strewn across the bench she spoke, voice quavering, "I went foraging, to make tinctures and dried herbs. To start my work. But… but… they are all different. I couldn't find one that I recognised. So I grabbed those that looked most likely and brought them home. But that maid…"

She cut off, glaring out the doorway towards Mary's room. "She knows nothing. Nothing!"

"Kez, dear, why did you go foraging? That is no longer necessary. I make good money. You don't need to work. Not anymore. Your place is here, at home with Chesten."

"But I have to work," Kerensa insisted. "I must have my own means. What if… what if…" She swallowed, "Things can always go wrong."

Understanding washed over Gerens. The end of the fish run in Porth Gwynn. The death of the men. Losing everything she had ever known. It was natural that she would be afraid. Especially now, as a mother.

Believing he saw the whole of her fear, he drew her to him again, "I understand, Kez, I do," he said softly into her wayward hair. "But that time is past." He pulled back so he could look into her eyes. "My brother was a good man. He'd have been a wonderful father too. But his work, it was unreliable and dangerous. That was the reality of life in Porth Gwynn. But not here, not for us. I am safe in my office on the docks, and my salary is secure. We have money in savings and our own roof over our heads. We will not be destitute. That won't happen again."

"But what of Chesten? What if her husband…"

"Chesten's husband will be a good man. Someone who also works in an office. We will make sure of it. Come, Kez, please relax. I promise you, these worries, they are the past. Not our future."

Slowly Kerensa nodded and allowed Gerens to embrace her once more. Though the tension didn't fully leave her body.

Later that night, after Gerens had gone to bed, she took out her sewing kit and crafted a small pouch from a length of dark pink linen. From that week on she set aside a small portion of her weekly shopping money.

Just in case.

Kerensa pushed a plump and wide-eyed Chesten in her perambulator, another gift from Gerens, on a walk down to the docks to visit him at work. The trio enjoyed lunch together watching the life of the dock. Sitting on Gerens' knee Chesten laughed and pointed at the tall masts of the sailboats, clapping when the gulls ventured close in an attempt to steal her cake crumbs. Kerensa watched as Gerens hugged her daughter tight, Chesten's blonde curls bobbing and catching the sun, love softening Gerens' features and felt her chest, so long caged by tension, expand out to the world around her.

"Yes," she whispered to herself that night, "I can build a life here." Rolling onto her side she watched the curtains swaying gently in the cooling sea breeze and breathed deeply of the familiar scent of salt and the new tang of pine. As sleep swept up to claim her for another night, she thought of Chesten's rosy cheeks and pudgy legs, of the kind faces of the townsfolk, the nods of acknowledgement as they passed her in the street. No whispers of curses or bad omens breathed behind her back. Of Gerens' smile, pure and true. And as her mind let go of conscious thought, Kerensa fell into a deep and peaceful sleep, untroubled by nightmares. Just Kerensa and the darkness until Chesten's hungry cry drew her back the next morning. To St John's. To her new life.

Mending

The sun was high overhead, the gulls soaring on a light morning breeze as Kerensa walked her daughter to her first day at school. At her side, small hand in hers, Chesten skipped, her fair curls shining in the morning sun. Kerensa smiled down at her daughter, her heart swelling with love for this little life she had created.

Soon the school gates came into view and Kerensa felt her daughter slow. Gone was the buoyant skip, and carefree smile, replaced by a slouch and dragging feet. Kerensa's throat tightened, but she refused to show her own trepidation and kept their pace towards the school grounds. Around them, groups of children gathered, some running to greet each other, shrieking with excitement, others gripping tightly to their mother's skirts. At the open gate Chesten stopped dead.

"Come love," Kerensa said, tugging gently on her daughter's hand.

But Chesten had frozen, her blue eyes wide with fear as she took in the yard of children before her and the tall wooden structure of the school house.

Kerensa knelt down before her child and gently turned her face so they were eye to eye. The reality of their pending separation clutched at her heart and tears threatened to form in her eyes.

So silly, she thought to herself. *It's only a few hours.*

Unbidden memories of her own childhood flooded her mind. Of nights alone in Meliora's small hut with only the winds for company. How did her mother stand it? The days apart from her? When here, faced with but a morning Kerensa felt her heart would break. Sadness and gratitude filled her chest in equal measure. How harsh her mother's life had been. How blessed had her own become.

Firmly pulling herself from the past, Kerensa focused her attention back to the nervous child before her. Chesten watched her with eyes full of hesitation, her bottom lip wobbling precariously along the edge of breaking into sobs. This would not do.

Straightening her shoulders Kerensa held her head high and gifted Chesten her warmest smile.

"What an exciting day this is!" She began. "I remember my first day at school…"

"What was it like?" Chesten asked.

"I was very nervous at first. Just as I imagine you are feeling now,' Kerensa answered honestly. "But then…" Kerensa grinned at her daughter, filling her voice with light and love. "I met another little girl named Derwa who became my best friend. And after that, everyday was filled with play and adventures!"

Derwa's dark smile and high laugh swam in her mind's-eye. Her truest friend would never leave her heart.

Chesten frowned, looking at her mother dubiously. "Will the other children like me?"

Kerensa's smile softened, "Not everyone will like you sweetheart. But that doesn't matter. You will find other boys and girls just like you and they will be your friends and that is all that is important."

"Like you and father?"

"Exactly."

A bell sounded and mother and daughter turned to see an older woman standing in the entranceway swinging a hand bell to call the children in.

"Time to go," Kerensa said and pulled her child in for a firm hug.

The warmth of Chesten spread across her chest and she breathed her scent in deeply; rose and lily, willing herself to be strong.

Breaking the hug, Kerensa held Chesten before her, "Go on, love. Have a wonderful day."

Chesten looked up at her mother, resolve wavering, tears threatening. Then determination came over her tiny features and, straightening her back just as her mother often did, she turned and strode purposefully through the school gates.

Kerensa stood up and watched as her child walked to the school house. Her little body still seemed impossibly small for this large task before her. A single sob escaped her lips and she held her hand to her mouth willing herself to stay strong. *This is a good thing*, she reminded herself, firmly. Albeit that she had never liked school, having friends had been the joy of her youth. Chesten played with Peter and the other children of Kerensa's friends, but she needed some her own age too.

Just then, a girl with long dark hair came up alongside Chesten and leaned close, whispering something to her daughter. Kerensa stiffened in anticipation, eyes watching the interaction keenly.

There was a pause, as if time stood still for the two little girls as they met. Then Kerensa watched as Chesten turned to the dark-haired girl and beamed her brightest smile as they linked arms and skipped the remaining distance into the school house.

Watching the two small figures, one dark and one light, walk up the steps and disappear into the building, the tears finally won the battle. Kerensa felt them coursing down her cheeks as she remembered two other little girls on the other side of the ocean who'd loved each other fiercely. Derwa would always remain in her heart.

"I want a new dress," Chesten announced, small hands fisted on her hips.

Kerensa, sitting mending socks by the fire, did not look up, just continued with her work. Gerens placed his book on his side table and opened his arms to the child.

Grinning broadly, Chesten skipped to his arms and allowed herself to be enveloped in a warm embrace. Kissing the top of her head he asked, "What kind of new dress would you like?"

"One with ribbons, like the other girls have."

"Well, I don't see why not," Gerens smiled indulgently at Chesten and released her from his arms back into the room.

The girl hopped happily from his lap, believing her request done with.

Eyes still on her mending, Kerensa spoke, her voice floating gently over the crackle of the fireplace.

"You've no need of a new dress Chesten. Yours are just fine. A small adjustment before the summer comes and they will get you through another season at the least."

Chesten pulled a face, "But mother, they are old..." she groaned.

"Surely a new dress is something we can accommodate, right Kez?" Gerens ventured.

Chesten straightened her stance confidently, now assured that her father was on her side.

"I am sure their dresses are very nice, Chesten. But so are yours. We don't waste things in this house."

"But mother, Emma got a new dress last week and Margaret's coat came on the train."

"Is your name 'Emma' or 'Margaret'?"

"No," Chesten frowned, unsure of where her mother was taking this conversation.

"Then I don't see what their dresses have to do with you," Kerensa stated firmly. Placing her mending in her lap she looked up at her daughter, the lines of her face smoothing as she looked at her child. *The child I made,* she thought with a familiar warmth and wonder.

But she would not give in to that rush of emotion. Chesten needed to learn how to survive in this world, it was Kerensa's job to teach her.

"Your dresses are fine Chesten, they fit you well. I will not have waste in this house."

Chesten opened her mouth to protest but Kerensa held up a hand to still her.

"But," she continued, "that doesn't mean we can't make them a little more fancy. Go to the cupboard by the hall and bring me the basket within."

Curiosity and hope mixed together as Chesten dutifully made her way to fetch the basket as requested.

"Now, come sit by me."

Gerens watched from his seat as Chesten curled up on the couch by her mother, basket in her lap."

"Open the basket."

She did.

Reaching into the basket, Kerensa drew out a bright red ribbon, smoothing its silky length between her fingers. Holding it up to Chesten's face she said, "As I suspected. Just your colour. Shall we sew it into the collar? A beautiful ribbon for my beautiful daughter? What do you think?"

Chesten took the ribbon from her mother and ran it through her hands. Looking up at Kerensa she beamed. "Yes!"

"Good, now fetch your sewing kit and let me show you how it is done."

Gerens wiped tears from his eyes.

Like with sewing, Kerensa's insistence helped to ensure that their daughter learned to read and write and do sums, just like her father. When the women's mending was done and Kerensa moved on to patching Gerens' trousers, Gerens would sit Chesten on his knee and read to her of great adventures and pirates and romance, all from books, not from his memory. Kerensa watched on as though in a dream, feeling the love and care of a father for a daughter as it emanated from her friend, a love and security she had never known. Together they guided Chesten as she grew and watched with pure joy as she traversed the joys and little trials of childhood and friendships. Together they built a life.

One night as the cool promise of winter washed over St John's, Kerensa tucked Chesten snuggled into bed, then, instead of heading straight for her own chambers, padded softly down the stairs. She found Gerens in the sitting room, reading by the light of a lamp, glass of whiskey in his hand.

In silence she went to him and took his hand in hers. Their eyes met in the firelight.

"Thank you," she whispered.

Tears sprang into Gerens' eyes as he watched her beautiful face before him. He nodded, unable to speak. Their eyes met. Something between them shifted, and Gerens swallowed hard. Smiling softly, Kerensa drew him to his feet and led him upstairs to her room. They never spent another night apart.

Cinnamon and Nutmeg

The snow was falling softly outside the window, the fading light framing the white wisps in a golden glow. Christmas was near. Chesten, now 18, was out shopping with her beau Peter. The two had been inseparable since Chesten's birth. But in the last few months that youthful friendship had taken on a rather more serious shade. They'd not said as much, but both Morwenna and Kerensa secretly hoped to soon be burning three candles for a wedding.

She put her mind to the Christmas pudding she was to bake for the festive tea she was hosting for the wives of the Port. Kerensa made a point of welcoming all the women of the town into her home for the season. So many new families had moved to St John's over the years, drawn by the thriving commerce of the docks and growing town. As a result Kerensa's friendship circle had changed somewhat since those first days bonding over shared tales of working the fish, as more and more women who'd never known manual work came to town with their families and hopes of success. But Kerensa had never lost those original connections, the unspoken understanding from former fishwives that no matter what came, together they would face it.

She was imagining the scents of cinnamon and nutmeg floating through the kitchen, when she felt his warmth come up behind her. She closed her eyes and leaned back into his embrace as he wrapped his arms about her waist, still tiny, despite the fortunate life she now led.

"Not long now before she returns for the eve," Gerens whispered in her ear. "You will be pleased to know that I still don't mind sharing you with our daughter."

"I should hope not!" Kerensa laughed turning in his arms to slap his shoulder playfully.

214

Gerens looked down at her. The years had drawn fine lines across his brow and alongside his mouth, lines she knew were mirrored on her own face. But his eyes still shone with warmth and love. His lips curved in a smile. For a moment the light fell just right to cast the face of another, much younger man across his visage. Kerensa pressed her eyes together and buried her head in Gerens' chest, allowing herself a moment with the memory of his brother, her true husband. Despite the years and this new love she had unexpectedly found with her friend, a part of Kerensa's heart would always belong to Rewan.

Nevertheless she loved her life here with Gerens and her daughter. It was warm, safe and comfortable; all things she had longed for in her own childhood. But sometimes, like a rock lodged in the neck of a gull, that comfort stuck in her throat. The heavy emotion of guilt swelling up inside, punishing her for being happy without Rewan by her side. It was a burden she would carry, for her child.

Besides, it would not be long now.

"Kez, are you all right?" Gerens ran a hand down her back in a gentle caress.

Kerensa shook her head and looked up into his eyes. "Yes, I am just happy. That is all."

She smiled to reassure him before turning back to the window, eyes watching the grey waves crest the coastline behind the veil of snow.

"Do you miss it, still?"

Kerensa knew what he meant. Placing her hands over his where they rested against her belly she squeezed. "Porth Gwynn was my childhood home," she began. "It was such a large part of my life." She paused, eyes closed, mind sailing across the miles of ocean that separated her from the shores of Cornwall. She remembered her mother's little hut, the warm glow of the cloam oven, the soft coo of a sleeping Eia, the humid breeze off the sea, the scent of thyme and sage and lavender. Her eyes opened. The sun was setting fast now, its light fading, revealing the image of her, wrapped in Gerens' arms, in the window's reflection.

She focused on his reflected eyes and smiled. "But this is where I became a mother, this is where my daughter lives."

She rested her head back against his shoulder, savouring the warmth of him, determined to enjoy this moment and all those to come. There would not be many left to enjoy.

The white lie came easily, it was right to spare him. Truth was relative after all, only some parts needed to be shared. Meliora had taught her that.

"This is my home now. Here, in St John's. With you."

"I will take you back. Perhaps next summer. To visit and show our daughter."

Kerensa blinked rapidly to hold back the tears. She knew it was a journey she would never make. She swallowed hard and forced her body to relax.

Gerens rested his head atop hers and pulled her closer, tight against his chest.

Kerensa's breath caught as the motion caused a sharp pain to fire deep within her belly. She winced.

"Kez?" Gerens asked, voice concerned.

"I am well my love. All is well," she said, gripping his hands tighter to her, breathing slowly, pushing away the flare of fear that pierced her chest. Fear had no place when you already knew what was coming.

After a while she released Gerens' hands, making her way to the kitchen and the brandy soaked raisins and spices that would soon fill the house with the scent of yule.

Interlude

You are beautiful my child, more beautiful than I can even imagine, still.

I am not ready to leave you, but my husband calls me back to the sea, to swim beneath the waves and rest in his arms.

And rest I must, for I am so weary.

Mine has not been a long life, but it has been full. Of pain, of sorrow, of truest love.

You will be safe though, my child. Your father will care for you. Though you are not of his body, he loves you just the same. My mother was wrong about that, at least.

As I press the small pink pouch into your hand, I watch the confusion flash across your eyes. I know your father would never leave you. Gerens will protect you for as long as he is able, as he has from before you were born. But leaving is not always a choice. I know that better than most. So just in case I leave this to you, for you and you alone.

I will watch over you, from where I rest with my husband. My heart finally at peace.

Take care my child. Live and love and laugh always.

I will remain on the salty breezes that race across the currents of my home. Resting. Happy. Safe at last.

***

Because of you I am.

You were an amazing woman, a powerful woman, strong. You held me up, kept me safe, made me who I am.

Seeing you now, so small, so frail; it doesn't suit you. As you sleep your body seems to crumple inwards, shrinking into death. But when you wake and smile at me your eyes light with love and hope and that fierce determination I know so well. Then I see you once again.

You are sick. Too sick. Your stomach swells and rots with cancer, as your own mother's did long ago. You are young, too young for this. It isn't fair.

Life rarely is, you tell me.

I reject that. You stood against injustice throughout your life. Ignoring the curses and slurs of ignorant townsfolk, overcoming pain and loss to build a new life, here across the seas. You forced fairness into your world, and mine.

The least the world could do was be fair back.

Outside is pouring rain, bitterly cold. The winds from the north are whipping the port. I can hear the groans of the wooden boats, the snapping of ropes in the gale. The sky is black with clouds, no gulls fly above.

But here is warm, beside the fire.

Father has set you up in a cot downstairs, you cannot manage the stairs alone anymore. He argued he would carry you up and down but you refused to be completely at his mercy. It makes me laugh, quietly to myself. Inside I also cry.

Brave and strong. Small and fierce.

Now diminished.

But only in stature, not in spirit.

The night is deep and black, but we remain by your side.

I read to you, you always love it when I do, I hope it gives you peace now. It was one thing you insisted I learnt. Something you never did and seem now to regret. Father reads and writes, every day. It's part of his job. I wonder why you don't?

The fire is almost out now.

And you are fading, your mind wandering. You forget we are in St John's. Who you are married to. It is another man's name on your lips this night, not father's. But it doesn't matter. We are here beside you, father and me. And we will hold you in our hearts forever.

The Gulls Cry

Chesten stepped off the plank onto Plymouth Harbor docks, her father by her side.

Around her the port bustled with life. It was an energy she was familiar with, growing up along the wooden beams of St John's Harbor, watching as her father managed the cargo shipments, taxes and regulations.

She breathed deeply, savouring the salt of the air, the tang of seaweed, the acrid burn of hot metal drifting from the repair sheds. On the other side of the Atlantic, and yet also coming home.

Gerens stepped beside her, offering his arm and led her to the waiting carriage he had hired. They still had a long way to go to reach their destination.

Chesten climbed into the carriage, adjusted her flowing skirts, pressed a hand to the firm bodice of the dress and looked out her window. Smoke rose up in long columns from the chimneys of the houses surrounding the port, the sounds of city life just beyond the reach of her ears.

She turned to her father.

"Thank you for bringing me here," she said.

He smiled back at his daughter, though his light brown eyes remained sad. She wondered if they would ever sparkle with their usual warmth again, now that mother was gone.

He knocked on the roof of the carriage and they set off.

Their journey up the West Coast of England took several days, stopping at boarding houses along the way. At each place the reaction was the same.

"That's a lovely accent dear."

"Thank you, I was raised in Newfoundland, across the Atlantic."

"And what brings you to our shores?"

"I've come to see the town of my mother's birth, Porth Gwynn."

A sharp intake of breath, followed by the sign of the cross, then, whispered in a low hush, "The town that died."

Chesten knew the story of course. Her father had told her of the dwindling fish stocks, the impending financial ruin of the town of his and her mother's birth. Of the coming winter, the low food supplies, sickness and injury. And of the storm on the Sabbath that claimed the life of her mother's first husband, Rewan, her father's brother.

The region was pummelled by ice and sleet and winds for days, flooding farms and valleys, felling trees and drowning all the men of Porth Gwynn. The Sabbath saved the other local ports, who had not been out that fateful day. Rewan was not so lucky. The storm scuttled the fleet. No man survived. He and the rest of the town's fishermen perished in the greatest storm in living memory. Nearby fishermen searched for survivors for days, few bodies were found.

After, the women slowly left, and the town was abandoned. No one had returned, the superstitious nature of the Cornish people kept them away. Too many ghosts.

Years later an official Lifeboat Service had been established in the neighbouring town of Port Isaac. Too late for her mother's home.

But Chesten wanted to see it. The home of her mother, her father and the man named Rewan.

"I can still see the bay, Chesten," her mother had whispered, voice raw with fatigue and sickness, "when I close my eyes. I still hear the call of the gulls, feel the salty breeze on my face, the scent of sage on my hands. I can still feel his arms around me, the musk of the ocean on his skin..."

Holding her mother's hand, her skin paper-thin, Chesten had listened as Kerensa spoke of her life in Porth Gwynn, before father, before her. It had been a tragic story, but also beautiful. The tale pulled Chesten into a different place and time, a different world. She could smell the fish, the thyme, feel the rough rock of the cove, the sand between her bare toes, see Rewan's deep brown eyes.

Gerens truly loved her mother. He always had.

And she loved him too. But Chesten knew his brother owned a part of her heart.

He didn't seem to mind. Whatever was left of her mother's love after Rewan drowned was enough for him.

The day Kerensa died he held her close, kissed her lips as she took her last breath. She passed in his arms, surrounded by his love and his protection, as she had been in life.

Her funeral filled the little church on the hillside of St John's, the only Methodist church nearby. It was as if the whole of the town came out to pay their respects to Kerensa. Chesten had stood in silence beside her father and cried. Face empty, her father had stared forward, saying nothing.

Later, when they'd returned to the empty house, so quiet now without her mother's laughing voice, her busy presence, her scent already fading from the rooms, he'd poured a whiskey and flopped into his usual chair by the fireplace, staring in silence at the flames.

"So many people came," Chesten had said, voice breaking with emotion.

Her father had smiled sadly, looking up at her, "That was your mother. Everyone always loved her. Everyone..." his voice had cracked, tears flowing from his eyes. She'd crossed the lounge to him and hugged him close, nestled in his lap as she had as a little child. It was the first and only time she had ever seen him cry.

When she'd announced she wanted to travel to England, to see the town of their childhood, she'd expected him to resist.

"I can pay!" She'd declared, anticipating his rejection of her idea.

Surprise rose his eyebrows.

"Mother, she left me some money. Here..." she'd handed over the dark pink purse, perfectly edged. "She said it was mine, to ensure I was safe. To be free."

A sad laugh escaped her father's lips as he fingered the faded linen pouch. "I should have known I won that argument too easily," he sighed.

Chesten frowned in confusion.

"Save your money, daughter, your mother wanted it for you and you alone," Gerens said and handed her back the purse. "I will purchase the passage for us to England. It has been too long." His throat bobbed, "I always promised her we would return, one day." Turning away he'd walked to the window, watching the mournful clouds sweeping across the bay, shoulders slumped in regret.

Now they were here, in England, and after days of travel, today was the day.

Chesten walked out into a mild spring morning, pale sunlight peaking between fluffy white clouds. Her father was waiting by the carriage, his suit freshly pressed.

"Ready?"

"Yes."

They climbed aboard and the carriage began a bumping progress through the cobbled streets of Padstow. They soon quit the town, the rows of stone homes giving way to rolling green hills and newly sprouting crops. Cows glanced up from their chewing to watch them pass. Overhead birds circled on the currents that swept along the valleys. About an hour later the cart turned left starting a rocking descent. Chesten sat rigid, face pressed against the glass of the carriage, scanning. Then she saw it, her first glimpse of the cove glittering in the morning light.

"Is that it?" she asked her father, "Is that Porth Gwynn?"

He didn't even turn to look, eyes staring at the back of the carriage.

"Yes," he whispered.

The driver took them right down the hillside, stopping on an uneven street that ran along the waterfront. Chesten descended the carriage and looked out over the bay.

It was small, tucked between two tall cliffs. To the right sat a collection of stone cottages, white paint peeling from the stone. Behind her the hill rose up, a few more cottages dotted along its side.

Overhead a lone gull called to the sea, its wings wide as it rode the currents that rushed up the cliff face.

"The gulls sound different here," Chesten murmured to herself.

"Which one was hers?"

"Come," her father said, and led her up a narrow path, out past the rows of cottages to a small hut on the very edge of the town, weathered thatch sliding from its roof. Chesten opened the door, it swung on a creaking hinge. Light from the open entrance illuminated a dark room, the oven built into the wall on one side. Through an opening on the right she spied an old bed, covered in stains, presumably from where mice had made use of it for a nest.

Gerens stepped in behind her.

"It's so small," she whispered.

"Yes," he sighed, reaching up to touch an exposed beam of the ceiling. A sad smile played over his lips. "In the spring she would forage. These beams, they were covered with drying herbs. The scent filled the room: thyme, sage, nettle, fennel." He took a deep breath. "Even after we left, she always smelled of herbs to me. When people were sick they came to her, not the doctor. She saved a man's life more than once."

It was a version of her mother Chesten did not recognise. Baking, making pies and pasties she knew were skills of her mother, and sewing and repair. But a woman bent in the garden, making potions?

The woman Chesten knew ran the household, supervised her lessons and arranged afternoon teas, their lounge room back in St John's, filled with ladies in gloves and heels, dainty cupcakes in hand. Thinking on it now, her mother had always looked somewhat out of place on those afternoons, so small and delicate next to the robust girth of her friends. Her presence was always so much bigger than her diminutive frame suggested, yet she seemed to rattle around their modest townhouse, as if lost in its size. But this little cottage, this seemed perfect for Kerensa. Chesten believed she could picture her mother here, chopping herbs and brewing tinctures, helping the sick.

Chesten squeezed her father's arm and crossed the room, walking through a door leaning open on a broken hinge, out into the backyard. She stopped in astonishment. Calling back to her father, she walked out along a little pebble path now overrun with weeds. Gerens stepped out behind her. All around them vegetables grew wild. Garlic, onions, potatoes, tall, short, wilted and fresh, in all stages of growth and decay.

Gerens gave a small laugh, "It still grows," he said, a veil of wonder in his eyes. He lunged forward, picking off a sprig of purple lavender from an unruly bush and rubbing his fingers together. He brought the crushed petals to his nose, breathing deeply. Tears tracked down his face.

Chesten walked to his side, slipping her arms about his waist. Together they stood alone, surrounded by a tangle of weeds and vegetables and looked out over the bay of Porth Gwynn. The waters washed gently up the beach, caressing the rocks that lined the shore. A soft, salty breeze brushed through their hair carrying the smell of seaweed and freedom.

Later they walked up the cliff. Along the way her father stooped to pluck a posy of little white flowers with yellow centres, a secret smile dancing on his lips as he did. At the top of the cliff they watched the waves breaking over the cliff base, the gulls soaring overhead, their call loud and urgent.

Her father reached out and threw the flowers to the breeze. The winds that swept up out of the bay caught them and spread their little bursts of colour out over the waves.

And Chesten breathed.

"Thank you mother," she whispered to the winds.

Epilogue

It's been two months since we returned from Cornwall. It's strange how I feel even closer to you now, despite our separation. Peter has been so supportive and understanding since you passed. He practically ordered me to visit your homeland. He knew it was something I needed to do.

But of course, we wed as soon as I returned. Recent events have made our union feel even more important. Life is short and we are in love. Why wait?

The wedding was simple, at our church. I had never been so excited and nervous both at once. I can't tell you which emotion held me most firmly in its grasp. After, as we celebrated with Peter's family I thought I saw you smiling at me across the room. I know it was a silly fancy, but I believe some part of you is still here with me.

I wish you could have been here to share it. You would have been so happy. But I must not dwell on what could not be. You taught me that.

Morwenna was wonderful. She helped me to adjust one of your dresses to suit me. Father cried when he saw me in it, said I was the spitting image of you.

He is doing well.

The sorrow is still there in the lines of his mouth, but he keeps busy. He planted a lavender bush in the garden. For you, I am sure, though he never said as much. He tends it daily, and has set up a chair beside it where he whiles away the hours reading on Sundays.

Don't worry, my married home is not far and I am sure to check in on him regularly.

Peter has taken up a position working with father, learning how to manage the docks in preparation to take over when father retires. It is a good job, with secure pay. But I am always sure to put a little aside, every week.

And I have news. You are the first to know, aside from Peter of course. We have suspected for a few weeks now, but this morning I am sure. I am with child! Soon there will be a new little one to occupy us all and bring father's smile to his eyes once more.

We've already been talking names, Peter and I. Though of course it is far too soon to be so confident, I feel sure it is a little girl who stirs within me.

I must go now, Peter is due home soon and the winds are picking up with the coming eve. There will be a storm tonight. But I wanted to visit you and share our news. It is both joyous and terrifying to know I am to be a mother. Life feels so uncertain and fragile and I long to sit with you by the fire, mending socks and talking of all that rests within my mind.

But I want you to know that whatever the future holds, I will be strong enough to face it. To stand tall and firm. To shape a path through it.

The world is harsh and dark and cold. But it is also sunshine and joy and love. And that is what I choose to carry with me.

For however long I get to walk this earth, I will do so filled with hope.

So rest well mother, turn your light to yourself and be at peace. Be assured that I am well, safe and happy. And I will keep your grand-daughter safe too, and bring her up as you did me, strong and independent.

One day, years from now, or maybe less, I will walk beside you once again and we can sing on the winds of the coast and swim beneath the waves, keeping watch over those we love.

Until then, sleep peacefully, wrapped in the arms of your love.

And I will continue on.

Note to readers

The idea for this story came to me, as most of my ideas do, when on holiday, this time in Cornwall. My husband and I travelled to Port Isaac, Port Gaverne and Port Quin on the north west coast of England for a week. It was an enchanting trip - stunning coastline, ragged, rough and breathtakingly beautiful.

While there, we heard a local 'legend' of the demise of Port Quinn, a once profitable and successful fishing-town that was abandoned in the late 1800s. Once, the town boasted upwards of 26 houses, now only a few cottages remain. Most are rented out for holiday-makers. It is a truly beautiful spot though.

Hearing this tale and being in the region, inspired me to research more about life on the Cornish coast, particularly for fishermen and their families. It was a tough existence. Hard, long days and full reliance on the success of the catch. As the fish stocks began to dwindle from overfishing, and the desire for 'Cornish Sardines' (pilchards) waned in Europe, the men and women of the fishing villages struggled to make ends meet and over time moved away to find other income and sustenance.

Out of this exodus grew the legends of great storms that decimated entire fleets of fishermen. There is no doubt that the storms off the Atlantic coast can be brutal and deadly, and many a man certainly lost his life to the seas. But economics was probably more the driving force behind the migration of people from the small fishing towns.

In writing this story I wanted to explore what life would have been like in such a village, the reality of day-to-day existence, the work, the fears, the joys. I have aimed to include relevant Cornish traditions, superstitions, foods and culture and have done my best to be faithful in all respects.

This is not a historical document. It is a fiction, drawing from many stories, legends, beliefs and hopes of the Cornish land that I have researched. If I have erred in my depictions it has been honestly done.

I loved researching for this novel, and hope that you have enjoyed exploring the world of mid-1800s coastal life with me!

Thank you

So many wonderful folk to thank for helping me bring this novel to life.

Firstly, as always, to my Jazzy-Pud, my 'writing buddy'. Your warm snuggles and comforting purrs brighten the most grinding of editing days.

To my amazing beta-readers for working through the initial drafts and giving me honest and forthright feedback that helped shape this into something far better than it could ever have otherwise been.

Next to my editor Lucy Skoulding for her time and patience working through my final draft (we finally got to meet during this one too!) And also to my mother-in-law and to the incredibly talented Mohamed-Nour Akalay, thank you for adding your editing skills to the mix, bringing out an extra polish.

A massive shout out to the incredibly talented Kimberly McMahon of @creatively_kimberly for the cover artwork. I am still in awe of your skill and remain stunned by the beauty of the image you created. A cover I will treasure forever. As you said to me, 'Look what we created together!' Love you always, my dearest friend.

To my funny, relaxed and easy-going hubby. Thank you for supporting me through another novel. Your constant humour and understanding get me through every time. Your belief in me holds me up more than you know. You are truly my infinite love.

And finally, to everyone who picked up this novel and gave an indie author a go - thank you! Your support means the world and helps me keep going with this passion that fills my days with purpose.

I hope I can fill yours with interest and enjoyment for years to come.

Sincerely,

Lelita

Did you enjoy Where the Gulls Fall Silent?

Please leave a review

Amazon: https://www.amazon.co.uk/dp/ B09HJH1TG6

Good Reads: https://www.goodreads.com/ book/show/59115862-where-the-gulls-fall-silent

Keep in touch with Lelita Baldock

Sign up to her newsletter for writing updates, free content and more:

https://www.lelitabaldock.com/writing-newsletter

Printed in Great Britain
by Amazon